The Unmaking

The Rayne Whitmore Series

Book I

Alanna J. Faison

The Unmaking

Alanna J. Faison

Published 2014

ISBN 978-0615961385

Cover model Brittiney Faison

Published through www.Createspace.com

This is a work of fiction. All names, establishments, locations, and incidents are used fictitiously, and are strictly from the author's imagination. Any resemblance to individuals living or dead is completely coincidental.

The Unmaking

Chapter One

"**G**reat, don't tell me that it's time already for your weird vampire show fixation. What is it this time?" My favorite/ only sister is standing in front of the television, dyed auburn hair cut short with a bang to the left side, nearly covering her eye. The latest brand name jeans are hugging her too-quickly-for-my-liking developing body. She asks, abruptly ending my silent Buffy time that is a monthly ritual of mine. I hadn't heard her enter the den area connected to my bedroom as I was occupied watching my favorite episodes.

I roll my eyes at her, pretending to be irritated as I pause the episode just as Spike is getting ready to sing his musical number to Buffy. "Do not go there. These shows are sacred and Buffy is a classic." She smacks her lips in irritation and I give her a smirk.

I look into her almond shaped hazel eyes and then at her cherry glossed full lips that match mine as if we are twins and not six years apart. My sister is very much the type to do her own thing. She has plenty of friends, every type of social networking account imaginable, and access to a private driver that would take her to any of the approved places my parents had given. So, for her to come bother me means that something just has to be going on in her young teen world that needs the advice of her big sister.

We get along extremely well, but we have a mutual understanding that given our age difference, our lives will probably go in different directions. I'm proud of the fact that my sister is independent and does not want to live up under my shadow. Still, if she needs me, I will gladly make time for her no matter what. I'll do anything for Jasmine. I scoot over on the couch to make room for her and her drama. She looks at me with those gorgeous hazel eyes that we both inherited from our mother and inhales as if she's going to blow out a 60 candle birthday cake. Twenty minutes later, I know all about Justin Bridges and his quest to have sex with my thirteen year old, hottest eighth grader in the city, apparently, sister. Then, I'm definitely the one to take a deep breath. Then another.

◊◊◊

After about two minutes of silence, soulful deliberation, and thoughts of murder-by-hire, I decide, "How about we go for a ride, get some ice cream, and talk about this away from where mom and dad might hear?" *I am not going to be the one trying to keep my father, the government security and arms dealer, from unloading a grenade launcher from an unmarked vehicle and pointing it at a fourteen year old boy,'* I think to myself.

"Sounds good to me, but you have to promise not to tell your girlfriend about this. She'll just encourage you to get one of dad's men to beat him up. Please Rayne, I know that was your first idea," Jasmine begs me, her bottom lip poking out. I try to look shocked at her request, but we both know that tomorrow I was going to be waiting outside the school with a couple of my dad's men to pay this Justin a visit. I was only going to scare him a little, geeze. She's right, Selene would encourage it too. In the six months that we've been together, she's become extremely protective of Jasmine. That is just one thing I love about her, along with her wonderful taste in pumps.

I put my arm around Jasmine and realize that she has relaxed tremendously after telling me her dilemma. These are the kind of things that sisters do for one another. Besides, if mom knew about this, she'd probably find a way to blame it on me being a lesbian, saying something like, *"Your sister is seeing the deviant lifestyle you are living and is trying to have sex in order to compensate for all the ideas you are putting into her mind."* Yep, that sounds about right. Boy, do I love my mom. Yay.

Jasmine waits for me outside my door as I grab my favorite half jacket, all black with rhinestones on the back and silver accents, and fish my keys out of the drawer. I take a quick glance in the mirror to make sure my make-up is still decent. Once I approve, I tuck one side of my long jet black hair behind my ear and head out. Two divas on an ice cream date. As we hop inside my white Aston Martin, I patiently wait until Jasmine is all buckled in before starting the car. Safety first.

"Where do you wanna go, Ms. Lady?" I ask, slowly turning up the volume on my music, then quickly changing the song when "Freek'n You" by Jodeci starts to play. Great, just great; a sex song is not what we need right now. Jasmine, bless her heart pretends not to hear.

I leisurely pull out of our drive and through the high security gates as Jasmine contemplates, then, finally decides on Bingham's lake. I smile and nod. Good choice Jazzy. Bingham's lake is where daddy would take us on boat rides and for fishing whenever we were feeling sad. It has been a long time since it was just the two of us out here alone. There's a nice view of the water through the trees at this spot where I got my first kiss. I was about the same age as her when I kissed the girl I liked. I'll take her there to talk things through.

Thinking back on that time, smiling, I know that I've come a long way. I had loved the way her long blonde hair was always in her face. I was always willing to touch it and put it up in a ponytail for her. That day, I pulled her through the trees to the perfect spot and told her in a whisper, even though no one else was around, that I liked her as more than a friend. I had planned my confession for weeks. How forward I was, and before she could even respond, I had closed the gap between us and kissed her on the lips.

When I opened my eyes and pulled back, she was staring at me blinking, so unsure, yet so, happy that I had done that. I saw it in her eyes, but she still ran away. We never spoke again, but she also never told anyone. Neither had I, as her movie star friends at the time would have probably disowned her. I still remember the sadness I felt waiting for her to return any of my calls.

Do I know movie stars? About a handful, because with money comes exclusive perks, but none that I've ever really bragged about or taken complete advantage of, to my mother's discontent. I have other plans and they don't involve simply being successful just because of who I know. I have faith that I'm capable of more than that.

Alanna J. Faison   The Unmaking

Sometime in between my trip down memory lane and parking, Jazzy had put on a pair of designer sunglasses and rebrushed her hair back into place. Stealing a quick glance at her, I picture all the boys in her school falling over her, adoring her naturally athletic build, small waist, and beautiful smile, much prettier than mine, as she was blessed with naturally straight teeth and I had needed invisalign. When she gets to high school next year, daddy will have to buy her a taser to keep in her purse.

Daddy is a tall, about 6'2", caramel skinned man with a big grin, short, curly hair, and full lips; mom is white with those astonishing hazel eyes, long brunette hair, athletic shape, and beautiful dimples. Somehow, Jasmine got the very best of both of them. She's on track to be on the World's Most Beautiful People list before she even makes it out of her teens and I'm not exaggerating. My little sister is as friendly as she is beautiful, and that, these days is truly rare.

She and I look a lot alike, but where she has dimples, I have none. Her lips are less full than mine and as I said before, her smile, better. I have more of my father's nose and hers is slightly narrower. Her face is rounder due to her still losing those childlike features and her skin tone is closer to my dad's. She prefers to wear her hair short and always with some reddish tint to it while I love my long, natural wavy hair. Both of us are beautiful and we know it in our own way.

Jasmine is still growing into her confidence and I had already found mine when I was her age. Where she hesitates, I never would have. Where she smiles and tells people she's fine, I tell them point by point why I am not.

We both get out and I push the remote to lock the car and set the alarm. Then, I start down the trail to the spot by the trees with Jasmine trailing behind, clearly thinking. The trees arch over us as if hiding us from the rest of the world. The scent of pine cones and tree flowers fill my nose. There's hardly any wind and the sun is slightly hidden by the clouds as if trying to play peek-a-boo with a baby. The warmth of the day feels good against my face, and I take a deep breath to enjoy the air near the water as I wait for Jasmine to collect her tangle of thoughts.

Kicking up rocks as we go, she finally finds her courage and asks, "Rayne, did you have sex when you were my age?" Instead of looking back at her I decide to continue walking as I acknowledge the question so that I won't embarrass her.

"Well," I start, close my mouth choosing my next words carefully, then, say honestly, "No. I knew that even though sometimes my body really, really wanted to; I knew that my heart wasn't ready."

"When?" she whispers without saying the rest.

"I was sixteen, a couple months before I was seventeen and trust me Jazzy, I was scared to death at first because I was still kind of unsure if I was truly ready." By this time, we reach my favorite spot and take a seat beneath the trees to gaze upon the shimmering water. Geese quacking and fish jumping become our soundtrack for this drama.

"I guess maybe, I wasn't then, huh, but I don't regret it. It was special to me and I thought I was in love," I admit.

I didn't really think about my first time too much. After I did it, by the time I had had my seventeenth birthday, that love I thought I felt had been erased partly because after my first time, all she wanted to do was have sex with me. No conversations, no dates, just sex. The other part of me simply cared more about my activities I was involved in such as swimming, track, and of course dancing.

"But what if I want to now?"

Silence. Even the animals seem to quiet down waiting on my response.

"Rayne, what if I'm ready? Maybe not in love, but just ready, to know how it feels?" she asks, searching for the words.

I have to sit here and think, let the words sink in.

"Baby girl, then all I can say is you're going to do what you want in the end regardless of what I say here now." I reach my arm out and pull her closer to me. "But for someone at your age, it's not going to feel the way it will when you're older. It can't. There's too much inexperience there and if you're lucky, you'll get a whole two minutes out of it. Do you really want to waste your first time on two minutes?" There's really no point in going with the *save your body for the right one, love will conquer all speech*. She's too smart for that. I have to be logical. "Besides, there are other ways to deal with that need and if not, just don't put yourself in those situations."

Jasmine picks her head up off of my chest and look at me sideways. Lips turned to the side, she barks out a laugh. "You can't be serious. Touch myself like an internet perv?"

I giggle at the comparison. "It's nothing like that and nothing wrong with it either. Many people do it and hell, I do it sometimes."

She stays quiet for a second then answers, "Maybe I'll try it, but what if I still want to do it with Justin? What if I can't trust myself?"

"You are going to still want to do it, but it'll help those urges. You're human, you're hormonal," I shrug. "The thing is to recognize situations that may put you at a greater risk to make a mistake and then to not make those decisions to be in those situations."

We continue to talk for another hour or so about her life as well as mine. By the time I buy us ice cream, I really feel good about myself. I have to make more dates to spend time with her because if I don't, someone will take advantage of her beauty and hormonal teenage lust.

Chapter Two

By 9:00p.m., I'm changing into my swimsuit getting ready for my nightly swim workout before my daddy comes home to practice a bit of martial arts with me. I had never really learned them growing up and that was something that he regretted not teaching me. I had always felt I was too girly for martial arts and wanted to dance instead. At the time, we compromised by me getting into the water. Now, he wonders why he even compromised with a four year old in the first place. My dad, he could hold his own among businessmen and even the president, but up against me, there had never been any contest.

My routine is to do three miles at the very least, and depending on my stress level, I sometimes do more. I always make sure one of the staff is on-site just in case something happens. That was a promise I made to my mom, knowing full well if I didn't keep it, she'd drain the pool in a heartbeat. No, my mom and I do not see eye to eye on a lot of things, but I never doubt her love for me or her need for my safety. We just live in two separate worlds and in hers, appearances are everything.

I can care less what people think about me. It has never kept me from having friends and even when I came out at school my sophomore year; no one ever treated me differently, at least, not that I can remember. Hell, I think I made more friends when I came out. I certainly had more date offers from girls and even guys. I do know that not everyone is as lucky in that regard as I am, so I don't take it for granted either.

I think one of the biggest fears my mother has is that I'm going to start dressing and acting differently, which has not been the case. All she clings to is her gay stereotypes. I'm a femme who loves my femmes and I don't see that changing. Mom has always said that she wants what's best for me, but by her actions, she only wants what's best for her and her image. I'm nineteen years old and I want to mold that image for myself, not through her eyes. Until she understands that, we can't be close anymore. Besides, I'm getting ready to travel abroad for three months before I come back and go to school. I'm sure the gap between us will be even wider if our issues don't get resolved soon.

I dip my toe in the water like I'd seen in movies. It is my ritual. Then, I dive in. The water is room temperature and it feels amazing. Daddy had this room built just for me with the ceiling painted with all my favorite constellations. I love to lie on my back and simply look at my faux stars. I'm not a brat, though. We all have our own special spaces in the house. Jasmine has her own art studio and we both share a love for dance so we have space for that too. We have a big house; understatement of the year, maybe. I float there a few more minutes, thankful for the blessings we were given and vowing to have my dad build me a house similar to this one, customized for all my needs. Spoiled, not a brat.

The work has been put in and it's time for me to exit the pool. Muscles pleasantly sore, I nod to my staff, David. He turns off the wave machine and points to where he has a towel and bottle of water waiting for me. After I wrap the towel around myself, down the water and start to head to my shower, I stop and turn before David shut the lights off. David has been on staff for about two years now and I only remember having about a handful of conversations with him. He's average looking, average build, and about four years older than me. I wondered how he got so lucky to land a job here.

"David," I say.

He stops what he's doing immediately and turns. "Yes, Ms. Whitmore?"

Ew. I hate that. "Rayne. It's just Rayne."

He looks around, unsure. Clearly this is someone who does not like to break the rules and I'm sure it was my mom who instilled the cost of breaking the rules into him. "Um, yes, Rayne?" It comes out awkward and fearful.

I smile at him. He's looking as if I am some newly discovered species. It's pretty amusing. "Do you like to swim?"

He looks longingly at the pool and sighs. "I love swimming. I used to live in Virginia Beach and went swimming all the time before my parents, divorced," he bites off the last word with a bitterness that I can't understand. I leave it alone because it's not my place to comment on memories that are clearly supposed to be suppressed.

Instead, I say, "That is a shame to hear, and I'm deeply sorry. If it will make you feel better, I give my permission for you to swim here once a week, but only after I'm done with my laps, okay."

I don't wait for an answer, as I turn and walk away while adding, "I will let my mom know that you have my permission, so don't worry, she won't bite your head off."

"Um, thank you Ms-er... Rayne. I appreciate it," he stammers behind me.

"No problem David," I call back, waving.

Then, it hits me. Maybe we should have an employee day where they get to enjoy some of the luxuries of our home since they work day in and day out but never get to be on the other side. Even though I'm sure some of them probably sneak every once in a while and help themselves to a massage chair or the home theater room. I'll run it by daddy later.

After the shower, I check my phone to see that I have a new text message from the beautiful Selene Marquez. All I can do is smile when I see the pic she sent me of a pillow with the caption: *It's getting a little lonely over here.*

I text her back, *As soon as I can baby.*

◊◊◊

I met Selene about a year ago when I was club hopping with a few of my friends. That is one perk of having lots of money; no one cares if you are underage as long as George and his friends are around.

It didn't take long at all for me to see her. I looked, then looked again. Then, at her ass. Hey, I liked what I saw. Her hair was dark, a shadow that swung all around her, straight and beautiful. She had a stunning skin tone, I could tell from where I sat. I thought she'd probably loved to be outdoors. Her body, Lord, all I thought about was how she had to walk around naked frequently. With a body like hers, it'd be a crime not to. She moved as if, as if she was music itself. It was mesmerizing. I watched her for a while until she finally noticed me.

Then, I smiled, made eye contact, and walked away. Now she knew I was there and that was all I needed. By the end of the night, I found her sitting alone by the bar. She looked out of place there, still and peaceful, around all the noise and movement. I walked up to her and asked, "What's your favorite song?"

She looked up at me standing next to her and locked eyes with mine. I could smell her perfume as I leaned in close to hear. She smelled wonderful, earthy, like cinnamon and vanilla. "Why?" She asked, not too interested, but curious just the same. I looked into her eyes and discovered that they were forest green and all I wanted to do was keep gazing.

"Because I'd like to dance with you to a song that has meaning, so that neither one of us forget this dance." Damn, I wanted to be close to her. I had never felt that way about someone I just met. No, it wasn't love, but a deep intrigue. It was a pull, gravity.

She liked that and decided to play along, this time, really looking at me. I could tell in her eyes she saw something she liked. Instead, she said, "You can't dance with me, but I'll tell you my favorite canción." That's when I caught the slight hum of an accent. It sounded deep, ingrained into her core, one of those accents that would never completely go away no matter how much practice she put in. I loved it and needed to hear more from this enchanting woman.

"Why?" I asked, now curious.

She stood up straighter, her leg now touching mine and said, "Because, as beautiful as you are, I can tell that you are too young to be in here. If I dance with you now, it would just encourage you to come back, and I can't promote bad behavior."

I looked at her, now amused. "I bet that the real reason you don't want to dance with me is that you know that if you do, you'll want to be as bad as possible."

She laughed at that and I knew it was the truth.

I continued, "I am younger than you, I'm sure, but, one dance, or even one conversation with me will change your mind. I promise that I have much to offer. You can't be more than five years older than me anyway and do you really want to miss out on something that could be... special?"

She leaned back and contemplated that for a few minutes then told me, "Tell the dj to put on something slow. You're gonna have to work at getting to know anything about me and I'll be the judge of that by how you dance."

That night, we danced to four songs in a row, sweating, with me fighting the urge to touch her, feel her skin against mine. I didn't want it to end and I refused to leave the club without knowing her phone number. After the way we moved together, it wasn't hard to get it because she wanted to see me again too. A week later, my driver was picking her up in my Aston Martin, to her surprise, and dropping her off at my favorite restaurant.

We continued to spend time together, her slow to trust, me doing what I could to earn it. Months later, we finally made it official in more ways than one. It was the best night of my life; the way she touched me as if she had the power to pull a climax from me just by brushing her fingertips against my skin. There was electricity there, it had to be. I felt the shocks spread through my body as I gave her more than I even knew I had. That night, I learned more about making love than I'm sure even the most practiced experts knew.

To this day, the memory of it still makes my body quiver. Selene was so absolutely thorough and sure of herself that even the confidence that I normally give off in waves was waning. I had trembled under her and all I wanted to do was make her feel half of what I felt.

Thinking back on those wonderful memories, all I want to do now is hurry and rush to see her. I'm going to make this workout with my dad as quick as possible. I throw on some grey sweats, a black tank top, my grey and white Nikes, and trek downstairs to find my dad. As I'm walking past the main hallway to reach the basement stairs, my daddy's best friend and business partner Damien, is standing at the end of the hallway, all black designer business suit on, hair in a fresh brush cut, clearly waiting for me. I look at the medium height dark skinned man and wave. There's obviously some kind of change in plans for tonight if Damien is here. I stop a few feet in front of him and cross my arms.

"What's up D?" I ask, head tilted to the side. Although Damien is my daddy's best friend, he's more of a big brother to me than an uncle and has always been one of the first people I would talk to if I needed to clean up any mess I made. He is absolutely reliable and whatever he does with my father and the business makes him a valuable asset.

"I need you to take a ride with me. Get your jacket, Jason's waiting for you." He may sound cool and collected, but I can still see through his relaxed demeanor and tell that he's not too happy with my father right now. But, I know enough not to ask him about it until we are on our way.

"Um, ok. Just, give me a sec," I tell him as I head back upstairs to my room to grab a light jacket and ponder where we could possibly be going.

D holds the door for me as I slide in his silver Camaro. The leather seats are cool against my back, the recently detailed interior sparkles, and his car freshener reminds me of strawberries. I buckle up and he does the same before speeding off into the night. I reach for my phone, slightly disappointed at the prospect of not seeing Selene until even later tonight. I sigh heavily.

Sumn's up wit my dad. I'll let u kno asap when I'm comin thru, I text.

Ok. I guess I'll jus take a long shower then. Alone, she responds.

I sigh even louder this time. *Ass.*

Lol. I kno. I can't help it, I've learned frm the best.

I shake my head, put my phone back in my jacket pocket, and turn my attention to Damien who is weaving through traffic, clearly even more irritated than before. Road rage, I assume. From the landmarks around us, it seems safe to say that we're headed to my daddy's company, but the manufacturing warehouses in the business district, not the corporate office downtown.

"D, what's the deal?" I ask him.

We turn a corner and then Damien answers carefully, "Since you're going to start being a part of the business, there are some things you need to see first."

"Okay," I say knowing that there is obviously something more to the story than that or he wouldn't be having this scowl on his face. "So, what's wrong with that?"

"I just don't think this is the right way to go about it. He should talk to you about these things first, not just throw it on you." Boy... that was telling. Damien grips the steering wheel tighter as if he could crush it into a thousand pieces.

"You guys deal with weaponry. I know that it can't be all rainbows and sunshine," I say, slightly offended at his insinuation that I can't handle it or am oblivious to what is going on.

"No," he nearly snaps. "No, Rayne. Your father should have been telling you these things a long time ago, and now he just wants to throw you into it. I don't think it's right."

"I think you're exaggerating D," I say as I turn back to look at the road, the buildings are nothing but blurs as we zip by.

"Dammit Rayne, you just don't get it. You'll see." We both sit silently for the rest of the drive, irritated at each other for different reasons. Five minutes later, we pull up to a security gate. The guard comes up to the car, points his flashlight inside and then waits for Damien to roll down the window.

Damien flashes his id and then the guard hands him some kind of computer speaker type thing. Damien speaks his deep, dominant voice into it. "Damien Carson. Charlie Zero Gamma X-ray X-ray Beta."

There's a pause, then a masculine voice comes through the speaker, "Voice recognition confirmed. Damien Carson. Password confirmed. Welcome back sir." Damien hands the device back to the guard who walks back into the security office. We wait patiently for the gates to open and then close behind us, one by one, three in all. I have never been here and I'm already intrigued at the heavy security around the lot.

Chapter Three

We pull up to the farthest building out of the five that are inside the gated area and Damien stops the car. Each building is a different size and none of them have windows in front. All of them have garages as well as doors except for the one we stop at. It's all white as far as I can tell from the lighting and seems to be the smallest of all the buildings. "Wait here for a second Rayne," he tells me as he walks up to the door, knocks and then says a few words to someone behind the door. Less than a minute later, he's waving me to come to him.

I get out of the car, surprised by the chill in the air as well as the silence. There are other cars around, but very few, and I wonder if there's more parking on the other side of the building. My steps are quick as a wave of fear quickly washes over me, then, goes away. What is that about? When I reach Damien, he puts his hand on the middle of my back, opens the door, and guides me inside.

It may be the smallest of the buildings, but the inside is huge, and astonishingly clean. As our footsteps echo against the gray tiled floor, I take in the expensive looking equipment and picture this place as if it were during the day. I visualize people with white coats standing over the machines and monitors, nodding their heads and collecting their data. But, there is none of that now. Now, there is simply enormous emptiness from the very top where the railings and walkways hang and steps, but after that, only darkness. The smell inside here is that of ammonia as if something dangerous had spilled and needed gallons upon gallons of cleaner to wipe it up. It becomes more overpowering to the point that my head begins to feel dizzy.

I'm grateful when we reach an elevator. Damien removes his hand from my back and then presses up on some kind of scanning device. Next, he swipes his badge and the doors open. When we step on the elevator, I realize that there are only two buttons. It's strange for there to only be two floors to go to, seeing that this place is incredibly huge. It must be a special clearance one.

Even after the card swipe and the hand scan, Damien presses another button and the same voice as before speaks, startling me, "Prepare for eye scan." Damien steps up to the panel with the buttons on it and remains still, unblinking. "Confirmed. Damien Carson." After another second, the voice says, "There is another occupant with you, identity has not been confirmed. Shall I override, Mr. Carson?"

I look at Damien and ask, "So, what am I supposed to do?" At this point, I'm afraid I'm going to have to go through an x-ray body scan.

"State your full name and then say confirm identity," he tells me calmly.

I sigh. All of this is becoming a little too unnecessary for my liking. What is there to hide down here? I'll play along for a little while longer though. "Rayne Danielle Whitmore. Confirm identity." I tried to sound as authoritative as D had sounded.

"Rayne Danielle Whitmore. Identity confirmed. Prepare for eye scan." Surprised, I hesitantly stand where Damien had stood and hold my eyes open, not knowing if there'll be a lazer pointed in my eye that could blind me if I wasn't who they thought I was.

Thankfully, the voice says, "Analysis complete. Rayne Danielle Whitmore, daughter of Jason Anthony Whitmore. Identity has been confirmed. It is good to finally see you Ms. Whitmore."

I take a deep breath as the elevator finally begins to move with a slight jolt and a humming sound.

"So," I say, extremely curious. "What does it do if you are not who you say you are?"

"Well, it accesses your perceived threat level, and from there it either gasses you to sleep while it calls security, or it," he pauses, but I already know the answer. "Can kill you."

I don't ask any more questions. I think I'm starting to understand why Damien had wanted my daddy to talk to me about these things first. Whatever is down here clearly needs to be protected and now all I can think about is how many people may have died trying to get to the lower level.

When the doors open, I finally see my dad standing in front of the doors waiting patiently for our arrival. At first glance, other than the fact that he has on dress slacks with just a wife beater, nothing seems out of place. Then, as I glance again before his chiseled arms embrace me, I can tell something is off. Even though this had been his idea to bring me down here, he obviously is having second thoughts about it. Hmmm.

"Hey, sunshine," he says warmly. I had always thought it was amusing that he called me that, since he was the one who named me Rayne.

"Hey, daddy," I reply with a smile.

He and Damien exchange brief looks and I can almost hear the argument they surely had before now.

I try to break the awkward silence. "The technology is beasty dad. I need to put one of your security locks on my phone in case someone tries to steal all the naughty pics on it."

That does the trick as Damien bites back a laugh and my dad attempts to completely ignore what was just said by shaking his head and pretending to clean out his ears with his finger tips. Dad then starts to walk away, his demeanor all business. Damien motions for me to follow. I walk closely behind them ogling all the cases of weapon after weapon that are hanging on each side of the wall as we go down a corridor. Interesting. I'd never seen so many different types of knives, swords, spears, bows, or even guns. My dad has to have every single hand wielded weapon known to man down here. This would have been a ninja's wet dream.

"As you know, we contract with the government to make weapons of all sorts, but that's not all. Sometimes I sell weapons to collectors or even overseas to small rebel groups if the price is right. We have the most brilliant minds at work here and those minds are just as valuable as the weapons we make. They, above all must be protected Rayne," my dad tells me, his mood becoming much more sour by the way his body language shifts as we get closer to a room.

He stops just short of the door, reaches for the handle then stops, before turning to me frowning. "There are consequences for those who threaten the safety of my family, my friends, and my valued scientists." As he says the last part, he looks me in the eyes, a cold ruthlessness behind them that I've never seen before from him.

"Show me," I tell him, needing to understand what it is that has changed my father in this way.

Damien steps in front of us and opens the door. Agonizing moans hit my ears, coming from across the room. I step inside. A white man is strapped to a chair, arms behind him, head bowed, and shirt ripped open in the front to reveal deep bruises and blood. Without seeing his face I know that it is in the same condition. On the floor is a bloody towel lying next to my father's suit jacket. He cleaned himself up before I got here. My father had done this to this man. Why did he need me to see this?

I try not to turn and run away as I study the room to see brass knuckles, spread on a table, a hammer, and other items that I care not to name. My stomach starts to hurt and my knees begin to tremble. As if he can feel my fear, the man lifts his swollen face slowly, looks up at me, and smiles through bloodied gums and missing teeth. One eye is completely swollen shut and the other eye reveals something dark and sinister inside it. It is almost as if he's enjoying the pain that he's been put through in a twisted sort of way. How can a man who has been beaten like this still look as if he's the one in charge? At this point, I am more afraid of him than all the weapons in the room. Instinctually, I take a step back and the battered man looks amused by my reaction.

I can hold my gaze no longer and stand closer to Damien as I tuck my hair behind my ears nervously. My heart is pounding and goose bumps form on my flesh. "What's wrong with that man?" I ask quietly.

Completely understanding my meaning, my father answers loudly, "This man is a sociopath. He kidnapped two of my best researchers and tortured them to get our secrets. All I'm doing is returning the favor."

The man laughs. It sounds like tires screeching.

"Where are they now?" I ask, afraid of the answer.

"Dead," the man hisses, sounding nothing like a human being. "I mailed them back when I was done."

I use my hand to cover the sound of disbelief. I imagine my father opening a package to find broken body parts, decomposed, staring back at him. How could this be business? How could my daddy, no, how could anyone play this game?

Damien puts a hand around my waist to balance me, and I cannot meet his eyes. He says nothing and so, my father continues.

"A perspective associate had been fishing around our sites for some time now. Ever since we began to expand certain types of weaponry that has proven very successful in some of our field tests, we'd begun to start peaking the interest of this client. So, he started to send his errand boy here over to my offices trying to broker a deal to sell some of my secrets. However, that man deals in the black market. We refused and he didn't like the answer." My daddy picks up random things off the table inspecting each one until he finds that he likes the tire iron the best. "We make weapons to kill things and we make security technology to protect secrets, but I would never sell those things to people like you. In the hands of your kind, the world would fall."

His kind? Before I can ask what that means, there's a blitz of speed and then a crack that fills the room. The man howls in misery as his leg twists in ways that it should never go. I have seen enough. My stomach has seen enough and I know what the outcome of this game is. Dad said he would return the favor and I know that only death awaits this man.

How do I feel about that? To know that my father who's always taught me to be moral and upstanding is a murderer. I don't know. I had looked at that man for only a couple minutes, but I can tell that inside of him is something twisted and evil. Still, does that mean that what my father is doing is justice? How many times has my father given out this type of justice? Am I expected to do the same?

My dad had once told me that reputation was as much of a weapon as anything else and now I understand what he meant. He has appearances to uphold just as my mom had told me many times before. I wonder if she knows, if she truly knows the man that she had fallen in love with so many years ago. How does my dad transform from this to the kind and gentle man that he is at home? If this is the price that must be paid to keep our family and assets safe, I'm not so sure that I want it anymore.

My head hurts, and all I want to do now is be with Selene. I need to be around something good and warm. I need something right, to hold on to. Selene is right, she is kind, and I need her. This is something I will never let Jasmine see. I promise myself. Never will she have to see the violence and torture. Inside those doors, more muffled screams are being drawn out. I slide down the wall crying silently for the loss of the scientists and for the loss of my ignorance.

Five minutes later, Damien stalks down the hallway to sit next to me on the floor, his hands on his head. We sit there silently for about five minutes before I finally ask, "Is he dead?"

"No," he responds, surprising me. "Your father isn't done with him yet."

"Wow. How thorough he is," I spit. "How many have you killed?"

"None. Jason doesn't want both of us to go down that road. He says that watching and actually having to physically carry it out are two different things."

I almost laugh at that. My daddy, the virtuous one, always taking one for the team.

"Rayne-"

I cut him off.

"Don't Damien. I'm not ready to talk about anything else right now. I don't want to know anything else. I'm on overload and I just want to see Selene," I practically beg, feeling the full weight of exhaustion that stress can put on you.

"Ok. I won't argue with you, but there is more that you need to know sooner than later now."

Those are the last words spoken between us as he drops me off at Selene's. I am deflated. I had told her that I was coming and that I was staying the night about twenty minutes before I arrived, then I had texted mom to let her know where I was too. I figure by this time, she'd start to worry a bit.

When we pull up at her house, my body is numb and my thoughts are a tangled mess. I had always prided myself on doing the right thing and maybe I had only seen the world the way I wanted to see it up until now. Maybe my dad is doing the right thing, even if it seemed wrong to me. My dad is not an evil man and clearly, he has an empire to protect. How else are you supposed to protect an empire? Damn. What wouldn't my dad do if pushed?

Right when the car stops, I hop out before Damien can say anything and Selene flicks on the porch light. She had been waiting for me. I have to practically fight with my legs to not run the rest of the distance to the door. She opens it as soon as I hit the first of four steps; and once I see her face, a wave of relief floods me.

I'm safe now, I tell myself. We stand in the doorway and hug as I listen for the sound of Damien's car driving off. Then, after a soft, much needed kiss, Selene pulls me inside.

Chapter Four

Selene's home is tastefully modern with creams and dark accents as well as wonderful artwork throughout. She loves mirrors, pictures of foreign landscapes as well as beautifully painted naked bodies of men and women alike in various poses and positions. It makes for an interesting blend throughout the entire house. Even the furniture is shaped with curious angles that look uncomfortable until you actually have a seat. Add in throw pillows and rugs and you have awesome splashes of color. Her entire house is like this, even the bedroom furniture is like being transported to a different place. She has throw blankets and pillows on the bed coordinated to match the walls, a nightstand design that is connected to the bed frame and a comfortable chaise lounge on the other side of the room.

The thing that really melts my heart is the picture Jasmine painted for her a month ago of two women, backs turned, holding hands, and facing a body of water. For her to have placed it in her bedroom where she'd see it every day makes me happy. Jasmine has talent and I know Selene really loves it.

The one place that is not filled with the bold splashes of color and décor is her kitchen. That place is Selene's sanctuary and it seems as if she wants to keep that area as untainted as possible. It always remains pristine with the stainless steel appliances sparkling, her spices and herbs are always neatly labeled and organized, and her dishes are always immediately washed, dried, and put away. She has a dishwasher, but I've never seen her use it once. I also know that even though Selene may not be as rich as I am, she has to have some type of trust fund or something because none of the things in her house come cheap, I would know. Even this quiet suburban area is fairly pricey. Her home always smells warm and inviting too. Earthy scents usually fill the air and today, I smell patchouli.

Selene is dressed in a Brazilian track jacket in support of her home country and some loose fitting jeans. She still makes nice and casual look model-like. Her long silky black and blonde ombre hair is braided all the way back into a ponytail, and she has a flower in her hair that matches the jacket. From the looks of it, it seems like she just came home from a walk rather than the shower that she teased me about earlier.

In the back of Selene's home is a small wooded area and she says that she loves to walk around and enjoy the nature. That's why she chose this area to live in. She once said to me me that the land around here is respected, whatever that meant. Selene's different in that way, kept plants, whispered to animals as if they were human, and only used as many organic items as possible. She'd said that there was a price for defiling nature and that if we listened close enough, we could hear the plants weep at how we treat the earth. That's my Selene.

As I plop on the couch and take off my shoes, Selene goes into the kitchen and brings me back some herbal tea and a sandwich. She had told me once before that the tea would help calm my energy and restore my muscles. I don't argue with her because I enjoy the taste of vanilla and honey. I thank her and once she's satisfied, she sits down next to me and runs her fingers through my hair. It's probably still slightly wet from my shower earlier. It feels good to have her touch me and I relax even more as she whispers something inaudible.

"Better now, beautiful?" she asks in her sweet song of a voice.

"Better," I say, meaning it completely. I am so much better that I don't even want to talk about what I had seen and risk the chance that I would not feel how I'm feeling at this moment again.

"So," she begins, still playing in my hair. She loved to do that. "Do you want to tell me what's wrong or are we going to pretend that nothing has happened and watch a movie or something?"

Geeze, when she put it like that, it seemed as if I was a coward running away from my problems. Ok, maybe I could be a coward for a few more minutes. No, I know she's right to word it how she did. The sooner I got it out in the open and worked out in my head, the better off I'd be. She already knows me too well, it's kind of creepy. "We can talk about it, but you have to promise not to say anything until I finish the entire story. No interrupting with gasps and frowned up faces either."

"You've never heard me gasp," she defends, and then laughs realizing full well that that wasn't true. There were many times I had touched her in just the right spot and...

I roll my eyes. "Stop making me think of those things when I'm trying to be serious," I warn and lean away from her and her now wandering hands.

She laughs seductively, scoots away from me and pretends to zip her lips.

Two deep breaths later, I tell her about my entire night, from the time I meet Damien in the hallway until he drops me off. We sit with the distance between us and the silence after I finish speaking makes it seem even further. Selene is clearly searching for words to make me feel better about the burden that has just been revealed to me, but she's having some trouble. It almost makes me feel even worse as if she is doing her best not to judge. But I still wait, needing to hear what her next words will be.

Finally, she scoots back close to me and rests my head on her chest. Together we sigh, and then, she whispers, "Power has a price. That will never change."

"But what if that price is just too damn high?" I ask quietly, fighting tears.

"Then, there will always be someone else willing to pay that cost love." Selene then gets up and starts pacing. I watch as she bites her lip, carefully choosing her next words. I sit up straighter, trying to remain patient, but I'm afraid that she will tell me to call the police or something on my dad.

"Baby," I finally say, breaking Selene from her daze.

She turns towards me and gives me a sad smile. I almost get up to hug her, but she waves me off. "I'm fine. I just was thinking of home."

"Does home have anything to do with my situation?" I ask, sounding much more asshole-ish than I intended. I cringe.

Selene pretends not to notice and responds, "Actually love, it does." Her accent rolls sweetly off of her tongue as she says, "I have never told you about my family and how they tried to force me to be with a man who not only I had no attraction to, but I did not even know." I flinch reflexively at her words, both stunned and confused as to why she never told me this.

Through my silence, she continues, speaking as if she's telling another's story and not her own. "His name was Sergio Cardoso and he was deeply connected to my family. I disliked him from the second I met him. The arrogance he possessed flowed off of him in waves..." Selene's face turns up into a scowl, and I swear I feel her anger hit me too. I begin to frown as I try to ignore the feeling.

"He was a bastard. The son of a bitch told my father that if I married him, not only would he "cure" my dyke-ish ways, but our children would be born into power and honor, and of course money." Finally, she sits back down, but on the other cream couch. "My father craved power and every time he obtained more of it, it was never enough."

"How?" I beg. "How did things end? And why…"

"No, Rayne. I care about you, but don't you dare start to accuse me of not telling you sooner. This is my life and I am entitled to keep certain secrets until I am comfortable with confiding in you. This is not harm to our relationship and if you treat it like it is and start making things all about you, I won't tell you shit else," she says as stingingly as a slap to the face.

All I can do is nod as I stare at this woman, the woman who right now, in my eyes, actually looks the years older than me that she is. I feel like a jealous brat and mentally kick myself. When I see tears forming in her deep, green eyes, I automatically start to stand up, but she beats me to it and begins to pace again. There's something eating her up inside and all I can do is sit patiently and wait. I think about how Selene has always told me that her trust is not a gift that is easily given and I know that whatever is going on inside her mind is part of the reason why.

"Rayne, in my culture, you honor your parents and their wishes above your own. My father wanted our bloodline to be assured; there was no other alternative for him. Sergio kidnapped me as I was walking home from the market one night. He tied me up, drugged me, screamed in my face, spat on me and called me a whore. Then, then he raped me. For three days he raped me." By this time, Selene's words have become sobs and I am so stunned that it seems that my body has been paralyzed.

Sickness was on the verge of taking over after what I had witnessed with my father, but this, this is just too much. Breaking out of my stupor, I sprint for the restroom and barely lift the toilet seat up in time to empty all my stomach's contents as well as dry heave for minutes still. When I finally finish, the anger comes as well as sadness that I never was there when that man hurt and defiled the woman that I am falling hopelessly in love with more every day.

As I study myself in the mirror and reach in the drawer to find my extra toothbrush to scrub away the taste of bile, I see a reflection looking back at me that I hardly recognize. There is borderline hatred in my eyes and I'm so horrified of what I see that I quickly rinse my face, and then leave the mirror behind. I feel as though that reflection is still standing there, staring me down as I walk away.

I now understand what my dad has done tonight, even if I don't yet condone it. His business, his possessions, his family is everything to him, and to protect that, he will do the unthinkable. A few seconds ago, I had become my daddy, obsessed with revenge on a man I had never met over something that he had done years ago before I met Selene. I can't fathom what I would attempt to do if this had been something that had happened to her when I'd been a part of her life. Fuck! I want to call in a few favors right now and have Sergio dealt with.

I walk back in the living room where Selene is still standing, but no longer pacing. Her eyes are red and puffy yearning for comfort, and yet, I still can't bring myself to touch her. Not from disgust, but right now, she just seems so fragile as if she would break from the slightest touch. I want to apologize for Sergio's actions, to tell her that I will never allow anyone to break her down again, but before I say another word, she begins again.

"And you know what the most fucked up thing about the whole situation was? Not that I had to save myself, or that I had to have major surgery because of the damage he did inside of me. That I almost lost my chance to ever have kids. The most fucked up part of the whole thing is that my father *told* him to do it."

I nearly fall to the floor this time, but somehow, I manage to make it to Selene's side, pull her down to the floor with me and cry with her for what seems like eternity. My soul is reeling and both of our shirts are covered in tears and snot. I don't care, all I want to do is make all of her pain go away, erase her past and free her of the prison of lies and distrust.

I make a vow to myself silently that I will protect Selene, my Selene and get her any help that she could ever need. "Is that why you left?" I whisper.

"Among other things, yes. But right now, that is all you need to know." Selene's voice is nearly back to normal and I wonder how she can separate herself from what went on. I want to ask her how many years ago had this happened, what happened with Sergio, how did she find out about her father's role in it. There are so many questions that her revelation had created, but now I know the true extent of the trust issue and that I will have to work to prove to Selene that I can be her safety net, and the woman she could trust.

"Selene, baby," I start, choosing my words carefully, wanting to be as honest as possible.

"Selene, I love you. I do. I love who I am with you and that I feel completely safe with you. I just wish that I could make you feel that way with me. Maybe one day you will; maybe one day you will feel like you can tell me anything in the world and know that I won't judge you and that you will still be the same person in my eyes."

She lifts her head up and smiles longingly at me as if she wishes that it could be just as I said, but knows that it isn't true. My heart drops and I know that Selene is not ready to tell me she loves me back.

"Baby, it's okay. Don't feel obligated to say anything you aren't ready for. I know that you're almost there. I know that you have strong feelings for me too. Even if it's not love, yet," I try to assure her.

"Thank you beautiful, but there are many things about me that might make you rethink those words. We were both born into power. The power that my family possesses is much different than yours, and you may not like what that means," Selene says somberly.

"But hell, Selene, that doesn't change that I love you now, today; and today, I mean the words that I said."

She sighs. "Ok, Rayne. I believe you and I truly want to be an open book with you, but I'm just not ready. I'm sorry that I piled all of this on you after what you learned about your dad. It was selfish of me in a way, but I wanted you to understand that people's circumstances can cause them to do uncharacteristic things, whether right or wrong, all in the name of power and control, or in the battle to obtain it."

I let her words run through me. "I get that. When you told me what happened, I wanted to do the things my father was doing to that man to Sergio. I wanted to go back in time and kill him for you." I watch Selene flinch slightly at my revelation, but I continue. "I didn't know you to protect you, but I still feel, responsible," I admit.

Selene puts her hand in mine and tears cause her eyes to sparkle. "Baby, don't. What is done can never be changed. Every day I am moving on from that betrayal, and believe it or not, having you in my life has made that transition so much easier. Rayne, I'm almost there. I may even be there now, but I just can't say those words."

"I'm okay with that. My heart knows that you're mine," I say with a smile on my face. "I'm going to learn all I can about you, and hopefully, I will learn more about myself too."

Selene takes my face in her hands and brushes my hair out of my eyes with her thumb. Then, she leans in and I can smell the soft scent of lavender in her hair as I breathe deep. Selene leans in and waits for me to close the rest of the distance before her soft, warm lips meet mine and her tongue pushes through my parted lips to explore my eager mouth. She's gentle in her approach, hesitant as if she'll expect me to pull away. I drown her worries as I deepen the kiss and climb on her lap, wrapping my legs around her waist.

Selene quietly moans in my mouth as she tries to rub herself against me and reach under my shirt to softly scratch my back. Soon, her lean, femininely muscled body is lifting me in her arms, my legs still wrapped around her as she carries me to her room, trying never to break our kiss. My body begins to tingle with excitement and I feel the hairs on the back of my neck start to rise. My eyes begin to adjust to the darkness of the room.

"Please," I beg Selene as she lays me firmly on the bed. Desire burning between us, reflecting in her eyes, I continue speaking quietly knowing full well that she can hear me. "I only want to feel you. I don't want anything else to matter right now."

"Shh," she coos. "I need this too baby."

Where Selene is usually gentle and filling, she becomes rough and consuming. Her kisses leave a trail of burning liquid passion to my center. My pants come off with a fierceness that leaves my own desire wet and throbbing. Selene stands up and undresses slowly in front of me. When she strips off her bra, her round, grapefruit-sized breasts bounce in excitement and her hard, caramel nipples practically beg me to wrap my warm mouth around them.

I can't contain myself and I begin to rub my clit in slow, small circles.

"Stop," Selene commands, startling me. "It's mine. No touching." I smirk and raise an eyebrow at her.

"Then, come take it, Selene," I say, my voice becoming raspy with need. I finish undressing myself and swing my hair back so that Selene can get a good look at all of me. She bites her lip and motions for me to turn around. I oblige, perking my ass in the air as I hear Selene's breath catch at the sight of me and my love dripping down.

Slowly, methodically, Selene licks. Strong powerful strokes cause my body to shudder as she attends to every drop that has run down my legs. Then, she takes one long, painfully slow lick from my opening to my clit. Just as I'm gasping for breath, I feel her press two wonderful, long, expert fingers inside of me. Selene continues her assault on my clit, somehow sliding under me as my hips buck from the pleasure.

It isn't long before my world is exploding and my center is pressed harder against Selene's mouth. "More," I somehow manage to demand. Selene acknowledges me by telling me to again turn around. As I do, she pushes my head down and tells me quietly to taste her. I shudder again at the anticipation and happily let my tongue enter her body, exploring, tasting, teasing, as she screams my name and climaxes under me.

We find more and more ways to please each other as we allow our body's need to drown out our pain. Even though I'm sure we could have explored our passion even further, sleep finally overcomes us. We lay huddled together in sweat and bliss.

◊◊◊

I wake up first and bask in the warmth and numbness that I feel. I sit and stare at Selene for a few minutes before I have to search for something to eat. I decide on oatmeal, fruit, and a slice of toast. I read 10:15 on the clock as I make enough for Selene. I set her portions on the table just as there's a soft knock at the door. I quickly go back in Selene's room where, thankfully, she's still sleeping. I reach in her drawer and pull out a big jersey that she likes to sleep in and a pair of boxers before I answer the door. Yes, I had cooked naked. I enjoy the freedom since I can never do that at my house. The person knocks again, a little louder this time and I rush to look out of the window and discover that it's Damien.

I open the door and purposely roll my eyes while pretending to look at my imaginary watch on my wrist. Damien ignores my rudeness, takes in my clothes, wild hair, and laughs. "Boy, you are one lucky woman," he tells me.

"Hmm, don't I know it," I agree as I think about all the love we made, and how Selene finally opened up to me. "I love her Damien," I confess again, willing to shout it to whoever will listen.

Damien punches me lightly on the arm and tells me, "Well then you need to start bringing her around more so I can see what you love so much about her."

"I don't know D. I can't have you falling in love with my woman."

He laughs for a couple seconds, then switches subjects. "Yeah, yeah, Ray Ray. Your taste is so much better than mine right? Please, you got your taste from me. I'm the master. But, anyway, how are you feeling now after everything?"

Damien pulls me down to the porch swing and stands protectively with his arms crossed, over me. His dark sunglasses make his eyes unreadable, but I know that if he were to remove them, they would be dark with concern.

I wipe nonexistent sweat from my forehead as I replay everything I saw last night. I also remember D's last words to me, that there was still more that I needed to know. When enough time had passed, I answer, "I have mixed emotions about it, but I think that I understand why he does it, even if I don't agree. I mean, if that is the reputation that daddy needs to uphold, then when does it stop? Shit Damien, I might as well have a mob boss for a father. He's playing a dangerous game and if he loses, then what are we left with?"

"You're right. It is a dangerous game and it's one that Jason has been playing for a long time. People respect and fear him. He,"

"If he's so respected, then how the fuck did his people get mailed back to him in pieces!" I have to lower my voice as I continue. "There will always be someone else willing to do what it takes to obtain power," I finish angrily as I understand what Selene was telling me about her brutal rape. Her father's lust for power was so great that he sacrificed his own daughter. In the end, what would my own dad be capable of?

"I'm sorry Rayne. I shouldn't have tried to come over here convincing you of something you know to be untrue." He sits down beside me. "I really did want to make sure you were okay. You know I love you, but I can't protect you from everything, and there are things you still need to know."

I laugh almost hysterically and D gives me a frown, but I don't care if he thinks I'm crazy. "Look man, I'm really not ready for any more revelations. Seriously, I need a couple days before I hear everything else."

"Rayne-" he starts, then shuts himself up.

"It's becoming obvious to me that daddy is not transparent when it comes to his business dealings and also the technology that he's making. If he wants me to see weapons of death and destruction and have me learn about shady business dealings, then he can tell me himself. You don't need to be doing his dirty work."

"There's more to it than that. There are things that you need to know about what's going on in the world if you are to be safe." With that, Damien looks up toward the door as Selene opens it gently.

Selene steps out on the porch looking every bit like a Brazilian model. Adriana Lima doesn't stand a chance. I'd expected Damien to be giving her the same eye as me, but when I turn to face him, prepped to say something smart, I see that he's taken off his sunglasses and is sporting a judgmental frown. It's hard to understand the point of the staring contest between him and Selene and as I get ready to speak, Selene opens her mouth.

"Good morning, Damien. I see that you're one that stole my Rayne from me. When I woke up alone, I was worried, especially after all that had been revealed last night." Her accent is thick with curiosity, questioning toward Damien as if she knows something I do not.

I don't like it. There's tension here and to me it feels like there is something going on between them. But, that can't be right, D would never lie to me about something like that and I knew that Selene doesn't like men at all, so it couldn't be any sexual history between them. Still, what I'm sensing is making me uncomfortable. I shift in my seat.

"Sorry about that Selene. I won't keep her from you any longer. But-" Damien pauses as he put back on his sunglasses. "Perhaps, since you seem to be well traveled, you can fill our Rayne in on some of the dangers of the world."

Huh? What was that? Was D assuming she was taking advantage of me?

"Damien, don't be rude," I chastise him.

He leans down and kisses my cheek. I smell the Sean John cologne that he loves to wear so much. "I'm sorry Ray Ray. I'll be good. You just be sure that you are careful. Use good judgment, with your heart and mind."

"I'm not going to hurt her, Damien," Selene tells him.

He doesn't turn around as he takes off down the walkway. "You may not mean to, but sometimes the world has other plans."

I look up at Selene and I swear I see something shift in her eyes. Yet, my attention turns back to Damien as he yells, "Fuck!" when he pulls on the door handle to his car, removes his hand quickly, and starts blowing on it. With one more quick look up towards us, he gets back in the car and speeds off.

I open my mouth to ask just what the heck is going on, but Selene reaches for my hand and helps me up before saying, "Thank you for the breakfast."

I kiss her cheek and lead her back into the house. "Thanks for last night, sexy." She laughs and smacks me on my ass.

I don't let it go that easily though. "So, what was that about with D? Have you two ever had a conversation that I didn't know about?"

She scowls but quickly tries to amend her expression. "No, but he thinks he knows my type, that much is obvious."

"Hmmm, well if that type is super attractive, funny, loving, and wonderfully skilled in bed, then yes, he's got your type alright," I tell her as I follow her into the bedroom and she starts the shower.

Selene laughs and to add an exclamation point to what I just said, pulls her shirt off over her head and stands naked in front of me, gracing me with the presence of flawless, smooth, lightly bronzed skin. I don't think I can ever get tired of the view in front of me.

"Well, Ray Ray," Selene starts, mocking the nickname that only Damien calls me. "If I fit that type, then, he really has no idea. Look how sexually repressed he seems to be. Huge muscles, sunglasses, permanent frown. He needs some sex like yesterday."

I laugh and shake my head as Selene steps into the shower and closes the curtain. After a few seconds of thought, I get up and go shower in the main bathroom down the hall. By the time I finish, I hear Selene bumping Usher's *8701* album through her system and I watch quietly as she washes our dishes in a red half shirt and black, laced, boy-short panties. Compared to me, Selene has more of a curvy body. Her hair is a dark veil that is much longer than mine. She's an inch or two taller than my 5'6" frame, and her breasts are a little larger than my 36 b cups. I take it all in, breathing deep as I examine my love. How'd I get to be so lucky?

Chapter Five

By nightfall, I realize that I haven't even bothered to check my phone. So consumed in the bubble of peaceful bliss that surrounded Selene and I as we took her black Dodge Charger to a movie, out to eat, then walked around downtown enjoying the sights and sounds, I never even noticed that my phone wasn't on me. Back in Selene's bedroom, I reach for my phone on the charger and find ten missed calls and three voicemails.

The most recent voicemail pops up and is from Jazzy. Normally, I don't do voicemails, but since it's from her and she usually texts, I decide to see what's up.

"Rayne… Rayne… please, don't come home, something's…" three seconds of Jasmine whispering those words into the line, fearful, pleading, before I hear the most gut-wrenching scream ripped from her. I drop the phone on the hard floor and hear it crack. Part of me recognizes that Selene is next to me, shaking me, questioning me.

There's a knot in my stomach and I know that something's wrong. I should call the police, I should… "Take me home Selene, right now," I demand as I run out the door. I can hear Selene behind me rushing to the driveway, keys jingling. The twenty five minute drive to my house seems to take an eternity even with Selene running lights and speeding for my sake. I try to reach my dad, mom, Jazzy, nothing.

'It's a practical joke' I tell myself. I don't know how many times I repeat it. Not enough I guess, because I never end up believing the words.

We reach the grounds' front gate and the first thing I see is the entrance's bars ripped from its hinges. As Selene carefully drives around, I notice that one of the help is lying under the broken gate, the spiked decorations piercing through his body. Before Selene is even stopped, I jump out the car and start sprinting to my house. Somehow, Selene manages to catch me, showing speed I would have never known she possessed. She grabs my arm firmly, forcing me to a standstill. I attempt to pull away from her giving her a stare that could frighten death itself.

"If you don't want me to break your arm now, you will let me go Selene."

"Stop," she commands, ignoring my own. She continues to keep an iron grip on my arm and I begin to feel weaker under her grip. Selene looks toward the house, obviously frightened and takes two steps back. "This feels wrong. I can feel the evil inside," she whispers, her voice trembling.

"Selene, please," I plead. "Let me go. I have to see."

"If I let you go, you have to promise me that you will stay by my side Rayne. I won't be able to protect you if you don't."

"Yes, yes, okay, just let me go," I agree just so there won't be any more time wasted. Together, we run straight into my home because this door too is ripped off the hinges and is lying a good twenty feet from the door way. Why isn't the security system working? Immediately I try to turn on a light and call for someone to answer me. There is no response or power to the house and a profound fear truly sets in this time.

"Call the police Rayne," my clouded mind registers Selene tell me.

"No. Not until I know." I have to find my sister, my mom, my dad.

As I walk deeper and more carefully in the house, I begin to smell two disturbing things. First, I smell gunpowder and as I look closely at the walls, I see a mess of bullet holes piercing paintings and shattered glass. Next, I smell death. I actually smell death. It takes all my might for me not to gag and continue to press on.

We reach the stairs and I hear the sound 'drip, drip' coming from above me. I begin to look up but Selene shields my eyes. "No. Do not look. If you want to find Jasmine, do not look." I hesitate, wanting to see what is making the sound.

"Tell me then, what is it?"

"There are bodies of your help hanging. Please Rayne, don't look."

I start to shake. Who could have done this? Who could have gotten through the security guards and the front gate quickly enough to have not given them time to call the police, to shut the power grid and security system down, but had enough time to cause this much death? My thoughts flash to the man my dad was torturing and I know deep in my gut that this is no coincidence. My dad had called him a sociopath, said something about his kind. He knew people. They'd want revenge.

"Selene, I'm afraid," I confess.

"Do you want to go back outside or are you going to look for your sister?"

I try to take a deep breath to steel myself. Then, I start up the stairs, trying to ignore the 'drip, drip' above me, the broken banister, shattered paintings, and I know my world is crashing in. Somehow, I find the strength to run to Jasmine's room. I call her name quietly, but there is no one inside. Further down the hall, I glance to see a blood streaked trail along the wall. It looks as if someone was attempting to hold themselves up while running away from whoever was attacking them. At the end of the trail, there's a body hanging halfway out of the window. Without closing the twenty feet of distance, I know that it's my mom. A cry of utter disbelief escapes my throat as I stare at the designer heels that she's still wearing and the way her body is unnaturally bent out of the window. Did she try to jump but never make it?

My knees shake and soon my whole body follows suit. I can't go any closer to her even though I want to help her. I know I can't leave her like that. Selene grabs my hand and whispers something that I can't understand. My strength returns, giving me the confidence to move forward.

One step becomes two, and then I finally close the distance. My mother's neck is broken and blood covers the side of her mouth. In the moonlight I can see a couple more bodies near the pool, dead, in unnatural positions.

"Call the police Selene," I say brokenly.

"Rayne, I already tried. Somehow, there's no service at all. I'm sorry, but we need to get out of here. I don't think Jasmine…" Selene doesn't finish the sentence; she just places a hand on my back as I struggle to rest my mom's body on the floor. Then, I weep, not caring about anything else, but needing to mourn for my mother.

"Mommy, I'm so sorry. I'm so sorry that all I ever did was argue with you. I need you to forgive me." I wait for two minutes, but those words that I desperately need to hear never come. When I finally think of Jazzy again, I stand up and head to my parent's room, now understanding and hoping that my mother tried to bide some time for Jasmine to get inside the safe room located in the far wall of my parent's room.

I know my mom died protecting my baby sister and I know that Jazzy may have died while trying to warn me. What I don't know is how absolutely horrible her death could be.

◊◊◊

"We need to go. Don't let your last images of your family be like this. Whatever is going on here is evil and I think it's still here. I can feel it," Selene cautions.

I ignore her as I press forward to my little sister. I want to hold her one last time, to apologize because I couldn't protect her even as she did her best to protect me. I step inside my parent's room and I swear the temperature drops a few degrees. The bed and two dressers are overturned causing me to stumble a couple times over various broken items. In the middle of the floor, I see Jazzy's phone broken in pieces. Behind me, Selene is whispering something else but I shut her out. Keeping my eyes forward, eight feet in front of me is my baby sister. The panel to the safe room is broken and open. I can almost picture her getting inside and trying to close it before it was too late. There are drag marks in the thick, once white carpet from her nails.

Tears threaten to disable my vision and all I can do is shake my head as I reach Jasmine's side. There she is. Lying there, in what seems like too much blood for anyone; let alone an eighth grader to bleed is my Jazzy. Her throat is slit so viciously that her neck is barely still connected to her head. Her stomach too is sliced open, her intestines no longer where they should be. This time, I can't help myself. I vomit again and again and again as I choke on my tears and bang my hand on the floor until it's raw.

Selene finally grabs my hand to stop me, but I shove her so hard that she falls over. Later, I would regret doing that. Later, is not right now though. Jasmine can't be dead, she can't be dead, she can't be. My mind sees the truth, but my heart, it knows it cannot bear this awful certainity. I try to touch her, as if by my touch she will wake up and be made whole. If only…

Alanna J. Faison   The Unmaking

This time, I start to find the words that I need to say. But, before I can say anything, Selene is pulling me into the closet and shutting it, covering my mouth with an iron grip. I start to protest and fight, but she just grips tighter. "You need to trust me and be as quiet and as still as possible, because our lives may depend on it."

I relax in her grip, but she still doesn't let go. Selene begins to shake against me as I follow her eyes through the slits of the closet door. My eyes go wide as I take in the image that I'm seeing. I blink once, twice, as this massive thing strides across the floor. The smell of death that I noticed earlier is coming from, It. Whatever It is, is at least 6 and a half feet tall and nearly as wide. It has no eyes, only empty eye sockets, three mouths and talon-like claws.

I want to look at Selene to see if she is just as petrified as I am, but I can't tear my eyes off of this... Demon. I say the word in my mind and know the truth of it. The feel of evil radiates off of its being. I can almost taste it in my mouth, so potent is its energy. Then, It walks over to my sister and leans over her body. I see one of its mouths start to open and...

There's a scream, sharp and breaking me from my frozen state. "No!" I barely register that the scream comes from my body before I realize that I am no longer in the closet and the Demon is no longer focused on Jasmine. Its soulless, sightless sockets are now focused on me. Another mouth opens in a disgusting gurgle and I find my resolve quickly evaporating. I nearly fall over from the terror I feel as the Demon takes a step towards me.

However, before I faint, fall over, or worse, Selene jumps in front of me, arms stretched out, and palms glowing.

She looks back at me and speaks softly as if there are other people she doesn't want to hear her words, her voice filled with power and sorrow, "I'm sorry Rayne, I didn't want you to find out like this." Her hair starts to flow around her in an invisible wind and the air around us starts to crackle.

I take one step back away from Selene and barely notice that the Demon has done the same. Then, a low growl escapes one of its mouths just as Selene slams her hands together, creating a boom and something that can only be described as a large burst of energy that engulfs the entire room. I fall to the ground, covering my head with both hands, as pieces of the ceiling collapse all around me.

The avalanche of debris pauses and as I begin to regain my footing, I see that Selene is the only one of us standing. Part of me wonders if it is she that I should fear. There are goose bumps on my arms and tiny drops of blood running down my forehead. Quickly, I wipe it away, just in time to see the thing rush Selene with a speed that should be impossible for something of its size. Selene barely has enough time to register what's going on before the thing is on her. Yet, somehow, she manages to dive away. I feel my heart beating forcefully, threatening to escape from my chest as I watch this scene unfold in front of me.

Popping up swiftly, Selene opens her hands once more and begins to speak quickly and quietly. It isn't quick enough and I can only watch as the Demon descends on Selene again with the power of a Mack truck. I hear the crunch of Selene's body hitting the wall before my mind registers what I just saw: Selene's eyes going wide, her arms bracing herself, and her lips moving before the Demon lands a blow so hard that it causes Selene to fly into the wall, pieces of wood splintering everywhere. When I see that Selene is unmoving, I break from my stupor.

She doesn't deserve to die here; this isn't her fault. My sister died trying to protect me and here I am simply watching as Selene is dying in front of my eyes, trying to shield me as well. How could I tell her that I loved her and yet do nothing? If we aren't going to make it out of here alive, then I might as well fight for the little time I had left. I run towards the Demon despite the stench of death it is carrying, screaming my lungs out for It to stop. I did not want it to take another step toward Selene who was now struggling to move even an inch.

"No! You son of a bitch, you murdered my family, but I won't let you hurt her too." I stand my ground despite the fact that my bowels were threatening to release at any moment. I stand my ground despite the fact that the floor starts to shake with every slow step it takes after turning back towards me.

I try my best to slow my heart beat, to find some peace in the last seconds of my life. I take one more look at Selene and my heart is relieved to see her sitting up. She mouths some words to me, but they take a second to register. By the time they do, the Demon has closed the gap and slices my left arm from the shoulder to my wrist before I manage to get out the way.

I scream in pain as a burning sensation like nothing I've ever felt in my life settles in. The pain is so overwhelming that I want to rip my own arm off so the pain will stop. I nearly black out from the pain. Hesitantly, I glance at the damage and see bone. I can still somehow move my arm, but it wouldn't do me much good. I know that I won't be able to last against something that can slice me open at any second. Selene's words hit me again as I do the only thing that I can think of to save at least her. *'Buy me time,'* she said. Praying to God that this works, hoping that the Demon will choose to follow me, the easy prey instead of Selene who clearly knows how to defend herself. I crash through the second story window, glass pieces cutting into me, roll off the roof and land on the hard ground underneath.

Another scream rips through me as the thing slams down on my ankle. The crunch itself of broken, shattered bone is enough to have me dry heaving as my back arches from the impact and pain. I don't remain that way for long as It grabs me by my throat, all three mouths opening at once. I kick and wiggle as much as I can as pools of tears roll down my eyes. I know I am in danger of passing out at any second and as I fight, I wonder why it doesn't just finish the job quickly.

Then, I stop struggling and choose to fight the battle another way. If the Demon is going to kill me, I am going to stare it down for as long as it takes for it to be finished. I will no longer give this thing the satisfaction of watching me struggle helplessly. The only thing that is left for me to do is defy it. I just hope Selene understands my sacrifice and makes it out of here. Alive. Then, I will rejoin my family in the next life.

One of its mouths closes and I feel the Demon's grip on me loosen, but still, I don't stop my death stare. Out of one of the other mouths, a long, jagged tongue snakes out and slices against my face. I hiss in pain, but don't stop staring. The Demon hisses in frustration and shakes me. Then, as if I'm painful to touch, it drops me to the ground. The gurgling noise that it made earlier becomes louder and begins to sound painful. Looking between the Demon's legs, I find that Selene is standing behind the Demon looking like a vengeful goddess.

The monster falls to the ground, body smoking. The stench of death is thick in the air as its flesh begins to sizzle. I hear Selene taking closer steps to the monster, and speaking words, at least I think they are words, quickly. Her hair is floating, the front of her shirt torn, exposing part of her bra, and she is trying to compensate for a limp. That same spark I saw in her eyes when Damien burned his hand earlier today is there again and I know, this time, I'm not imagining things.

"Taloq Rukem, mocre balim, jaloq yrvik," over and over she repeats. Her voice becomes louder and I realize that it's because she is standing over me protectively, her back now towards me. My vision comes and goes and I have to blink repeatedly in order to stop seeing double. Soon, there are no more screams.

"Shh," I can hear her cooing to me. "Rest now. I will keep you safe."

I try to sit up, but the pain is overwhelming my senses. Dizziness is the least of my worries as the adrenaline begins to leave my body. It ignites a firestorm of pain unlike anything I've felt before. As my consciousness fades, I make an attempt to call out to Selene. Then, darkness swallows me.

Chapter Six

Despair, confusion, anger, fear, pain. I feel all of these at once as I make an attempt to open my eyes, but become afraid of what I might find when I do.

"You're safe Rayne. I promise. Please, come back to me now." I can hear the pleading in her voice and I want to feel sorry for her, but I can't because, I remember. I'm the one who just lost everything. For a second I stop breathing. I don't even remember how to inhale air into my lungs.

Still, I choose to open my eyes and find that even though the only light in the room is from the drawn curtains, it still takes an effort for my eyes to adjust. Then, I become thirsty, very thirsty as if I've swallowed a gallon of sand. I start to open my mouth to ask for something, but as if she's reading my mind, Selene tilts a cup to my mouth.

"Here, drink this."

I close my eyes again and take a sip from the cup, only to spit out the bitter tasting liquid, now knowing the truth of it all, that Selene intends to poison me.

No, no, that can't be right. My mind is foggy and I can't shake away the clouds of confusion. I love Selene, she wouldn't harm me.

But the world may have other plans. Who said that? I don't remember.

Frustration, hatred, defeat. It all floods my heart.

"I'm sorry Rayne. I keep screwing up. I should have told you what it was before you drank it. It is water laced with a special Brazilian medicinal herb. It will numb your pain," Selene explains.

Which pain will it numb? Certainly not my missing heart that has left a black hole in its place, swallowing me. I'm left empty.

"Just water," I demand, my voice raw and raspy, sounding nothing like me.

Selene nods and leaves the room. When she comes back she is holding a sealed water bottle in her hand and makes an effort to show that it has not been tampered with. I drink the whole bottle and then we both sit quietly, her waiting for me to speak. The clock on the wall's ticking sounds like a drum beating against our silence. I observe the room finally and discover that I am not in the hospital as I first assumed.

The room is a normal bedroom, plain and empty of anything but the clock, bed, and a nightstand. I also see that I am not hooked up to any monitors. Yet, when I look at my left arm, recalling my injury, the slice down to the bone, I see that it is bandaged and the pain decides to make itself known all over again. Although, what I'm feeling now is nothing like the pain from last night. I don't even want to think about my ankle which I don't seem to feel at all. Weird.

Tears fall freely down my face and Selene starts to reach for me but stops. Good. I don't want to be touched, to be consoled, I just want my life back. Impossible, I know, but it will take a while for my mind to grasp that my entire world has exploded so much that there may never be any pieces left to pick up. I don't even know where to begin, so many questions go through my mind and they may have answers that I don't want to hear.

Fuck it. What can be worse than the horror I just witnessed?

"Is it dead?" I surprise myself when the question falls out of my mouth. I guess hatred is the first emotion to rule.

"I'm sorry Rayne, but I wasn't strong enough. That's why we're here, in hiding," Selene answers me sadly.

"Hiding?"

"Yes. We are in a safe house that Damien arranged. I was able to contact him before the police arrived. He knew what to do in case something like this happened and he has bought us your safety." The answer only creates more questions.

Angrily, I spit, "What the hell are you Selene? And what do you mean in case something like this happened? What do you know? Does this have something to do with what's going on between you and Damien? How can I trust you after what I saw you do? What did I see you do Selene?" I want to cry but I can't. I'm afraid and confused and I have more questions that need to be answered.

Selene takes a deep breath and I see that tears are threatening to fall from her green eyes as well. "Never in a million years did I think I would have to be the one to tell you this Rayne. I think I know what your father wanted you to know but was afraid to tell you. I will get to that in a minute, because you're right, you need to know what I am."

With a sad smile that I was getting too used to seeing on her face, Selene admits, "I am witch born, Rayne. Next in line to be high priestess of my people. The magic is my birthright."

I look over at the empty water bottle, examine the top for tampering, and read the label slowly. Surely, she found a way to lace it with something. I can tell when I look back at Selene that she knows I don't believe her. She continues anyway.

"There are things Rayne, that you cannot begin to understand. Accept it and you will be stronger because of it. You saw that thing and you saw what I did to it. Do not doubt the power of others simply because it is new to you." A compelling argument, one that as of now, I can't dispute.

"So if you are, 'witch born', as you say, what does that mean and what was that, thing?"

"You know what it was. I can see it in your eyes." She crosses her arms, determined.

"Demon. It wasn't just a monster, it was a demon," I say automatically, knowing the truth in my words, again. Evil. Filth. Destruction.

"You are correct. And from what I understand now, it wasn't just any demon, it was a Devourer. It was sent, no, summoned there for a purpose, clearly revenge. Devourers feed off of three things and that is why it has three mouths: flesh, fear, and souls. As for why it was sent, I will get to that later. I know this is too much to take in, but believe me; I will help you and protect you now more than ever. Now that you know what I am, I can do that to the fullest," Selene assures me even though I don't know if I'm ready to believe that.

"As for what it means to be witch born is simply as the name suggests. I am not a normal human that dabbles in magic. We true witches are our own race. We can have children with normal humans, but the magic may or may not pass on. When true witches have children with other true witches, our children will always be witch born. I control the magic inside me and the type of power I specifically possess, I get from the elements."

I rub my forehead as I process this information and Selene gives me a small smile before continuing.

"Others may be healers, necromancers which are those who can speak with or even control the dead, seers who can see somewhat into the future or even more, or someone simply able to convene with nature and animals. There are many witch born talents just like people who can swim really well or jump really high. But, our gift is limited only to that power we are born with. I will never be a healer for example, but the fact that my power is elemental means that I am vastly much stronger than many others."

Selene's voice rises in excitement as she scoots forward in her chair, brushing some unruly strands of her silky hair back with her left hand. "This is why I was supposed to be a high priestess and why my father wanted me to marry Sergio. He too was a witch and he was an elemental like me. Our type is probably the most common even though it seems as if we're special, but the strength comes from how much magic we can hold, our chakra or chi if you will. I am special because of those limits. In sports terms, most elementals would be considered sprinters, but I would be more of a cross country runner," Selene admits.

Relief flows through her as she finally tells her secret. I believe her. I see the truth in her words. Even if I didn't believe her, the ball of light she's now forming in her hand would be enough to convince me.

I also caught something she said. "What do you mean was? What is Sergio now?" I ask curiously, for a second, forgetting about my own issues.

She puts out her light ball and says, "Now, he's dead. I couldn't tell you this before Rayne, but there's another reason I understood your father. After Sergio raped me, I told you that I had escaped on my own. I did, I escaped only because I killed him. No, that's not true. I could probably have escaped without killing him, but I just didn't want to at the time. How he made me feel, what he did to me, I had to make him pay. I needed revenge and I delivered it to him myself. He drugged me so that my chi flow was disrupted, like the flu for a magic user, but my body burned the poison out much faster than he'd imagined. That mistake cost him his life."

I pause at that thought. Revenge. It comes full circle to me now. My dad's researchers were taken and tortured, he got revenge on that man, that man who had a look in his eyes that was evil and wrong. I was afraid of him because I knew immediately that he wasn't normal. He had to be 'other,' maybe not Demon and maybe not like Selene, but he was something. I can feel it now and I become more fearful as the truth finds me on its own. No, not on its own, my eyes were forced open.

Revenge. This is all a destructive cycle that must have begun to moment my father built his reputation by doing the unthinkable. My father tortured and killed that man and then whoever he worked for sent that Devourer to our home to murder my family. Daddy had to know about witches and demons, certainly Damien did and that's what he was hinting to Selene about. That's what he wanted to tell me. When my dad said to the man something about 'his kind' I didn't know what he was referring to, but now I know. That man wanted something of my father's that he wasn't willing to give up and now they were all dead because of it. I would be just as dead if I had been home, if I wasn't so angry with my father that I stayed the entire day hiding out at Selene's. I shudder at the thought, not necessarily thankful because I would switch places with Jasmine in a second if I could.

I barely lean over in time to vomit in the trash can on the side of my bed as I picture Jazzy lying dead on the floor with her throat slashed, that thing, that Devourer coming back to feed on her flesh. The way my mom's broken body had hung out the window, neck broken sends chills through me. How many times had I vomited in the past few days? I start to hyperventilate and I want to run away and hope that I can outrun my pain. Before Selene can come to my side, I fling the cover off of me and try to stand up, completely forgetting that my ankle is broken.

Immediately, I fall to the ground and let out a scream similar to the one last night when I felt my ankle being crushed.

Selene lets out a curse and then lifts me up, back on the bed. Next, she empties the now full trash can in another room before coming back to sit beside me, upset. "That damn healer told me that you shouldn't be in pain like that anymore. I've been giving you the damn herbs everyday like he said!"

"What do you mean every day?" I ask accusingly, panting as Selene tries to make me comfortable. Then she reaches for the drink she gave me earlier. This time, I drink it without spitting it out even though it tastes like dirt.

"Baby, it's been almost two weeks now."

Chapter Seven

I'm not sure that I hear her, so I blink a few times and let the words sink in before I say, "Huh." I am more lost than ever.

"You don't remember anything do you?" she asks in return, reaching for me again with a look full of pity. It's a look you'd give a stray puppy you've stared at in the pound.

"How could I? After I passed out at the house, I woke up here, just now. Just now Selene! Now is the next day, not two fucking weeks after my family and employees were murdered. Two weeks is fourteen fucking days. Two weeks is a lot to miss out on!" I want to scream at the top of my lungs, I want to break everything in this room, but instead I look at Selene with all the hate I have inside me. Something again shatters within me.

She flinches under my gaze and then looks away. I wish I knew what was running through her mind right now. What has she had to go through to get me here, keep me safe? She doesn't deserve to be the punching bag for my pain, but she's the only one here and I'm giving out the only emotion my heart is allowing me to feel right now. Maybe later I would feel bad about this, but as I'm feeling, maybe later, I'd be dead. After all, I'm only human and I'm sure a human heart can take only so much pain.

"Rayne, when you passed out, I carried you to the car and drove to meet up with Damien. I told him what happened and he sent men to the scene and they handled the police. They even had to change the scene some to look like humans had done it. It was terrible. They found your dad," Selene hesitates.

"Tell me," I demand.

"You don't need to know baby. It won't bring him back."

"I need to know! Did he fight back, was he protecting anyone? My dad wouldn't have just given up. Where was he?"

"He was found tied to a chair; his heart was ripped out, Rayne. But I don't think that the Demon tortured him. I think it was whoever summoned the Demon. They saved him for last," Selene tells me even though I thought she'd lie.

All I feel is numbness at her words. I unwisely play the scene in my head. Someone tied my dad up first and made him see and hear the screams of everyone. Then, after there was no hope, after torturing him physically and emotionally, that person murdered my father and gave the Demon his heart to feast on. It took the piece of him that was giving and loving and kind. I know I will have nightmares for the rest of my days. How could anyone heal from this?

"What else?" I manage to whisper.

"Baby, it can wait. Please."

"No!" I yell, then talk in a less loud tone. "No. You already said it's been nearly two weeks. I need to know."

"Ok," Selene agrees, her green eyes full of regret for me. "In order to protect you, they burned a couple bodies to make it look like you were among them but so it was too unrecognizable to completely i.d. Then, at the morgue they planted some of your DNA when the testing was done."

So, now other families had to have closed caskets or couldn't identify their loved ones, all to protect me.

"Damien made some calls and so did I. We were able to get you out of town and here to this safe house. I called in a healer whom I trusted. You kept fading in and out, screaming, fighting, and we had to sedate you over and over. When he began to heal your ankle as best as he could, you passed out and hadn't woken up for three days. You had to grow the bone back at a rapid rate, just in case we had to run again. It took a toll on your body. This is the most alert that you've been. I had to give you different herbs, make sure your arm wasn't infected, and clean you. I've been scared to death that you would never come back to me, that you would never be my Rayne again."

This time, Selene actually allows herself to cry, completely as if for the past couple weeks she's been trying to be strong for me. I owe her my life and probably more than I will ever be able to repay. I would never know where to begin, how to truly say thank you. Still, she's right about one thing, I don't think I'll ever be able to be the Rayne that she knew before this. She died that night too. I don't know who I am now. I try to form the words to say thank you, but they are not ready to appear.

"Where is Damien now? And don't worry about the explanation about my father and his business. I need to talk to Damien about that." I had some serious questions about what was going on with the business and what did it mean now that I was supposed to be dead.

"He's been working around the clock to keep everything contained while trying to keep himself safe and the business protected. It's all over the news. You're father was a powerful man."

He wasn't powerful enough to protect his family. If only he-. No, I wouldn't do that to myself, play the "what if" game. In order to be strong, I had to live in the now. "Is he in danger too?"

"I really don't think so. I think the message was clear enough and that the damage that was done was enough to make anyone else think twice about crossing that man again."

"What man?" I ask. I need to know the name of the man who ordered the death of my loved ones, the one who destroyed everything.

"Damien wouldn't tell me. He said that he doesn't know for sure who to point the finger at, but they are looking into it. The leads are just making him go around in circles, plus he has to use some underground channels that may draw dangerous attention to him which could make him vulnerable to an attack when he has no idea where it might be coming from. It seems like a lot of hiding behind other people is being done and I don't enough about that to tell you anything."

"It's okay, I'll get that information from him. I think I'm feeling better now. The pain has stopped," I admit. The physical pain at least.

She smiles. "Good. That means the drink is working." Selene looks around the room as if to make sure no one is around before she asks me, "So, how did you do it Rayne? How did you find the strength to fight to stay alive long enough for me to build my power?"

I sit up straighter as I try to remember what exactly I felt in those moments. I have to fight through the fogginess of my mind trying to protect myself from the whole ordeal. Finally, I speak. "I fought to buy you time and also because I didn't want my final moments to be full of fear. I couldn't let that thing steal that from me too. When it grabbed me by the throat one of its mouths closed and it got frustrated as I kept staring it down. I didn't understand it then, but I do now. You said that the Devourer feeds on fear and I wasn't feeling any at the time. The only emotion I was feeling was defiance."

Selene shakes her head quickly as if I slapped her and I look at her sideways. "What?" I ask, confused as to why, she herself, looked puzzled.

"You said you stared it down and it couldn't kill you?"

"Yeah," I say slowly. "I guess so."

Selene stares deeply into my eyes for a few seconds and I finally turn away feeling uncomfortable. Finally, she whispers, "It's you, I know it is."

Huh? At this point I am completely perplexed and also fearful to ask any more questions, but I force myself to ask anyway. "I am what?"

Selene mumbles something to herself and then her entire demeanor becomes perkier, almost scaring me. She nearly jumps out of her seat as she gets up so fast, hair swinging wildly as she hurries out of the room, calling behind her. "You will know everything soon enough. Just relax baby!"

I stare out at the door and realize that I have to go to the bathroom. As I glance to the side of me, I see an empty bedpan and I groan.

Chapter Eight

After I stop feeling self-conscious and just use the stupid bedpan, I feel much better and drift back to sleep. I don't know how long I'm out, but when I awaken, I hear Selene plus another voice in one of the other rooms. The voice is feminine and commanding. I almost wince at the power behind it from here. Then, I almost become angry as I realize that Selene is pleading with the other person to come see me.

"Please… special…she can be…"

The voices are muffled as if they are walking away and Selene is following behind, trying to get this other person to stay.

"Diana… Please just see…"

I've had enough of this. I don't like to hear Selene beg, especially not on my account. Plus, I have to find out who this person is that's too good to apparently even come look at me. This time, I remember that even though my bones have been spelled to grow back quickly, my ankle is still in terrible condition. I make sure I get out of the bed much easier than I did before. I make it to the door without putting hardly any pressure on the ankle but I still feel slight stabs of pain come and go. Out in the hallway, I see a light coming from what I assume is the living room and I see Selene's head nodding emphatically.

"I just know it Diana. I would have never summoned you here without the proper tributes if this wasn't a matter of urgency. Please, you don't have to believe me, but once you see her you will know the truth. You will know that I'm right," Selene says to the mystery woman quickly and passionately.

Finally, I hear the other woman's voice clearly. "And if you are not right, you will pay the price young witch. You must know your place and I will be more than glad to teach it to you." Her voice is like a cold shower, shocking and lacking any warmth at all. It echoes all around me as if it is coming from different directions and I almost look behind me to make sure there aren't any speakers on the wall, magnifying the sound. Even though her voice is filled with icy power, it is the most beautiful sound my ears have ever heard and I have to see who it belongs to.

I round the corner, limping foolishly and then come to a stop. The woman known as Diana is facing me, looking directly at me and I have to bite my lip to keep my jaw from dropping. Diana is about 6'4" with long blonde hair that is so light that it almost looks white. Her skin is incredibly smooth and is slightly glowing. Her eyes are the lightest blue I have ever seen in my life and her lips, small and pink, are frowning. Still, it doesn't take away from her other-worldly beauty.

She is wearing a long, one strapped dress that hangs modestly over her chest, showing nothing, but still managing to look attractive. There are no shoes on her feet and I'm sure that she hardly wears any at all, despite having perfect feet as well.

It takes all my energy to look away from this woman, who by no means would ever be mistaken for human. But, I have to show her where my heart lies as I look toward Selene.

"Are you okay baby?" I ask her.

Selene looks almost horrified at my blatant disregard of the woman across from me. "Um, you're asking me if I'm okay? Rayne, you shouldn't be out of bed," she tries to chastise me. Her voice is thick with the accent I love so much as her nervousness comes to the forefront.

"I had to check on you. I heard you speaking and it sounded like something was wrong." I start to wobble slightly and lean against the wall before I topple over while still trying to look serious and protective.

Selene notices my mini struggle and smirks. Then, she catches her composure and looks back to Diana who is staring at me with a raised eyebrow.

"You'd try to come to the aid of your witch while in your condition, human." It's not a question but I answer her anyway, trying to ignore the way her voice resonates all around me and the goose bumps that are forming on my skin.

"Yes, as you said, she is my witch. I love her." I try to sound confident, have my voice contain power like hers, but I know that's impossible.

"Interesting. Come to me child," Diana coaxes me. My body seems to move on its own toward her.

As I get closer, I notice that her skin truly has not one flaw to it. There is no visible mark or scar, no extra hairs poking out, nothing. She is what make-up tries to imitate. Diana lifts up my chin, taking me in as if I am a science project. Her hand is warm and delicate, but part of me still wants to pull away from her as if she is a ticking time bomb. Yet, I force myself not to pull away as we lock eyes.

Suddenly, I'm gasping before I realize it and I quickly turn my head. What I've seen, I can't explain. There is a power behind her eyes, frightening and beautiful all at once and a look that says that she's seen and done more than I ever will. Her stare made me feel as though I was drowning. Waves of a tempest crashing down onto my chest, filling my lungs.

"It's okay child, don't be ashamed. It is not often that one can look into the eyes of an Immortal the first time meeting one." She smiles at me. "You are beautiful. Young witch, you have chosen well." Diana says; her hand now on my shoulder, her height just as intimidating as her supernatural eyes.

I blink twice at her words. Immortal? This is just getting better and better. I examine Diana's appearance. She doesn't look to be much older than mid-thirty's, but clearly, I needed to add at least a couple zeros to her age. Apparently there are a lot of things that I need to be brought up to speed on. I definitely don't like feeling like I'm at the bottom of the food chain either. No wonder why her damn skin glowed. Jesus.

"Thank you Diana. Are you now willing to look?" Selene responds, a slight desperation in her voice.

"I will look only if you agree to pay the cost. If you are wrong, you will pay double that. These are my terms," she says, with finality.

"I will," Selene responds.

"Wait," I say backing away from both of them. "What cost? Look at what? If this is about me, I should know what you're talking about. And if you are going to have to pay something to a freaking Immortal I should at least have a say in it." I try not to sound whiny or fearful, but we were dealing with a real life, f'ing Immortal. I know that there is no way in hell they were talking about money.

"You will watch your tongue child. Although I am surprised that she did not explain to you why I am here, you should appreciate what she is doing for you."

'But, I don't even know what's going on,' I think to myself, distrusting my voice not to sound pouty.

"Rayne. There is a prophesy, no, more like an agreement that says that some humans will be given power from the immortals in order to protect themselves and their kind. Long, long ago before humans stopped believing in supernaturals or the 'awakened' as some of our kind calls themselves, they pledged themselves as servants of the immortals. The humans were being wiped out in waves with no true means or heroes to stop the attacks," Selene begins.

Diana continues for her, cutting her off with a wave of her hand, "In turn, if unique humans met certain, as you say, criteria, they could be marked by an immortal to become more than human. They would possess the means to destroy their enemies. If the human was worthy, they could become a protector of their kind. In this way, humans would not have to be completely powerless against the other races that walk the Earth. However, that was long ago and the pact that was made has been long since forgotten. As well, we immortals no longer walk this plane."

"Selene," I say, turning to her, ignoring the growing pain in my ankle. "What about me makes you think I could be one of these people?" I am extremely curious to know.

"Forgotten doesn't mean that it doesn't exist anymore either. One of the prophecies says that 'they will be destroyed, gaze upon evil, yet know no fear," Selene tells me excitedly. "Your family's death in a way was your destruction, they were your lifeline. When the Devourer came after you, you knew what it was and yet you stood up to it, unafraid. It is said that, that human who fulfills the prophesy and becomes marked will be a warrior that the world has never before seen. Rayne, there has not been one marked in over a generation. That seer was talking about you." Selene sounds so confident that I could be the one.

I look at Selene. She thinks that because that thing's mouth closed, I could be some kind of super-human. I start to shake my head, but I can't let Selene look like a fool in front of the immortal. What if she was right about me?

"So, when she improperly summoned me, Selene stated that your entire family was just murdered and that you fought against a Demon, a powerful one at that and it was unable to kill you. Is this the truth young warrior?"

Warrior? Me? I look back at Selene who smiles and gives me the confidence that I need. I step toward Diana again, nodding.

"Yes. I couldn't let that thing hurt Selene too even if it cost me my life. I refused to let it kill me knowing that I was afraid of it," I say, as truthfully as possible.

Diana nods in approval. "Those are the qualities of a protector. There could be power in you yet."

Before I can blink, Diana pulls me into her arms, grabs both sides of my cheeks and stares piercingly into my eyes. This time, I'm unable to look away and I swear I feel her pulling memories out of my mind. Birthdays, arguments, swimming, family time, the Demon, she sees it all. It's not really painful, but I feel a type of violation that I've never felt in my life. The memories of me making love to Selene play and I try to force myself to think of something else. Diana focuses of my passions, competitiveness, and morality. Finally, she pulls away from me and smiles.

"It's been over two hundred years since I've marked anyone. There is something remarkable inside you and you don't even know it. You have a strong urge to protect child, and I believe that with that strength, I can turn you into a weapon," Diana says satisfactorily.

I finally give in to my pain and limp to the couch. They both follow me without a word. So, I respond, "A weapon? To be used as I see fit, or as a tool for others?" Power comes at a cost; I was learning that the hard way.

"You are right child. You would owe me a service, but by no means would you be a slave. We immortals are oath bound to guide the chosen humans, not to rule them. Long ago when that pact was made, our eldest brother Alexander fell in love with the human race. He said that he saw qualities inside of your kind that no other race that walked the earth possessed. He never told us what the quality was and instead said that we must all look for ourselves."

"With that, he bound us all to human-kind and used his immortal life blood to send the power into every human alive. It merged with their dna and gave them the chance to be able to unlock the power that he had gifted them with. It cost our brother his life forever as he knew it would, but not before making us promise that we'd never enslave your men or women. He loved you so much that he sacrificed everything! Therefore, that is the quality I seek when I mark a human. Genuine self sacrifice for the thing called love. It is the one thing that I know cannot be taught. Either it is who you are or it does not exist."

Selene reaches for my hand and holds it tight. I squeeze it back.

"I want to protect you, but I see that there is something else in you that has the potential to be a force all on its own," Selene tells me.

I think about their words. "Will I be able to kill the demon that killed my family, or fight the man who started all of this?" I need to know if I will have that kind of power, and at this point if I owe Diana a service, I don't care what it is.

"Think wisely before you make any rash decisions, young one. I can feel it in the air that you are thinking of revenge. If you allow hate to rule your heart, I will not help you," Diana warns.

I turn, let go of Selene's hand, and look Diana squarely in the eyes, this time unflinchingly. "Diana. My family deserves justice and if I can be the blade that delivers that justice, then so be it. Still, that will not be my sole purpose in obtaining power. If I can grow strong to protect people so that they never have to go through what I just did, then I will do it. After what I witnessed, I never ever want to be weak again. If you refuse to help me, I will find another way."

Diana remains quiet for a couple seconds, then nods as she stands up, turning her back towards us. "So be it young warrior. I will mark you as one of mine and your journey will begin to become something more, something that has always been hidden inside you. I will help you unleash the power that you humans have lost." She turns back towards me and motions for me to stand up. I do so without hesitation. "This does not mean that you will succeed. And even if you do unlock the power within you, you may not be worthy of the title protector. Knowing this, knowing that this could possibly be the death of you, if you are still willing to go through with this endeavor, you will have three moons to finish your business in this world before you and your witch enter mine." She looks toward Selene in acknowledgement.

"Normally, I would not allow someone who was not marked or my cohort to enter my realm, but your persistence about me meeting your lover was admirable and I know you would not want to be separated from her in this great time." Diana smiles with flawless teeth.

Selene bows. "Thank you Diana. I am in your debt as well."

Diana turns back to me. "When you come to me, be prepared to forget all you once knew about right and wrong. You have lived in a world that is oblivious to its true self and therefore, you can no longer see things as you once did. I hope you understand that."

I nod.

"Now, take off your shirt."

I blink a couple times and get ready to open my mouth to question her, but quickly change my mind and do as she commands. Once my shirt is off, I swear I see a look of appreciation in her eyes as she gazes upon my round breasts. Hmmm.

With a motion so quick and fluid, I barely see a long knife materialize from the air and Diana grab it until I realize that she's sliced her hand down the middle. The knife goes back where it came from and Diana takes the pointer finger that isn't on her bloodied hand, rubs some of the blood, and draws a symbol right above my heart. When the symbol is complete, she says some unintelligible words and then slams her opposite hand into my chest right where she drew the symbols. My skin is being branded and I can't help myself as I hiss at the pain. When Diana releases her hand, the symbol is now a part of my flesh, tattoo-like. It glows brightly for a second, then, it disappears into my skin. Confusion paints my face.

"If the symbol stayed visible, supernaturals could find out you were marked and try to kill you," Diana explains as if reading my thoughts. "It will manifest itself when needed. Now, it is done. As I stated previously, you have three moons to summon me again."

Diana waves me away in her queen-like demeanor and motions for Selene to step forward. "I leave her in your hands. She is marked with my blood now, so keep her safe. Now, for my payment." Diana grabs Selene the same way that she grabbed me, but this time when she grabs Selene's face, she kisses Selene in a hard and demanding way.

Before I find words to make a fool of myself, I see that she's not really kissing Selene, but taking something from her. There is a white glow coming from Selene's mouth into Diana's. When Diana is finished, Selene falls to the ground. By the time I reach Selene on the floor, Diana is gone. I barely register the fact that my ankle is no longer in pain. Damn, what did she do?

Selene is able to get up on her own and forces me to go lay down on the couch while she makes us both something to eat. I don't even get to tell her that my injuries are healed. When she finishes, she sits beside me and we both eat in silence. Three moons? I have three nights to decide if this is what I really wanted. They say that life can change in only a matter of seconds, but damn, I am facing a hurricane of issues and wondering if before all this is over if I will drown in my own sorrow.

"What did Diana take from you?" I ask Selene as I try to get my mind off of death, destruction, and apocalypse.

"Well, I told you about chakra or chi right? There is also another part of that. Chakra is what is inside of us, but when it is on the outside it becomes our aura. It is an invisible field that surrounds us all. The stronger the individual, the more powerful the aura will be. It is our strength and our life force. Soon, you'll be able to feel the aura of others. What Diana did was pull some of my aura from me as payment for inappropriately summoning her to this plane without a proper tribute. Because of that, I cost her some of her own aura to travel and she was simply replacing what I made her lose. She had to do so in order to replace any weaknesses from traveling, jet lag if you will. Don't worry, she didn't take enough for it to be a danger to myself, it just made me light-headed. I owed her. I didn't realize how high maintenance the Immortals are."

"I see. So how do you know about Diana?"

"I really don't. She's the first immortal that I've ever met and I still don't know how she heard the call as opposed to someone else. It was actually a long shot, but one of my contacts was familiar with the spell. I'm really good with supernatural history. I know the stories behind the immortals and the humans so I just knew I had to bring one here to see you. You are what I think you are Rayne don't you doubt that. You're special. I'm just so fucking sorry that it had to take this for me to realize it." Selene seems to have her own what ifs going on and I try to stop her train of thought.

"Ok, so what else don't I know about? How many different types of things go bump in the night?" I ask. I've wanted to ask all night.

"You have no idea. Hell, I have no idea about them all, because a lot of the races, like the immortals, don't even walk this plane anymore and have to be summoned. Some, like the fae have died out, or so they say. Vampires, werewolves, and even angels are nothing like the stories. For instance, angels are not ones to fuck with. They are a race of true warriors that usually only live in the otherworld which is where you go when you pass on. If you see one here, that means war or apocalypse is about to break out. They are the balance keepers and from what I've heard or read, completely unstoppable, or at least as close it as one can get."

I listen intently and with mild shock as Selene reveals all this to me. I watch her mouth move and curl up into a smile at just how excited she's getting by telling me all of this. It's amazing how much of a secret her whole world has been to me and I start to wonder if I would have ever known about it otherwise.

"You've met a demon, and trust me, they get much nastier. Some are only incorporeal in this realm, but can wreak much havoc by feeding off of chaos or other things. Some can change forms and live among us. They can also breed with humans in some cases, but the offspring will always be male for some reason. Half demons are not always evil, but they are almost always volatile, terrible tempers. Other demons can…"

I stop Selene right there, even though I don't want to. "Okay, okay, so I have a lot to learn. My brain is definitely on overload right now. How about you just pick the main things that I need to know right now and teach me later?" I suggest.

"Ok, but there'll be a quiz at the end." Selene smirks and winks. "Let me run you a shower. It's been a while since you had one and in the morning you can contact Damien." She gets up and walks back toward the hallway where I came from. Seconds later, I hear water running. Then, Selene comes back and helps me to the bathroom.

When I reach the shower, I see that there's a stool for me to sit on. Selene helps me out of my clothes. I think about milking it for all it is worth because the attention she's giving me is awesome, but I finally give in and tell Selene that Diana somehow healed me. I get a punch in the arm for my confession.

"Well, you won't be needing this then," Selene tells me, snatching the stool out of the shower.

As Selene stalks out of the bathroom, shaking her head, I say, "Thank you," quietly. She freezes in place before shutting the door silently behind her.

Finally alone, I stand there as the hot water beats against my body. This is the first time since everything's happened that I can be truly alone with my thoughts. I'd never see my family again. I'd never hear my little sister's laugh or get to talk to her about that boy Justin that she liked. I'd never get to hug my mom and dad again. And, I'd never get to tell my mom that I was sorry for arguing with her and that I wanted us to have a better relationship.

Then, I think of all the employees who were just collateral damage, the girl whose body they burned because she resembled me, the torture of that man in my dad's building, the pain of having my ankle shattered. Suddenly, I don't feel so safe anymore and I look around suspiciously at the tiled walls and bright yellow shower curtain as if the demon with its horrible mouths and terrible stench will come through the door at any second. My breathing quickens as the walls feel as though they are closing in on me.

What had my sister felt? How did she find the courage to call me instead of just looking out for her own self? Why couldn't it have been me instead of her? Why, why why? I want to break something, pull my hair out, but I can't. I fall to the floor and bawl my eyes out, screaming at the top of my lungs. I want to be rid of all this pain. I want my cries to rip this feeling from my body, this helplessness, this…

I lie there crying, sobbing, shaking. The water has long gone cold but I don't care. Selene doesn't check on me, but I know she's outside of the door beating herself up, knowing she cannot help me right now. Knowing this is a battle that I have to fight alone. I cry, until tears are no longer able to fall. I mourn for the death of my family, the innocents that were our employees, and last for the woman that I once was, but will never be again.

Rest in peace.

Chapter Nine

After I finally reach for the strength to turn the water off, I stand and wrap a towel around my shaking body. I'm positive that I'll catch a cold from this, but that's the least of my problems. When I look in the mirror, I see a stranger in the reflection. Eyes puffy red with black circles under them, a frown that seems to be glued to my face, nose red as well. Quickly, I turn away, unable to bear another glance at myself.

I open the door and Selene is sitting on the floor across from me, her head in her hands. She's had to be so strong for me that I almost forget that she needs to do mourning of her own. At the very least, she loved Jazzy as if she were her own little sister.

Yet, Selene simply wipes her eyes on her sleeve and stands up trying her best to force a smile on her face for my sake. This is a woman that has done so much for me, but has yet to tell me that she loves me. It doesn't matter, she's proven it every step of the way. I smile back at her as I understand that between her and D, they're all I have left.

"Where have you been sleeping?" I ask Selene as I reach for her soft hands.

"In the room across the hall from yours."

"Well, take me there," I tell her.

She seems shocked at this as if she had expected me to not want to be near her yet, but it's just the opposite and that's what I say to her.

"Where else would I want to be Selene? You're my home now."

For the rest of the night, we cuddle and allow our closeness to compensate for the voids we feel in our hearts.

◊◊◊

By the time I reach Damien, he's already in some meetings but he'd been so shocked to hear from me that he cancelled the rest of his obligations for the day and drove straight to the safe house. As I open the door for him, he rushes in, scoops me up in his arms and refuses to let me go for at least five minutes. His broad chest heaves up and down in sobs as he whispers over and over how glad he is that I am okay.

It takes Selene reminding him gently about the need for people to breathe to get him to finally allow me back my personal space. Even then, he keeps a close distance as if I'm going to need him to come to the rescue at any second. After asking me about ten times, he finally accepts that I'm doing fine. Next, we spend half an hour explaining the visit we had from Diana, what an immortal is, and telling him that I will be leaving in two more nights to learn how to possess power that humans had long forgotten they had. He isn't happy about that at all, but at the same time, there is a hint of relief in his eyes that I can and will be safe.

"Is this something that you truly want to do, especially this quickly after this whole thing? Do you want to clear your head first, finish mourning?" Damien asks, even though he knows me well enough to know that my mind is already made up.

"This is not an opportunity I can wait on. If Diana is telling the truth, it has been over 200 years since someone has been marked, well at least by her. What that tells me is that she believes I am capable. Me lying in bed for more weeks crying will not change anything, even if I want to, and trust me, I want to so bad. I want to give up and just waste away, but I won't. I owe my family too much. I owe them justice," I answer D without a second thought. He can hear the passion in my voice and doesn't push. I watch as Selene goes to the other room to give us more privacy.

"Don't worry about your affairs Rayne. Even though it seems as if you are dead, your father has secretely been putting money aside for you for years in overseas accounts. You have more than enough to never even have to work again. Plus, I was able to transfer Jasmine's undisclosed money into your account as well. You can do as you wish with it. No one can touch it but you and me. As far as the company goes, I am in charge now and though I am going to make small changes, you will always have a say and hopefully, there will be a way to bring you back from the dead and you can run it yourself," Damien tells me.

"I don't want to run the company, that much I know, you can keep it as long I get updated on major issues and changes. All I want right now is to know what was so important that my family had to die. What was such a secret?"

D takes a deep breath and sighs heavily before leaning back and taking off his sunglasses that he loves so much. He rubs his face and says, "We were working on special weapons that would help combat supernatural threats in many ways. Modern technology doesn't really seem to have an effect on their kind, so we had to change our way of thinking. Bullets have no effect unless you shoot them repeatedly with kill shots and besides, most are too fast to even be shot. We've been studying their nature and developing new tools based on their perceived weaknesses."

"We had plans to sell it to the government. There's a branch that deals with the Supes but they are limited on their research because they are a new group and have only found out about the existence of supernaturals about fifty years ago. Even then, only a handful of higher ups are privy to this information. They'd very much like to keep exposure nonexistent as well as deal with the more dangerous of their kind quickly and quietly."

I nod and Damien continues, trying to quickly get through the background info. "Since then, it has been hard because many of the supes actually have been working in government and are even feeding misinformation to humans. They are doing their best to keep the accurate knowledge to a minimum. They've been extremely successful because most people don't know what their powers are or how to recognize someone as 'different' from the rest of us. Your father was a brilliant man however, and brought together the most excellent team, best contacts, and finest researchers out there because he felt that humans needed more protection against such a potentially dangerous threat. You see, when your father was in the military, he came across a werewolf that was on a rampage. His team was on a mission in the Ukraine and apparently the wolf had been recently turned without learning to control its urges. He was able to kill it only because it was too consumed with ripping apart the body of one of his comrades. That incident was covered up like many others."

"It wasn't hard to connect the dots. If one existed, then they probably all did. Jason was not prejudiced and didn't feel that they were monsters that needed to all be taken out, but that we mere humans needed extra security. As his research and business grew, so did his reputation. Jason started to attract the wrong kind of attention and many of the people in the supernatural community who had inside knowledge of his weapons wanted him to stop production, sell his products to them as well in order to use it against members of other 'races', or just for added protection for themselves. Small stuff, like security enhancements he didn't mind, but things that could be too dangerous in the wrong hands, he refused."

"His intention was to give the weapons to the government, the humans he wanted to protect. He even hoped that one day we could market them to the public under a guise like colored contacts that keep vampires from glamouring people for example. If the government had gotten a hold of some of these weapons, then I'm sure the same thing would have happened. They could have started a war themselves, and this is where Jason and I disagreed." Damien takes a small sip of the drink that Selene had given him once we sat down and then stares me down hard.

"Rayne, please understand. You are my family. No matter what I disagreed with, you have to know that I would have never stood by and let anyone or anything do that to Jason. I'm saying this because whoever is behind this hit, they felt the way I did and I know that it looks bad. When you saw your father torturing that man, it was because he had kidnapped those researchers to copy the work they were doing at the company. Your father refused to sell him anything and they did not want to take no for an answer. The man warned him that if he wouldn't sell to his employer, then he needed to shut down his research. Jason ignored his warnings as well as mine that what we were getting into was a dangerous road."

"I don't doubt for a second that you had nothing to do with this and I kind of see your point, but, there's more to this isn't there? There's a piece missing, I can feel it." I lean forward, enthralled in our conversation.

"Well, yes, other than the fact that I can't get any fucking information on who's behind this shit. You'd think they'd want to announce to the company what they did to prove a point not to fuck with them or not take their demands seriously. Right now, we are just watching our backs and reassessing every single person or company we've ever done business with. That could be their plan too, to throw us into chaos and confusion and I have to admit, it's kind of working. It's the same strategy that terrorists use. They are slowing our entire production down and some of our best people who know the truth have resigned."

Damien stands up, clearly stressed as he rubs a hand over his dark hair. "But, there has been talk that it is becoming more difficult not to risk exposure for the supes and that a type of governing body of their own may be forming if they haven't done so already. I don't think those people like that either and it seems that they may be trying to arm themselves for a type of power struggle. We already know that individually, each race has their own way of dealing with their kind, but now, they may be working together like never before."

He begins to pace with his hands behind his back while he speaks. It's a sign of nervousness that I don't often see from him. "That may spell trouble of a different kind if we push too hard. We may outnumber them in terms of bodies, but with their combined strength added to the fact that we have only myths and rumors to rely on, it could end tragically with a war unlike anything the world has ever known. The problem is, we can't trace anything and that's the problem with dealing with the supes, it's hard to find evidence when they truly don't want it to be found. They have ways of making people forget or see things that are untrue. The only thing we do know is that the person we are looking for is a magic user. Selene is the one that figured that one out."

We both look at Selene who doesn't seem ready to offer any more information, so I start.

"So, let me make sure I understand all of this. My father wanted to keep a special group in the government armed against supernatural threats. You, and this mystery person or group, both think that by doing so it could lead to unnecessary 'witch hunts' against anyone who is 'different.' This group wanted dad to either sell them the same weapons or stop production completely, for a price of course. My dad refused. So, this person had one of his men kidnap the researchers and then kill them as a message. When that message was received, dad retaliated by hunting the guy down and torturing him in revenge. Then, the same thing happened to my family."

I stop for a second as I figure something else out. I put my hand over my mouth in shock, but finally continue after Damien looks at me in confusion.

"It was all a game. You just said that supernaturals can keep things like identities and evidence from being discovered if they don't want it found, right? Well, I'm going to assume that that is only the case when dealing with humans, that we can't always find supernaturals, another reason why dad wanted these weaknesses compensated for. He probably got angry and thought that he was able to track the man who killed your researchers down through his own brilliance, but that's not the case."

"Whoever is behind this wanted that man to be found because as you said, my father had a reputation. That person knew, he knew that his own man would be killed and he was betting on that, using his death as an excuse to take out my father and even our family because he was too much of a threat to the supernaturals to live."

Damien looks at me as if he's been punched in the gut. He sits back down slowly. I look to Selene's disgusted face too as the air in the room seems to get heavier. I know I've hit a homerun. I have great analytical skills and it really didn't take much for me to figure it out once I got most of the evidence into place. I just can't believe it. My father was so much of a threat that whoever ordered his death felt as though it was the only option. Everyone played into this person's hands and that made him or her, a serious menace.

"I can't believe this shit. And in the meeting, I argued with Jason in front of the guy about how it may be a mistake selling to the government. He must have gone back and reported it. Oh my God, that's probably the only reason why I'm alive. I wasn't seen as a threat." Damien looks as if he's going to be sick, but if I'm honest, I'm sure I look the same way.

"Then whoever this person is has a lot of power and experience. They have to have a lot of followers who believe in his cause plus money to get things done. We already know he is witch born, that much I'm sure of. It has to be a male and he has to be over forty years old. That should narrow the field down to about twenty possible people. This is when the list gets scary. My advice would be to just let it go, but I know it would be disrespectful to your family to push that, so I will say instead, we must tread carefully. I can give you a name of an informant who may be able to point you in the right direction," Selene tells us firmly.

"Are you sure you have the right contacts and skills for this?" Damien asks.

"You have no idea who I am or what resources I have at my disposal. I may live modestly, but I can assure you I have plenty of means to get what I want. The problem is deciding what the price will be for the information we may obtain. My world is a dangerous place and in my world cost brings on a whole new meaning."

"And I," Damien begins.

"Will not put yourself in any unnecessary danger. Pay someone to get the information we need. Money is no object. You need to run the company. Will you make sure I have enough funds when I get back, a place to live, and arrange a way for me to see my family's graves tomorrow without me being followed? I need to say goodbye," I tell him much more authoritarian than I probably should.

He stands up slowly and puts back on his sunglasses so I can't see the emotions behind his eyes. Still, I could be blind and see the pain he's hiding. What a pair we are. Both of us cut more deeply than any knife could ever reach.

"Ok Ray Ray. I will pick you up at seven in the morning tomorrow. Be ready."

I get up and hug him tightly. "I will. I love you D."

"I love you too." Then, he kisses my forehead, waves to Selene and leaves, shutting the door quietly.

Deep breaths keep me from shedding any more tears.

Chapter Ten

I take a nap and when I awake I find that Selene is watching me, rubbing my head and whispering something quietly to herself in a musical tone. I think I am becoming more attuned to her magic because now I can feel the slight wind around me as she speaks. It calms me and I smile my 'thank you' to her. All those times I thought she was muttering to herself or when I felt a tiny spark of electricity, she was actually using her magic and I had no clue. Crazy.

"You were having a nightmare," she tells me.

I try to think back to my dream but I can't, which is probably just as well. I'm sure I can guess what it was probably about. "Well, I don't remember it, I just felt you and woke up."

"Good. It seemed like it was bad. I was worried."

Selene seems to be doing more than her fair share of worrying about me and now, it has to stop. I need to be able to do the worrying for myself.

"Soon you won't have to protect me. I will be able to do it on my own. I know Diana said that I may not survive it, but I know I will. There is no other option for me."

"I believe in you, but I will always worry about you. That's what people do when they're in love. They worry about the other person. You're my responsibility," Selene tells me honestly, lovingly, and my heart skips a beat.

"About damn time you said it," I smile.

"Well, you've known how I felt all along. I still have my issues, but I trust you Rayne, I do."

"And I will do my best not to give you any reason not to."

"Good. Now, can you do me a favor please?" Selene asks, as she pulls her hair back, out of her beautiful, sad face.

"What is it?" I ask quietly, enjoying our closeness.

"Can you just hold me for a while?" Selene asks, surprising me.

"Of course love," I say, understanding that she needs to be the one to feel safe after working overtime to make sure everything was fine with me. I wrap my arms tightly around her waist and pull her into me. Selene lays her head on my chest and I inhale to smell of vanilla in her hair. We lay together silently for hours, me never breaking my hold on her.

◊◊◊

Damien knocks three times on the door and I hurry to open it. As he steps in, Selene calls out behind me.

"Are you sure you don't want me to come with you?"

I had already had this conversation with Selene earlier about how I just wanted to say my goodbyes alone, that it was something that I needed to do. I feel sort of selfish because I know how much Selene loved Jazzy, but ultimately, I need this time to be exclusively mine. I can't do the next step with Diana until I take this trip by myself. I know Selene understands that, but I also know that her feelings are hurt.

"Yes, I'm sure. I have to do this alone," I say with finality.

Selene just nods and kisses me quickly on the lips before leaving the room, the hurt slowly filling her eyes even as she tries to hide it. I frown, but keep my resolve. Damien gives me a pat on the back and reaches for my hand. I decline. I can do this.

I get in the car and buckle up as Damien says something into the Bluetooth that he's wearing. Seconds later, he gets in, looks in his rearview for a few seconds, then pulls off. Five minutes later, he stops the car and tells me to get out. I don't question it, simply follow orders. Next, we get into a dark Suburban with tinted windows and a driver who I recognize as a man named Tanner. His salt and pepper hair and serious face is hard to forget, especially after I've given him hell a couple times in the past. This time, he doesn't even acknowledge my presence as I get in the car, probably afraid of any breakdown he thinks I may have.

The ride back into the city takes two hours and no words are hardly exchanged on the way, except for Damien telling Tanner to circle a street again or to get off of the main road and then get back on. I don't ask any questions as my mind thinks about how bad it would be for us if we were to be ambushed by someone who realized that I wasn't really dead, or if it even mattered that I wasn't. Wouldn't it be even better for the game knowing that I did live? Wouldn't that increase the fear and chaos? My mind asks these questions until we pull up to the cemetery. Then, Damien finally addresses me.

"Are you ready for this?" A loaded question. Five simple words.

I sigh and open the car door. "Which way?"

Damien gets out and points me toward the direction. "There, in between those two big oaks, and really close to that bench."

I look at the oak trees bowing over as if they're weeping for my family as well. I try to take a step forward, but my feet seem to be frozen. I look back at Damien with desperate eyes. "If I go over there and see their graves, then it's all true. This really isn't a bad dream," I say, fear creeping up into my throat, causing my voice to betray me.

"If you go over there, you will see that they are at peace. No more pain. They are just resting, waiting for you to join them again," Damien tells me trying to ease some of the unfairness of the whole situation, of life itself, and of this irrevocability.

"Ok," I whisper and find my feet again. I walk two hundred twenty three steps until I stop at the graves, until I see not only my family's, but of the unknown person who is occupying my spot. I bend down and touch that marker first, the one that bears my name and I say a prayer for her, for her family. Then, I touch my parent's.

"Hi," I say, not knowing where to begin, having never done this before. Definitely not thinking I would have to do this so soon. I sit there for a moment then look up to the sky. "Mom, I'm sorry that we hadn't really had a chance to work out our differences, but I did listen to your opinion. I did listen even when I pretended I didn't. I know that you always had my best interest in mind and that you loved me no matter what. I get a lot of my strength from you. If I could have told you this when you were here, maybe we could have been much closer. I hope that even though I didn't say it, I hope that deep down you knew it."

I turn and put my hand on my father's headstone, the wind picking up as if my family's spirit has come to listen in. "Daddy, I want you to know that I forgive you for your decisions and that I don't blame you for any of this. I talked with Selene and D about your business, your choices, and what you were trying to accomplish. I may not agree with you on everything, but I know you based your actions on what you felt like you were doing to help people. You are the greatest father in the world and you've always tried to protect me. I love you and mom both and I hope you're taking good care of Jazzy."

I turn to my sister's grave and think about all the promise she had in her, our last conversation, how independent she was and how brave she had been trying to keep me safe. I try to hold my tears in, but I can't, and I quickly give up trying as it becomes nearly impossible to breathe again.

"Jaz, I don't think I could have done what you did. I wouldn't have been able to think as fast, be as brave. I love you so much for what you tried to do to save me and I blame myself because maybe if you weren't thinking of me, you could have been safe. It should have been me, not my beautiful, smart, little sister. If I could take your place I would in a heartbeat Jazzy, I promise you that. But since I can't, I'm gonna do the next best thing, I'm going to get justice for you."

Tears flow freely onto my baby sister's grave. "I will fight as hard and as long as I can to find out the truth and to make sure they know who you were and what they took from me. I'm sorry that you won't be able to live your dreams and I will try everyday to keep you alive in my heart and mind. I can't believe this is really real and I don't know how I will be able to get up every single day knowing that I won't see you, but I will do my best because you would hate it if I just gave up, but it's going to be hard. I just hope that I'm strong enough."

After about an hour of conversing with my family, hoping they heard every word I said, I finally leave them behind, in the ground, where time doesn't matter anymore. I had told them everything I knew about what happened and even explained to them what I was getting ready to do with my life. When I said everything I felt that needed to be said on this visit, I actually felt slightly better. I felt as if they had all gathered me into their arms and told me that I was going to be okay. Part of me wants to believe it, and that will be the part I hold on to.

I look back one more time at their resting place and whisper another goodbye, knowing that I won't be able to come back here for a while and I don't want to forget where to go or how at peace the world looks from my vantage point at the moment. I have to hold on to the love that they had for me or else I will destroy myself with grief. I have a purpose now and I'm not allowed to break down anymore. I feel that; I understand that. Life would never be fair, easy, or simple. This is a truth that I need to hold fast to as well. Bottom line, regardless of what happens in this life, we must go on. My father taught me that.

"You look a lot better than you did going in," Damien observes as he opens my door for me.

"I feel a hell of a lot better too," I say as I slide in and he closes the door behind me.

When he goes around to the other side and hops in, Tanner immediately starts the car, but this time, I see him give me a little smile through his mirror. He was worried about me and now that my demeanor's changed, a sense of relief has washed itself through the entire SUV. I give him a nod in acknowledgement and he pulls off. It will be a battle with my pain, but now, I feel as if it's a battle that I can actually win.

"I need you to make a stop for me. Damien, can you make arrangements at another safe house that's close to here?"

Damien turns to me confused, trying to figure out what's on my mind. "Well, sure, but we can't stay long, I have a couple meetings," he answers.

"It won't be long. I just need you to grab a few things first."

◊◊◊

When Damien drops me back off to our original safe house, it's about seven hours later. Damien and I hug one last time, tightly, before he stretches our embrace out to arm's length and takes a long look at me. I watch one lonely tear fall from his eye, and I catch it and wipe it away.

"I know what you're thinking D, and I'm going to tell you not to worry about me. I will make it through this and I will be much stronger. I know I'm going to be gone a long time and won't be able to contact you, but the minute, no, the second that I can, you know I'm going to call. I love you," I try to assure him.

"Ray Ray, you've had to grow up really quickly and I'm so proud of you. I know you're who Selene says you are, because you've been that all along. You've always been brave and kind and protective. I just don't want this to change you into something you're not. You hold on to who you are. Do not let any power that you obtain corrupt you. Do you hear me? Don't seek out revenge, get strong so you can protect yourself," Damien speaks, his voice shaky. "I don't want to lose you too." I know he isn't just speaking in terms of death.

"I can only try," I tell him, not willing to promise him anything yet.

"You are your father's daughter," he responds after one final embrace. "I will see you later. No goodbyes." He waves at me and walks away, not turning back once as if I won't be there anymore if he does.

"Later." I call back, too late because the SUV is already driving off. I don't even stand there alone for two seconds because Selene is at the door trying extremely hard not to run to me.

"I was worried. It's been hours," she says instead.

"I know. I'm sorry, but I had to get some type of closure," I respond levelly.

Selene waves me in the house, then, really gets a good look at me. After about twenty seconds of staring, she smiles. "So, you decided to chop all your hair off and color it like Jasmine."

"Yeah," I smile back. "She would've loved to see me like this. I think I read somewhere that in some cultures when a family member dies, you cut your hair. Well, this is my version of it. It's so every day when I see myself in the mirror, I see her too. Not to mention when I train, it'll be more manageable."

"Well, you certainly look even more like twins now. I love it."

We smile simultaneously.

Then, I get serious. "So, this is the final evening we have together alone for a while and I don't want to spend it sad and afraid of what's next, but I do have some questions."

"Okay. Well come sit and I'll see if I can help you out," Selene says, sounding studious.

She pats the spot next to her on the couch and I sit close to her, collecting my thoughts. I don't know how much she'll be able to answer, but it doesn't hurt to ask. "So, what do you know about the training that I'm going to have to go through?"

Selene shrugs her shoulders. "Nothing really. I've never met someone who has gone through it, I just know the stories and that those who are successful went through hell." Selene sees my face turn up into a frown and changes tactics. "But don't worry. I would never ever in a million years have summoned Diana if I thought that you wouldn't be able to handle this. I've had my suspicions about your potential for a while now, but after the Devourer, I knew you were different."

"But, why? What have I done or shown you to make you even think that I could be eligible to have this 'mysterious' power that humans thousands of years ago negotiated with the Immortals?" Oh my God, saying it out aloud truly makes this sound like a sitcom. I put my hands over my face, bracing myself for her response, and expect to magically hear clapping from an invisible studio audience.

"Baby, listen to me. You have this force about you that you don't even see. Do you remember the time that we were out at the club and that poor guy was getting pushed around because that dude thought he was looking at him sexually? What did you do? You picked the guy up off the floor, wiped him off, marched up to that asshole and maced him all in his face."

I laugh. "Don't forget, then I kicked him in his nuts," I say as I remember the situation and how angry I was that no one else did anything to help him even though about one hundred people had seen what was going on.

"Right! You didn't even know that man, but you wanted to protect him. Seriously, even though you could've gotten hurt."

"Because what's wrong is wrong. That man had no right to do that to him just because he thought he was hitting on him. Shit like that just pisses me off."

"Rayne, that's not all. What about when we were at the swimming pool and you dove in, swam faster than the lifeguard and saved that little kid who was running, slipped, and fell into the deep end?"

"But, he was drowning, I just-" I try to diminish what I had done, but Selene abruptly cuts me off with a wave of her hand.

"But, there was a lifeguard who was right there. Someone who was trained to save people, someone who was more than capable to save the kid, but you couldn't handle it. You had to save that kid, because you knew that you would succeed and someone else might fail. And if that lifeguard would have failed you would have never forgiven yourself, so you put it all on yourself. You know I'm right Rayne. I know you, I know how you think. Don't you see? You have the qualities of someone who has the potential to do great things. You didn't let fear consume you then or with that demon. You *are* the prophesy Rayne and now the Immortals are going to equip you with the tools to be a force. Embrace it and don't second guess yourself," Selene tells me in a compelling way that makes me believe because she truly believes what she is telling me as well.

"Am I really that awesome?" I smile.

Selene leans in and kisses my forehead. "You saved my life when you had no idea what you were facing. I think you're pretty fucking awesome meu amor."

"Okay. I'll believe you then. But, what do you know that will be able to help me when all this goes down?"

"Well, you just have to keep believing that you can pass all the tests. You can't defeat yourself before whatever they throw at you has a chance to. So you have to go in there believing you are meant to do this, that this is who you have always been. Next, time does not run the same here as it does there. One month there could be about three months here. That's partly why the immortals chose to leave this plane. Eventually, they start to age and there it slows the process. Still, they only age about every couple hundred years give or take, so if you see an Immortal that looks like a child, do not treat them as such. They are probably thousands of years older than you."

"Wow. So they're not truly Immortal are they?"

"Yes and no. They will not die of old age, they ascend."

"Okay, explain. And what the hell is ascending?"

"It means that they reach the end of their lifespan and then go through a ritual where they are drained of their aura and then are reborn. It is almost like reincarnation, into yourself."

"Ok, wow, I don't think I want to know anymore about what that entails. Moving on. What else do I need to know?"

"Well, um. Let's just say, Immortals are not shy about their sexual needs and will take and share lovers with no problems," Selene says hesitantly, but still trying to hide a grin.

"Well, they can just count me out. I don't want a ten-year-old-looking-but-actually-thousand-year-old trying to take my goodies," I say.

"You say that now, but the Immortals are like uber sugar daddies. They shower their lovers with lots of gifts and rewards," Selene says as if to test my reaction.

"Ha. I think I'll pass. I will try to be as respectful as possible about it," I tell her.

Selene lifts an eyebrow. "Who said I was talking about you?"

I punch Selene softly and she chuckles making me feel relaxed. "I'm kidding Rayne. If I did that, they might forget all about training you," Selene shoots back.

"Don't make me leave you here Selene," I warn jokingly.

"Okay, okay. I couldn't deal with that. I'll stop," Selene promises, crossing her heart while her accent makes me shiver. "There's something else too. Although I'm not sure what other awakened groups live on that plane, you can be certain that the immortals are not the only inhabitants. So, we must be cautious because they may not all be kind."

"I understand, I'll be careful. Now come here. There's something much more important than talking that our lips could be doing." I pull her into a slow meaningful kiss that she gladly reciprocates.

Chapter Eleven

Before we realize it, it's dark outside. Both of us unwillingly peel ourselves off of each other, still locked in our embrace. I give Selene a quick kiss on her now swollen lips before I stretch and yawn. Judgment time.

"So, what's next?" I ask, feeling butterflies in my stomach.

"Take a quick shower and I'll get everything ready. I won't summon Diana until you're absolutely prepared," Selene assures me, putting a hand firmly on my shoulder, her naked body still calling to me. I mentally shake myself and touch my scarred arm so that I can remember why I'm getting ready to do this.

"Alright. I won't be long."

After I shower, I throw on a black tank top and some green yoga pants, since I'm a little short on a wardrobe right now. Besides, I don't know how I'm supposed to dress to go to the realm of the Immortals. I laugh a little inside at the thought that not only am I doing this, but I'm concerned about what kind of clothes I should be wearing to go to another dimension in. What in the hell am I getting myself into?

Finally, I bring myself to take the steps into the living room where Selene is standing, waiting patiently for me. She turns to face me and smiles and I can't help but do the same because of how sure she is about me. "Are you ready, Rayne?" she asks.

I nod, then say, "I'm ready. What do I need to do?" I close the gap between us and catch Selene with my gaze.

"Nothing. The candles are all lit and in place and we are already standing in the circle. I will just say the incantation, cut my hand for three drops of blood, and then call out to Diana. A gate will open and she will come for us," Selene explains as if she does this sort of thing every day.

"No," I tell her. "I will cut my hand. It's the least I can do. I'm the one marked so it should be my blood. You said that last time you didn't know what Immortal would show up, but if I do it, it will surely be Diana who comes," I say insistently.

"Hmm," Selene responds, studying me. "You might be right. We can try it your way then."

"Good," I say and then reach out my hand, ready to get this over with. Ready to start my life over again, to become more, someone who protects.

Selene places a gentle kiss on my lips and then steps back to grab the knife. I unconsciously gulp at the thought of the knife slicing my skin, but Selene doesn't seem to notice. She grabs my hand firmly and looks at me one more time before nodding. A second later, there's a slice, then a burning sensation as a little bit of blood begins to pool out of my cut.

"Don't do anything until I look at you and then drip three drops into the air like a triangle like this." Selene demonstrates in the air and I nod in understanding. Then, she continues, power dripping through her words, "Ah signum ma rah. Um Immortalis rekesch. Ah fidelis ad mah rah. Um tah rah Immortalis sanguine ad rekesch," She chants it three times before looking at me and then I do as she instructed making the drops of blood into a triangle in the air.

For a couple seconds nothing happens, then suddenly, my hand stops bleeding and I am in a vacuum. Where I put my blood, I feel a pull and I gasp as the air itself rips open and reveals some sort of portal. All the lights and candles behind us go out and then, even more so like a surround sound system, I hear Diana's voice swirling around us, demanding, and yet, amused.

"So, you've made your choice, child. Then, come. Step through the portal and begin your awakening. I am waiting here for you on the other side. But know this, you either succeed or you die. Step into the world only with the intent of triumph, because even the slightest hesitation can cause you to be lost forever, stuck in the grey between our worlds."

I gulp one last time and look back at Selene who now has locked her hand into mine. Without saying a word, we both step forward and into a world I never even fathomed could exist. The pull is strong and I find myself almost flying toward the exit and almost letting go of Selene's hand. I fall to the ground and barely get to catch my bearings. The air feels different as if it's heavier against my skin, tastes different because it is lacking the pollution of my world, and even smells different here like there are different species of flowers and animals. Everything seems brighter and as I try to shield my eyes, Diana's standing over me with a sadistic look in her inhumanly blue eyes. I try to scoot away, but powerful hands grab me.

"Un-make her," Diana orders the hands.

Before Selene or I can protest, before I even see who's clutching me, the bright lights of this world go out.

◊◊◊

Cold. Dizzy. I slowly open my eyes and visually explore my surroundings. It's dark, but not so much that I can't see anything. However, I feel like shit. My arms are killing me. My hands are chained above my head and as I try to pull myself free, a sense of fear creeps over my entire body. I'm on my knees and the heavy weight of the chains causes my arms to shake.

I realize that I do have enough give in them to be able to stand, but not much else. To do this, I have to shimmy up the wall scraping my back against the jagged rock. I'm completely naked, exposed, afraid. The chains won't budge and Selene is nowhere around. At least while I'm standing, the chains allow me to put my arms to my side. It's all very unpleasant still. The shackles upon my closer inspection are rigged so that if I try to pull them off, I could end up peeling off all my skin, if not scraping bone. If the tiny drops of blood forming on my wrists are any indication, I'd better be careful.

What's going on? I thought they were going to help me, not lock me up. Diana's words run through my head. 'Un-make her.' I become frantic and pull harder on the chains trying to free myself as I forget exactly what I just learned about the shackles. I learn my lesson with a sharp cut to my wrist. I break skin and hiss in pain. I call out Selene's name urgently, hoping that she will come to my rescue. Instead, someone else shows up, another Immortal.

He's tall, blond hair, with dangerous green eyes that are staring at me like a hungry lion. I study him as he stalks towards me, smirk on his face. Like Diana, he is nearly glowing, otherworldly. He has on no shirt and his grey bottoms look like a type of sarong. His body is that of a swimmer. Lean, muscular, but not overpowering. On earth, he'd give Brad Pitt a run for his money. Here, there is no doubt that he's a warrior. He lifts up my chin and studies me silently. That's when I notice the sword and try to pull away. I'm not familiar with blades, but it looks like a machete, only much sharper and older. He just laughs and turns his back to me, pacing for several seconds.

Finally, he says, "I'd been expecting you to ask a million questions by now. Why am I here? What are you going to do to me? Where is my lover? But you, young one are surprising." His voice is deep and commanding as it echoes from all over the room the same way Diana's did when I first met her. In this deep cavern or dungeon, it is even more eerie as his voice seems to even reach the high ceiling. Where Diana's voice is similar to someone who lived in England long ago, his voice sounds more modern, even if the same accent is still there.

I still stay silent, afraid that my voice will betray the fear inside.

He continues. "Well, I am Lawrence, the younger brother of Diana and the best weapon forger in the land. That will suffice for now. It has been a long time since there has been a human in our midst and I must say, I do not think you will be with us for too long."

"Why is that?" I ask quietly, flinching as the shackles eat into my skin.

Lawrence takes three long strides and is so close to my face that I think he's going to kiss me. "Because, young one, no human has ever survived being un-made by me."

Before I can even process what he's telling me, I am being impaled by his sword right through my diaphragm, upwards, until the sword exits nearly at the base of my neck. The pain explodes through my whole body and I am screaming inside, but no words form on my lips. Lawrence locks eyes with me and I cough up blood right in his face. Ignoring the splatter of blood on his brow, he smirks in pleasure at my pain.

He retrieves the sword and it's more painful going out than in as he slowly turns it inside of me. My vision wavers and I lose control of my bladder as reality sets in. Is that why they stripped me naked? Excruciating pain, humiliation, and paralyzing fear eat away at my soul. I can't even tug at the chains as my strength becomes nonexistent. I feel my life being cut away and confusion sets in. I don't understand this. I came here to get help, not to be murdered in cold blood, tied up, with no way to defend myself.

Suddenly, Lawrence slams his palm into my wound and the heat from his hand seeps into my skin. I feel the wounds inside me stitching themselves back up and I gasp for air with tears in my eyes. He's healing me and the pain recedes, leaving me more confused than I was in the beginning.

"Why?" I whisper, tasting blood on my tongue.

"Why? Now, you ask the questions after you have tasted the steel of my blade. Fool. Because you are weak and I do not think you are worthy of the mark that you wear. Because fear rules you and revenge calls to you. How anyone could think you could ever have any power inside you is unfathomable. I know you will not prove me wrong. I will break you, human. I will torture you, heal you, and then start all over again. When I'm done, you will beg for death to take you and I will gladly oblige. There's one other thing that I forgot to mention about myself. I apologize for not telling you this bit of information sooner, but I am the greatest master of torture our people have ever known," Lawrence tells me with such heat in his voice that I begin to sweat. I don't even have a chance to take another breath before I am impaled with his sword again, this time piercing a lung and causing me to black out from the pain.

I awaken after what seems like days upon days to find myself dripping with sweat. My hands are now raw, my lip bloody, and one eye is swollen shut. Lawrence has healed the worst of my injuries, but has left just enough pain so that I remember every slice, every punch, every broken bone. For three days he has come and assaulted me, tortured me, and mocked me. On the third day, I begged for him to stop, pleaded and cried that I wanted to go home. He told me that he would not only kill me, but Selene too. I spit in his face.

He laughed, unchained me, then strangled me with the chains. After that, he water boarded me. I think I went mad until he knocked me out. A small mercy. The worst part is the knowledge that I'm getting ready to feel unimaginable pain all over again, that I will only be able to remain chained like an animal and take it. And to what end? Even if Lawrence continues to heal my wounds, surely I'll die from the shock, hunger, or thirst soon enough.

Now, I hear footsteps returning and I panic. I cannot keep this up. I'll never be able to withstand another punishing hour of this. I am alone, weak, hungry, and so thirsty. I have to buy some time to get free of this. I pretend to be sleep as I listen to the footsteps get heavier with their closeness. Maybe then, he'll leave me alone for a little while longer so that I can think and rest.

Icy water splashes all over me and I yelp, then growl in pain from my sudden flinching. Now, I'm just fucking mad. I open my eyes and blink out the remaining water as I start to shiver. There's nothing left for me to lose now. My shivering from the cold becomes trembling with rage. Lawrence looks at me in amusement. I look back at him like I want to rip his head off. He pretends not to notice.

This only makes my anger grow. I'll repay his ass if I ever get out of here. I promise myself that.

"Rayne, is it?" he asks, saying my name for the first time. "I'm glad you're awake. Your lover Selene was asking about you. I told her that I didn't think you'd last much longer and she looked concerned. Maybe I should bring her here to say goodbye."

"Why?" I ask. "Where are you going?" Not the best comeback, I know.

A flash of surprise shines through his mischievous green eyes and then it disappears. "Was that a joke? Delightful."

"I just want to know if that's all you've got? Are you really threatening me now after all you've already done to me? I don't fear you or any of this anymore. Right now, I just want to destroy you," I tell him calmly. Fuck him and his glowing skin. I'll peel it right off of him and use it for a nightlight.

This time, he laughs a loud booming laugh. "Thank you Rayne. This is the most fun I've had in years. Then, he slices my upper left thigh and I hiss in pain. He raises his sword at me again, but I try to swing away, ignoring the protests of my too raw wrists. He misses and I try to counter with a kick that's nowhere near the target. Lawrence laughs again at my attempt to scramble away and head butts me something vicious until I see stars. Before I can shake off the blow, he comes at me again and slices my stomach. I stumble back into to wall and hit my head again.

I take a deep breath and stand as upright as possible with the blood beginning to pool on the ground around me. Then, I feel it. The power building up inside me, the will to survive, and it clicks. It is like an inferno roaring to life, a wall of water breaking through the dams. The minute I stopped being afraid and started to fight back is when the power started to flow. This whole time, he wanted me to feel helpless, hopeless, weak, and afraid. It isn't about just having the will to survive; it was about being able to be in a life or death situation and still being able to be courageous.

This test is meant to force me to find my power and awaken it. I had to remember my goals, my family, why I was here doing this. I had to forget all I once was, my weaknesses, and become something more. I had to be un-made. The entire world seems to slow down then speed back to normal as I see things as if for the first time. My new senses explode.

Lawrence comes at me again with a forward strike. This time, with new eyes, I'm able to follow his movements. This time, with new strength, I rip the chains free of the wall and wrap them around his neck pulling as fiercely as I can manage as he runs the blade through me again. It doesn't hurt like it did the first time and the surprise on his face gives me the ultimate satisfaction I need. I collapse in his arms after he pulls the sword out of my stomach and I loosen the chains on his neck. He scoops me up like a baby and pulls me close to his chest before kissing me on my forehead.

I grin stupidly as he says, "Well done child. Your mark is glowing. You have unlocked the secret to your power and you have been un-made."

Damn right.

Chapter Twelve

This time when I wake up, it's to the beautiful hum of Selene's voice. She's running her fingers through my hair and I put my hand on top of hers. We lock eyes and I see that she's been crying. Quickly I sit up and question the reason for the tears.

"I'm just so proud of you. I didn't know that you'd be tortured Rayne or else I never would have called on Diana. Please believe me. I would never put you through that." Selene spits out her apologies, but I silence her with a finger.

"None of that matters now. That part is done. I can feel the power inside me and it feels incredible. I pull aside the sheet that is wrapped around me and look at my body. No scars, no pain, it's amazing. I smile at Selene to show that I forgive her, that I never even blamed her.

"Lawrence healed you about six hours ago and said that you'd probably be out for a couple days, but I guess he underestimated your strength. They'll want to start to ceremony immediately then," Selene says.

"What ceremony?"

"Apparently after someone unlocks their power, there is a celebration and an introduction to the eldest of the Immortals. I don't know anything else about it."

"Well, okay then. Let's get this over with. I want to keep going with all this."

"Don't be in such a hurry for punishment Rayne. Lawrence is already excited about teaching you to fight with weapons."

I laugh. "He probably just wants payback for me choking him with the chains."

"Yeah, he's told everyone within hearing distance how you broke free and tried to choke him to death. He's very proud of you and wants to take you on as his lover," Selene tells me, extremely amused.

"Oh really now? Well do Immortals understand the concept of being a lesbian?"

"No, they understand the concept of bisexuality extremely well though, but exclusively attracted to only one sex, or only one partner, it's absolutely preposterous," Selene laughs. "Still, if you let him down gently, he'll probably leave you alone. He sees your willpower and it attracts him, that's all."

"Well, I'm flattered, and even though I have no interest in men, like that, maybe he can tell me more about this more than one lover thing," I joke.

"Ha ha, very funny. You wouldn't know what to do with two women in your bed."

I raise my eyebrow at Selene and smirk. "I'm sure I could find my way around just fine."

"Well, you're just going to keep imagining that, cuz this one right here does not share."

"I wouldn't ask you to," I tell her, kissing her lips.

"Good. Because if you did, I'd find a spell to cut you in half and then tell *you* to share."

We both laugh as Selene pulls me out of bed. "Come, let's go find Diana. I'm sure she's anxious to see you now."

We walk down a long corridor filled with beautiful marble columns that remind me of a Greek palace. Everything is elegant, bright, and warm. I feel like royalty as I stroll through and admire the tapestries of purple and gold, the elaborate paintings depicting naked men and women, epic battles, elegant feasts, and the unmatched architectural beauty that is this home. If I didn't have a job to do, I could get comfortable here for a long while and probably never have a care in the world. If only the circumstances were different. I shake myself from my wishful thinking as we reach a massive wooden door with gold trimmings. Selene knocks purposefully and seconds later, a familiar melodic voice answers us.

"You may enter."

Inside is a space that looks like a bedroom, but is so large that even I, who grew up with much more than most, have to do a double take. The bed itself can hold about four people comfortably, not to mention the furniture that is not only large, but looks soft and inviting in neutral colors. The art on the walls would make Da Vinci look like macaroni art. Then, there's Diana standing at the double glass doors which are open, leaning against the frame with both hands, her golden dress tied at her neck, but the back cut so low that I can almost see her ass. I have to clear my throat in order not to drop my jaw at her beauty. What a sight it is indeed.

I glance over at Selene to see if she's watching me, but it seems as if she's enjoying the vision in front of us as well. I don't feel as guilty. I take a couple more steps forward before Diana finally turns around, her hair swinging seductively in her face and I have to wonder if she's doing it on purpose.

"Rayne, it is a stunning surprise to find that you have unlocked what was hidden inside of you. My mark was the first part of the key and only by ridding yourself of fear and believing in your strength were you able to put the rest of the pieces together. Child, there are great things for you to achieve and here we will make you a powerful weapon. Now that you have been un-made, I can teach you the ways of the supernatural and extraordinary. Now, you will be able to see the world as it has always been. You are one of the awakened," Diana tells me, delighted. She touches my shoulder gently and the mark on my chest comes to life with a powerful glow. I feel excitement coursing through my veins and I say a silent prayer to my family.

Diana looks at Selene and states, "You may now take your leave, witch. I have business with the child and I have arranged for Kaede to go over some ancient writings with you that may be useful in the future." She dismisses Selene a little more rudely for my tastes, but I decide to leave it alone for a while.

Selene ignores her pride, thanks Diana and kisses me on my cheek before leaving us alone.

"I may not necessarily be a mind reader child, but I have lived long enough to pick up on the slightest hint of body language or facial expressions. If you do you not like how I treat your witch then say so. Speak up for yourself young warrior or you will not be heard," Diana tells me as she lifts up my chin, examining me like a doctor would a patient.

"Fine. I don't like how you dismissed Selene as if she were a servant. She's my girlfriend and if it wasn't for her, I wouldn't be here," I admit.

"I will try to be more kind in the future," Diana says, with slight humor in her voice.

"What is so funny?" I ask, starting to get upset with her attitude.

"You amuse me is all. It has been too long since I've been in the company of humans. Lesson one then Rayne. We are not human, you cannot expect us to always behave in the way that your kind does. Remember that will be the truth with other types of supernatural beings that you encounter as well. Many of us are more long lived than your kind and your cultural expectations are not always relevant or familiar to us."

"Well, maybe you shouldn't have given up on us," I say before thinking.

A flash of anger and something more deadly crosses Diana's expression, and then her calm demeanor returns. She ignores my statement and says, "So, Lawrence tells me that you have the spirit of a true warrior. He is quite taken with you."

"I can't say that I'm too fond of him yet, since I know more about the sword he carries than the man himself."

Diana laughs and motions for me to follow her through the double glass doors. We step out into a beautiful field of green, purple, blue, and pink, headed towards a small body of water. I breathe in the crisp air and realize that I can hear birds in the distance and voices farther down the way. A new found talent no doubt.

"Lawrence is one of the best warriors we have to offer. It is an honor to be held in such high regard by the likes of him. He even believes you will be a suitable lover." She glances back at me as we cross the sand near the water.

"Hmm, so I've heard. I think I'm suitable enough without his help thank you very much. This human has only one lover at a time," I tell her firmly, hoping she gets the hint.

"You are young yet. You will seek more hands," Diana tells me as if saying that the sky is blue.

I laugh. "Well, Lawrence doesn't have the right set of hands that I like," I respond.

Diana frowns. "This I do not understand."

"I have no interest in men," I say honestly.

"Oh, so you are waiting for my favor then." Diana nods.

I laugh uncomfortably. "Um, no, Diana. With all due respect, I need no one's favor. Selene is enough for me."

"Well, I can accept that, for now. But later, you may want to learn what a true lover is or maybe even both of you will reach out to me. After all, your witch is a beauty and force all her own as well. She will be a great high priestess if she chooses to work hard."

I stand there for a few seconds, my eyes going to her hard nipples and I try not to groan. It's hard not to be attracted to someone who literally radiates beauty, but I can be attracted to her and still be in love and faithful to Selene. That is what I'm going to do.

"Diana, if we ever have this conversation again, let it be on my terms," I plead, trying to tear my eyes away from her body. My senses are heightened right now and I really need to learn how to keep them in check. That is the only explanation as to why I am acting like this.

"Fine. You will see though that the power awakened inside of you will rouse different desires. With the flames of power, the flames of passion so too arises. You will seek it, crave it," Diana warns.

I will take my chances. For now, I am just passionate about ending this conversation. I change the subject as we continue to walk into a breeze, adjacent the shimmering water. "Diana, what kind of powers did I unlock? I want to understand what this all means."

"The amount of power may differ among humans, but it is obvious that you have a lot of strength inside you. For some people, even without the help of the mark and the un-making, a small amount of power comes through. Those are people who excel in the arts of fighting, are extremely fast, or even feel as if they can sense things that others cannot. If they were ever marked, they'd have remarkable power. You, are somewhere in between. You may not have exceeded the way some whose power had slightly manifested, but as your urge to protect grew, your power began to leak. I believe that is why your witch was able to recognize what you could be in the first place. She may not realize it, but she felt your power," Diana explains.

We stop at the edge of the water and it's so clear that I can see straight to the bottom. I reach down and touch the water. The temperature is perfect.

"So, how much power you have, I do not know, but I can guess that it's enough to make you not only a force, but a threat. You may become a target back in your world if you're not careful. Still, when you are through with this training, you will be more than able to protect yourself and those you hold dear. Depending on how hard you train, you powers can only grow. They are not at a set limit. What I can say assuredly is that your physical strength has improved, your reflexes are sharper, your speed has increased, and your emotions are now heightened. If you were of normal intelligence then your intelligence has just grown slightly, but if your mental abilities before were exceptional, then they are now even more so. Any assets that you used a great deal before will be even better now."

"I nod in understanding. Well, I was a fast swimmer before, so I should be even faster now. All those muscles that I'm used to working will work better then."

"Precisely, child. Would you like to try it out?"

I look out at the water and smile. "There aren't any sharks or some mythical creature out there that will eat me right?"

"Not to worry. There are no merpeople or shapeshifters in these lands. They dwell in the lands of the west," Diana responds seriously.

"Oh," I say. "Good to know." After all, I didn't want to be attacked by a mermaid on a Friday night. That would just ruin the rest of my evening. I wipe my face as I try to get used to hearing about all these things I never believed existed. This is my world now. The rest of the human race may have turned their backs on it a long time ago, but I am going to embrace it as much as I can, especially if it will help me find justice for my family.

I strip off my outer layer and stand there in my bra and panties that I received from them. Everything fit so perfectly. I'd have to thank the local tailor. Normally, I'm used to tying my hair back, but now that it's cut short, I don't have to worry about it which feels a little strange. Still, I walk out into the water until I can sort of dive in and I start to swim with long even strides.

I feel so free and normal that I don't even notice how far I've gone so quickly until I realize that I can't even see Diana anymore. Still, I don't turn around. I keep swimming, pushing my limits, faster and faster, until I reach about four small waterfalls. The water is pounding down loudly against the rocks below. I take in the hills on either side of me, the green contrasting so boldly with the blue of the water that I almost cry. There are hundreds of different types of fish swimming along with me. I can even see their colors clearly through my watery paradise. For a few minutes, I simply float on my back, admiring the beauty of this world.

"You could stay here forever, you know. But, I thought there was something you needed to do back in your world," Lawrence calls to me from the cliffs above.

I call back, "I was just remembering how I used to go to the lake with my sister. I wish she could have seen a place like this. She would have loved to paint it."

"Then paint it in your memory and tell her about it in the next life. You can tell her of your struggles among this peaceful background as I mold you into a warrior."

"We will train here then?" I ask, suddenly excited. The land itself seems to be feeding me power.

"If that is your wish, then yes. But now, we have to go back and prepare for the ceremony,"

Lawrence tells me, pointing me to a spot where I can climb out.

I reach him with surprising ease and then he pulls me upright. Lawrence gives me a look of pure pride and I smile back at him with the satisfaction of knowing that he thinks there is a potential inside of me to be a great warrior. Then, I also understand that he will absolutely push me to my breaking point in order to make me reach a level that is satisfactory to him. I'm in for a hell of a ride.

Lawrence pats me on my back. "Come. We will run back to the village. You will try to keep up," he orders.

"Fine," I say, knowing this is going to be interesting. He bolts in front of me before I even have a chance to gather myself. I can already tell that he's going to be a bit of a show-off.

It is interesting alright. What I didn't know, on top of me not having any kind of footwear, is that I'd be zig zagging through trees, running up hills, jumping across divides, and much more. I get lost once or twice when I can't keep up, but Lawrence comes back for me, encouraging me, or rather, pissing me off by laughing at me until I try harder, run faster and finally make it back to the village.

We traveled one hell of a distance in a short amount of time. My muscles feel amazing as if they are a brand new model. I begin to understand my strength and my speed, when to push it, when to keep it in check. My mind is quicker as if all my synapses have begun to fire; more of my brain is being used. This feels like the state I was meant to be in all along. The power is swirling through me as if it is finally free from a prison, long forgotten with no hope to ever be unbound. There are no longer any invisible chains holding me back. Only forward. One step at a time.

◊◊◊

"Let us prepare," Diana states as she appears from the entrance of her enormous home. I look around at all the homes in the village. They are all grand in some way, from the gold that trims them to the sheer size. Each one is built in a design from a different era, probably a time that each liked best. I see villa styles, Roman designs, temple-looking homes, and even some that look like small castles. I guess when you have nothing but time to acquire wealth, this is what you get. There is no excess dirt on the paved road, hardly any commotion, and everything seems to be in its place. This land has had a long run of peace.

"Kaede! Take her to her chamber. We will being at dusk," Diana orders.

I look around for this Kaede until I see a girl who looks no older than ten peek around the corner of the doorway. It creeps me out that in reality she's probably over 900 years old. She bows to Diana and then me. I do the same, not knowing the proper custom for greetings. Diana then looks towards me. "Go now child. There is much anticipation over you."

I nod and follow Kaede until I reach the room I woke up in. She follows me inside and points me to the bed where there is an elegant red robe with intricate black flame patterns covering it. There is also a black sports bra type thing and some type of spandex looking shorts. I pick each item of clothing up off of the bed and examine them. The quality is good and the material is breathable. Although I'm not digging the idea of these spandex shorts, I know that they serve a purpose.

Finally, Kaede speaks and I'm aware that I'm getting more used to the surround sound of their voices. Hers is more like a soft wind chime than the powerful melody of Diana or deep drum of Lawrence. "You must purify yourself first by bathing in our special herbs and salts. When you are done, you will dress and I will then escort you to the receiving chamber. When you arrive there, you will light all three candles and wait to be called upon. The rest of the ceremony will be easy to follow."

"Who will all be in attendance for this?" I ask as she walks me to the pre-made bath.

"The ceremony itself will consist of our twelve elders and maybe a few others. When the celebration begins, the numbers will be much more. It has been a couple hundred years since the last ceremony and I'm sure all are excited to see what makes you so special."

Great, so I will basically be put on display for the entire world to see. How fun.

"Where will Selene be?" I ask her.

"Your witch will be allowed entry into the chamber but I do not know if you will be allowed to converse with her or not," Kaede further explains.

I become slightly irritated. I will be extremely excited when I can do things on my own terms, especially seeing my girlfriend.

"Do not get upset young warrior. You must understand that you now have responsibilities that must be taken care of before pleasure. Is that not why you are here?"

I turn to face Kaede who is looking at me with a serious look on her face. I frown. "Did you just read my mind?"

"I cannot simply pull any thought from your consciousness; however, I am attuned to heightened emotions. My empathy can weaken the barriers of your mind and allow me to glimpse those deliberations," Kaede explains matter of factly.

My temper begins to flare at the violation as I recall how Diana had pulled thoughts from my mind, but I quickly put myself back into check for fear of being exposed once again. I will have to remember to be careful about what I'm projecting around these Immortals because if they discover something they decide they didn't like about me, I'll be in no position to do anything about it.

"That is an interesting gift Kaede, thank you for sharing that with me," I tell her as sincerely as possible.

"I will take my leave now. When you are ready, all you have to do is call. I will hear you." She bows once more and then disappears from the room leaving me standing alone and not entirely trusting of these Immortals.

For now though, I'd have to just stay on guard and learn all I need from them.

I hope I purified myself correctly by soaking, then submerging myself in the bath for a while. I don't feel any different and it isn't like it's something that I do on a regular basis. After putting on the under clothing, I drape myself in the robe. It feels soft and silky against my skin and for a second I feel as though I'm back at home in my robe getting ready to watch movies in my bed. My heart aches and I wonder if I will ever not feel the big gaping hole in my soul from the loss.

After a couple minutes, I call Kaede who appears just outside of the doorway. She motions for me to follow and I fall in step behind her as we travel through the halls, courtyard, the center of the village, and into a small arena. The sounds at night are much more alive than during the day or maybe it's because I am focusing harder this time. I can hear crickets chirping see lightning bugs dancing in the distance. The sound of the lake gently caressing the shore calms my nerves and the laughter of people preparing for my celebration in the distance makes me feel welcomed here.

Kaede points me to a door which must be the receiving room and I step through. The room is musky and dank and has the feel of a holding cell. I look around and find three different sized candles on a small round table. For a couple seconds I look around for something to light the candles with, but I quickly realize there is nothing. They must have forgotten the matches or something when they were prepping for the ceremony.

Then suddenly, it hits me as if I've had the knowledge the whole time. Reflexively, I walk to the first candle and state. "Life." It flickers to life right before my eyes and amazement washes over my entire being. I step to the second candle and say, "Death." Again, it begins to burn brightly. At the third candle, I smile, and think of my un-making, how I felt a new me had arisen. I begin to understand the cycle of the life of an Immortal and how it ties in to the test that I had endured. Loudly, I say, "Rebirth." The third candle shines brightest of all.

Chapter Thirteen

As I turn away from the three candles, attempting to still understand the knowledge that I was somehow gifted with, my mark begins to glow. I place my hand over it and feel the warmth radiating from it. Beneath it, I can feel my heart pounding excitedly for what's coming next. The wall in front of me slides away and I am facing the center of the arena, with twelve glowing faces looking down at me in a c-shape, from their seats above. I become still as the force of their power hits me, threatening to knock me over. I can tell that it is a purposeful thing and I know that I am still being tested. As I look around, I see Selene to my right, standing in anticipation.

"Rayne Whitmore. You have proven that you are indeed worthy of the promise we made to your kind many millennia ago. You may step forward young warrior," a voice prompts.

I step into the center of the floor and wait.

"You were able to reach inside yourself when death and defeat were claiming you as their own. You found you power, a power that was embedded deep within you, a power that was allowed to stir due to your mark, and that was broken free of its chains by your will. This is not something to take lightly. Power can create chaos and destruction in one's life if it is not cultivated in the correct way."

I nod and bow. I know full well the price that power could have on one's life.

"Now, show us what you can do," another one of the Immortals says, standing up and clapping his hands as if calling on something.

Selene walks up to me and kisses me on the cheek before taking off my robe. "We have a gift for you," Selene whispers to me, a fire in her beautiful eyes and I look around, wondering what it could possibly be.

I feel its presence before I see it. My mouth becomes dry and I have to lick my lips a few times. Lawrence appears with a longsword and hands it to me. I look him square in the eye, then he kisses me on the forehead.

"Destroy it. You have a fighter's instinct, just listen to your gut."

My heart rate quickens. I didn't think that revenge would come this soon or easily. I'm almost disappointed at that. Two more people, cohorts I'm assuming since they are not immortals, bring in the Devourer, chained and fighting back, its mouths snapping every which way. Its footsteps pound loudly against the stone floor and I clutch my sword tighter. I stare at its dirty, massive body that seems to be covered in years of grime and filth. I didn't notice that before, but now, I'm more aware of the smallest features this monster possesses. I watch its face turn towards me, saliva dripping down its fangs, two slits on its face sniffing the air. I hope it remembers me.

"Release it," demands Diana. The cohorts quickly unchain it and I steal one more glance at Selene before motioning the Demon to come and fight me, sword clutched in both hands, my stance low as I wait to strike like a viper waiting for its chance.

This time it's different. This time, the Devourer knows that it's not the predator and that it's fighting for its survival. The pure animalistic instinct kicks in as it lets out a thunderous roar that shakes the walls of the arena and comes barreling towards me with the size and speed of a small truck.

I think about my father's martial arts lessons and root myself firmly into my stance. As the Devourer gets closer, swinging its massive arms towards my face, I sidestep with a speed that matches its own and throw it off balance. The Demon crashes into a wall with pieces crumbling all around it. With fury, it grabs a large stone that broke off the wall on impact and hurls it towards me with such speed that I barely have time to raise my sword and react.

I swing fiercely and bat it away, but in no time, the Devourer closes the distance and lands a blow that has me skidding across the floor like a grounder in major league baseball. Finally, my back finds the wall and the wind is knocked out of me followed by stars in front of my eyes.

Then, I'm being slid up the wall by my neck and I barely get my hands up in time to block the blow that is directed at my face. I find enough leverage to push off of the wall to knock the Demon down and roll free of its grasp. It's clear to me that waiting for it to attack is not going to get me anywhere except for pummeled, so I go on the offense, trusting that my speed is superior to its own. I sprint toward the Devourer, sword raised, but at the last second switch my grip to land a slice right in the midsection of the monster.

It cries out in rage, but my rage is greater as I remember my mom's broken neck, my sister's bloodied body, how Selene said that my dad's heart was ripped out of his chest. I don't care if these Immortals can read my mind when my emotions are high. I want them to see the pain and suffering in my mind, the need for the justice that I am about to deliver. I want them to feel my resolve as I promise myself to never again be weak or afraid.

We exchange blows and blood pours from both of us. It doesn't matter though. I see clear enough to understand that the blood I shed will be no where equal to its own. It feels like the fight is lasting for hours as I feel my muscles grow tired, but I push on, giving as much as I'm getting, my face bloody, and painful. The Devourer manages to knock the sword from my hand. I think about scrambling to get it, but change my mind. I don't need it anymore as I can feel the Demon's strength weakening as it is the one who is now afraid. It probably has never had a human who fought this hard. I got away once and this time, this demon won't.

It lands another kick into my midsection but I manage to scramble out of the way before it can inflict any more damage. I dive under its legs as the Demon tries to tackle me. Next, I land a kick with so much force that it jars my whole body and sends the monster to the ground so hard that it bounces off the stone.

It doesn't get back up. I walk to the spot where the Demon had first broken the stone off the wall and pick up a nice large piece. The Devourer begins to stir as I reach the spot where it now lay. I stand over the Demon, victoriously and burn the image firmly into my memory. I study the thing that murdered all the family I had.

"I will find out who sent you, and then I will send him to hell to visit you," I promise, before I send the stone down on the Devourer's skull, over and over, until there is no skull left to shatter.

In that moment, I truly know that I will never ever be able to go back to the Rayne that I once was.

Chapter Fourteen

Drunk, happy, and naked, I lie in bed with Selene. Finally alone. After my ordeal with the Devourer, the Immortals, threw me a giant party the likes that I'm sure not even Charlie Sheen, Jay-Z, or Hugh Hefner has ever seen. There were naked men and women everywhere. Not just naked, but attractive, supermodel attractive, every last one of them. Plus, they were having so much sex it was insane. Their equivalent to alcohol is incredibly strong, tasty, and had me rethinking my monogamy as well as my sexual explorations.

Boy, did they know how to throw a party. And the best part, it was all because of me. Most of them had not seen a human for so long that all of them were willing to entertain me. Even the music, though a bit medieval for my tastes, had been in full swing the entire night. And people said that my generation practically had sex on the dance floor when we danced. Well, they literally had sex in the town square, while they danced. It's safe to say that Selene kept a close eye on me. I had to remind myself about twenty times that I had to eventually go back to our world.

"Come on Selene, it'll be the first time we've done it now that I got powers. We don't have to hold back. Plus I got more stamina," I tell her, rolling my hips seductively.

Selene looks at me and shakes her head. She's pretending to not be as drunk as me, but I know the truth. I saw her downing those drinks like a sailor. Is that even the right phrase? Who cares. "No. Your drunk ass will prolly jusss throw up on me," she tells me, slurring her words. Fake.

"Who's drunk? You are the one wobbling and s-slurring." I reach out, grab her arm, throw her on the bed, and claim her lips. She fights me for all of two seconds before returning the kiss, then deepening it. I moan quietly in her mouth and shift my body so that I'm on top of her.

"Do you. Still. Think. I'm sexy?" she asks me in between kisses.

I freeze just before I make my way to her neck and lift up so that I can look her in the eyes. I may be drunk, but I can be serious in order to assure her.

"You are incredibly sexy and I am so attracted to you. Yes, these Immortals are very good looking, but you have everything they have if not more." I tell her, head pounding.

"And what's the more?" she asks.

"Your personality. You are actually someone who knows how to brighten a room." I smile at her. I don't particularly like the temporary setback to my foreplay, but if I can make her feel good about herself, then it's just as well. "None of these Immortals know me like you know me. We have a bond and no matter how pretty someone is on the outside, if they can't make me smile or laugh the way you do, if they don't care about me the way you do, then it doesn't matter. I love you Selene. I'm in love with only you. Their looks don't have anything on what's real between us. You're here with me in this weird world because you care about me. No one can compete with that." I gauge her reaction and hope that she understands me.

She smiles and kisses me on the lips, but I pull away, needing to add one more thing.

"Plus, no one here has an ass like yours, and I need me a woman with some ass."

She laughs and flips me on my back. "Well then. I expect you to show me just how much you appreciate this ass."

"Oh, I will," I respond, getting turned on as she traces her electric fingers from my neck to my center. I feel her magic surround me and I moan in delight. "Thoroughly."

Selene then enters me with two fingers as she pushes a storm of power deep within my middle. I gasp and arch as I feel all my nerves come alive. The magic courses through my body until I'm shivering with desire and need. She then removes her fingers from inside me and I immediately feel their loss.

Licking her two fingers slowly, seductively, Selene whispers, "You've always tasted so good to me. Warm and sweet."

"Then, don't tease me. Why don't you just take it?" My voice is low and needy with anticipation. I watch her green eyes grow darker with desire just before she lowers her head to my dripping middle and takes a long, agonizing stroke from my clit to my opening. I can feel the controlled magic dancing on her tongue. The heat of her driving me crazy. My body threatens to explode all too quickly, the need to finish so great.

I roll my hips to adjust where I need her mouth the most, but she doesn't comply and I growl in frustration which just causes her to laugh.

"Be patient," Selene commands.

She slides her long fingers back inside me and begins her slow torment on me, pushing inside, licking me slowly, but purposefully. I run my fingers through her long hair and I whisper to her not to stop.

Her other hand explores my breasts, my nipples, my stomach, sending small surges of power through me until I can't even begin to tell where the pleasure is coming from. My entire body is one big nerve and every single spot she touches on me feels utterly amazing.

I feel my climax building up and I start to moan louder and breath heavier as it begins to break through the surface. Then, everything just stops. Selene pulls away from me, just before my eruption and I look at her in frustration, nearly growling again. Quickly, she claims my lips before I can announce my protests. She then repeats the entire process three more times, until I am nearly half insane with need.

"Please baby," I sob.

This time, Selene climbs on top of me, spreading herself open so that her clit is now rubbing against my extremely swollen one. I moan at the feel of her warmth and wetness and grip her back tightly as she begins to grind her body against mine with passionate roughness. Her slickness mixes with mine and my clit goes crazy under the pressure.

Selene pushes harder and moves faster until the pressure on my clit is too much and I explode, bucking under her. Still, she doesn't stop; she rides me until her own climax comes, powerful and sensual on top of me. We lay there unmoving for a few minutes before Selene finds the strength to roll off of me.

She's lying on her stomach and I begin to kiss every inch of her back. I make my way to her ear and bite gently before saying, "Now, let's test this stamina of mine."

◊◊◊

When I finally awaken, my body is pleasantly sore and I can still feel traces of Selene's magic on my skin. Seeing her lie there looking like a goddess makes me want to repeat every second of our pleasure right now. I lean down and press my lips softly against hers and to my surprise, she reciprocates, and pulls me down to her. Clearly, she had the same thing in mind. I smile and let my hand travel down her body. We begin to kiss with more urgency when there's a knock outside of the door.

"May I enter?" Diana's voice calls from outside.

I have half a notion to say no, but I finish my kiss, cover our bodies, and say, "Yes. You can enter Diana."

She steps inside and then takes in our appearance and then smiles. "I would love to let you continue with your lovemaking; however, from the looks of it, you would never get out of bed. Under different circumstances that would not be a bad thing, but considering what you accomplished last night, I figured that you'd want to get started as soon as possible so that you can start learning how to use your new strengths. Lawrence and I have both agreed that you seem like that type that is not easily broken. We shall push you to become great." Diana takes more steps toward us, her sheer dress revealing her nipples underneath and I try to look away without Diana noticing, but of course she does. She even gives me a look to let me know that she saw me watching. Super. Just super.

Diana turns her focus to Selene. "There are lessons for all of us to learn here. Some we may enjoy more thoroughly than others. Being pushed to our limits is an enlightening feeling."

Diana turns towards me. "Lawrence is waiting for you at the falls." She then leaves the room.

Selene and I stay silent for a couple of seconds, both interpreting what Diana just told us in our own way.

"She read your mind, didn't she?" I ask, already knowing the answer.

"She tried to, but I realized what she was doing and then she stopped. They are prideful beings, so much so that it may be dangerous. They need to feel like they possess you in some other kind of way and it frustrates her that you aren't going for it. Diana's trying to get to me and I was almost letting it work."

"But what is the point?" I ask growing irritated and confused.

Selene sighs. "These Immortals like to obtain valuable things. Strong magic users and some others can tell who I am by just feeling my aura. I would be of use to them too if they still lived on our plane, as it is, their magic is stronger than mine so I am of no use to them."

"So, if they want to possess me, do you think this whole thing may have been some sort of mistake?"

She hesitates. "No. Right now, I think it's just a game. Pretty soon, they will grow tired of playing and leave you alone. They are testing your will to see if your resolve is a true as you claim it to be."

Well, I sure hope so; after all, I am only human.

Since I don't really remember the run back from the falls, I swim there again. Being in the water just truly seems to refresh me. By the time I reach Lawrence, my mind is firmly set on my goal.

"Thank you for bringing me the Devourer. Selene told me that you hunted it for me even before I got to your realm. I can't believe that you were able to find it so quickly," I tell Lawrence.

Selene had told me that Diana informed Lawrence of my memories of that night in case he would need the information to break me. He thought that if I was able to be un-made, then having the Devourer be my first kill would be a fitting gift. I concurred.

"It was not a problem. I enjoyed the hunt almost as much as I enjoyed watching you destroy it. It has been an eon since I've traveled to a hell dimension, albeit a minor one. I had to use the blood of one of my cohorts that is familiar with some of the demon worlds. We went and traced the demonic signature from your home to the place he came from. After that, it was extremely simple. I did have to kill a couple demons myself, but it was well worth it. You have made things much more interesting for me Rayne Whitmore."

"Well, thanks. I'm glad I could help," I reply sarcastically.

He ignores my eye roll that went along with it. "You have a lot of fire inside you, young one. Now, I will teach you how to truly fight." With that, Lawrence kicks me so hard that I fly off the cliff and back into the water with a painful smack. A second later, he is pulling me further down. I barely manage to take a breath before I'm completely under water and doing my damndest to break free of the submission hold that he has me in. When it's clear that I won't be successful this time around, he allows me to swim up for air. I gasp for breath, gulping the air as if it's a sixteen ounce drink and wipe the water from my eyes.

"Lesson number one: when you fight, you do what it takes to stay alive. You need to be prepared to do battle in all kinds of scenarios, on many types of terrain, with many different handicaps. Do not panic. Allow yourself to overcome the obstacles so that it is always you who is still breathing. Think about your un-making. Why do you think that the first punishment I put you through was torture?" Lawrence floats close to me, pressing me for a response.

I already know the answer and as I finally catch my breath, he pulls me under again, holding me until the very last second that I can hold my breath. I want to kill him, but I force my rage down and try to remain calm as I suck in air. Getting upset will only make it worse. I won't be able to focus and I may not be able to hold my breath as long.

"Because it's the hardest thing to overcome. It's not only a severely painful experience, but it is a mentally devastating feeling too," I try to say quickly so that he won't pull me under again just yet. I think about my own experience and how I felt at the time. Even when you aren't feeling more pain than you can bear, you have to continue to tell yourself that death would not be a more welcome experience.

"Precisely. If you've known the greatest suffering, then, even if you fear it, you can be more prepared for it." With that, he reaches for me again, countering my block calmly, and pulls me down into the deep water, dragging me further below the depths.

Chapter Fifteen

Eight months have gone by since I'd been marked and entered the realm of the Immortals. Back on the mortal plane, it's been nearly two years since my family was murdered and I was stripped of the chance to grow up like a normal person. These days, I look at myself and barely even recognize the Rayne that I once was, the carefree, happy, young adult.

I've kept my hair short, but the red that I colored it to honor my sister has grown out greatly and my face shows the knowledge of a deeper pessimism of the world that I will soon return to. That young woman who was unsure and afraid of this power is now a distant memory.

As I stand before myself in the mirror now, I see a woman that will never hide from shadows, but someone who has become part of the shadows. The loss I feel for my family is still there, eating at the back of my heart and soul, but somehow I've managed to continue to move on, or at least I've learned to hide it from not only myself, but the ones around me.

Even Selene has changed. She's been working hard in secret, memorizing and mastering high level spells, weaving signs, and learning how to fight with her magic. From what I've heard from Kaede, Selene has become a force of her own. I'm proud and grateful that she has taken this step in order to be able to stand along with me in my quest to find justice. It's even better that she seems to have found herself as well.

Since I've been un-made, which is the awakening of the powers hidden inside humans, powers that were gifted to us by the Immortals thousands of years ago, I've had to be re-taught the truth of the world and the supernatural races that live in it. I've had to accept witches, vampires, werewolves, demons, Immortals, and even the elusive fae. I've had to learn how to recognize these creatures, how to defend myself against them, how to track them, their habits, and much more.

I've gone on hunts with the Immortals to protect the land from outsiders who have ventured through the gates of this realm, attempting to destroy what the Immortals have built, trying to claim their secrets, and rule their region. And I've killed without hesitation, without remorse.

Simple fact, I will kill again, and for better or for worse, it gets easier every time. I look down at my now rough hands and I try to remember how soft they were just eight months ago and I can't. I clinch both hands into a fist as I leave my reflection and push those memories to the past. I go to find Lawrence.

The Immortals do not exclusively live in the realm alone, which is why they have an army in the first place. Their home is more like a vast kingdom with about three towns that is valued for many of its resources. The resources must be protected not only for the sake of the Immortals themselves, but for the protection of many worlds. They hold secrets that many have thought lost for millennia. Each secret has been well worth killing for because the lives saved could never be measured.

Lawrence has been training me to be a killer and Diana has been grooming me to be an encyclopedia so that on the battlefield, I can make split second decisions, or even one day a Machaera or Sword, which is a Protector for the Immortals. Becoming a Machaera means to be granted immortality, to be given great responsibility, especially protecting those resources which are powerful artifacts and even keys of pure energy that can unleash some of the world's most deadly beings.

As of now, there are five Machaera alive. The oldest one has been around since 3 B.C. His name is Constantine and I am told that he once saved an entire village from a demon called Typhon that breathes fire. It is rumored to be trapped by magical bonds in Mount Etna this very day. Its eruptions are supposedly caused by the demon's rage. The other four are spread out in other realms, fighting the good fight and such. Three males and two females. The Immortals said that I could be the sixth, that I had that potential if I kept growing.

Yet, right now, all I'm focused on is finding the man who ordered my family to death and every single day I come closer to that goal. Every day I grow stronger and smarter. My training is almost coming to a close and soon I'll be back in my world where I can hunt him down. Diana has told me that learning about something in theory and actually doing it in the real world are two completely different tasks.

Even though I may be able to hold my own against some of the weaker or younger Immortals doesn't mean that I will be able to fight off a pack of wolves, especially when the moon is full. I need a cool and clear head at all times and I can't let the need for revenge or hatred take me over. It would be the death of me.

Creatures like the Luna Dasa, the moon's servants, as some of the older wolves call themselves, can be over five times stronger under the moon or if they are in moon rage and the beast inside them has gone mad. Especially if it is an alpha, the leader of the pack, who can pull even more strength from his pack from their pack-link if they are near, I may not stand a chance.

I won't even get on what a pure blood vamp could be capable of if they are in bloodlust. Plus, the longer lived a vampire, the more deadly and less human they can be. In other words, I may be able to put up a fight, but I can't cheat the facts.

As I head to my meeting place to speak with Lawrence, I spot Selene in a nearby garden, pulling some herbs in a long, flowy lace dress. Compared to me in my dark tunic, she looks like an angel. She notices me, smiles, and waves me over as she pulls her long dark veil of hair from her face. I step closer into the garden and can smell the various plants, flowers, and herbs. Selene has always tried to get me to remember the names, but I've never really been able to keep up on them. My knowledge extends to purple cone shaped plant, smelly, prickly leaf flower, and green thingy.

She has accomplished something that is made possible with her high priestess heritage where if she does a spell enough times successfully, it will imprint into her chakra and she will be able to weave a sign for the spell or simply say an incantation. From what I've heard from Diana, a high level spell done wrong is pretty draining and dangerous stuff because it will both consume your life force quickly and kill you when used too much, or you could succumb to dark forces in your weakened state.

However, since Selene is technically a high priestess, her chakra level is much higher than most and can exceed normal limits. Still, the more complex and powerful the spell, the more energy she expels. Because of this, Kaede has been forcing Selene to push her limits even more in her training and also teaching her how to make potions that may sustain her chakra longer as well as replenish it faster. I'm sure she's picking the herbs for them now. I call it the energy drink for witches.

Selene stands up and wipes off the excess dirt from her clothes. Today she looks a little ragged and tired. I notice the hint of bags under her beautiful green eyes and the off-coloring of her skin and I frown as I take her into my arms.

"Don't," Selene warns before I say anything. "I know what I look like and I'm going to take a break in a little while. I plan on sleeping and cuddling with you all day once I pick the herbs to help me make a potion to help my body heal."

"What kind of healing?" I ask protectively.

"It's to help me heal from the emotional pain of this lack of sex. I mean damn, it's been almost two weeks." Selene jokes, trying to keep me from worrying.

I play along. "Well, if that's the case, we can do this right now." I start to strip out of my shirt, but she grabs the bottom of my fabric tightly.

"Mine. Not for show," Selene growls.

"Wow, with that tone, one would mistake you for a Wolf," I tell her teasingly.

"They aren't the only possessive race I can promise you that. But seriously baby, don't worry about me right now. I just need to relax and heal. I'm working on high level spells that are pretty draining, but I will be refreshed tomorrow. Go do your task with Lawrence, and then tell him I said you are taking the rest of the day off to be with me, no arguments. And if he thinks he can test me, I will find him; better yet, I'd send Diana after him."

I laugh, then shudder at the thought, remembering when Lawrence had lost me in the hills on one of our training sessions. It took Diana three days to find me and when we finally met back up with Lawrence, she punished him something vicious. With all that anger, it was a wonder that Diana wasn't training me.

I travel through the trees, the wind blowing teasingly at my back, bringing the scent of the lake with it. After about a five minute trek through the growth, I squeeze through a few more trees until I come upon the workspace that Lawrence requested that I meet him at. He's standing, shirtless as usual looking as if he's in his late thirty's instead of the millennia that he really is. He once told me that they long ago stopped keeping track of their age. His glowing skin a flawless, permanent bronze that models would kill for and the shoulder-length blonde hair that he has been allowing to grow makes him look like a god from a Greek myth.

I don't have to be a straight woman to appreciate beauty like this when I see it. I'm also sure it frustrates him that he can't charm his way into my pants. The other day, he'd said that the passion of our lovemaking would be so strong that the earth itself would tremble. I trembled in laughter.

Lawrence is not like one of those guys at the bar who keeps on thinking that he can turn any lesbian straight with his spectacular bedroom moves. He is an Immortal, and that means to him that everyone is bisexual, that sex was a bond you share with people you respect, a celebration that only takes two beautiful people and opportunity. Sex for them also meant sharing their power and life force. It recharged them. It made sense to me that they would do it so frequently.

He definitely doesn't have a human point of view on sex, especially the bisexuality. Gay people and straight people alike just couldn't always accept that people could like both sexes. It was just that he couldn't understand how someone didn't like both sexes.

They are also strong advocates for threesomes. Diana had tried that angle with Selene and me. I wasn't as quick to refuse that offer as I had been when I first arrived. Selene and I both said no, but I have to admit, I did have some images running through my mind. I also think Diana knew I had considered it. Hell, she was absolutely beautiful, alluring, and powerful. So was Selene. It would have been mind blowing. To be able to taste their power together would have been ecstasy.

Once, I had walked in on Diana with a fae (one of the few left on this plane) by the name of Celeste. I actually don't think it was an accident; since Diana had a habit of summoning me during her sex sessions, I couldn't take my eyes off of the scene in front of me.

They both knew I was there. Hell, Diana had been the one to call me, but she had something to prove. Immortals are prideful beings and she wanted me to know what I was missing, the power trip I could have enjoyed. Let's just say, after that amazing performance, I rushed straight back to Selene and ripped her clothes off, literally. I never told her exactly why I'd been so eager that night. I'm glad she never asked.

"Rayne. It is especially good to see you this day," Lawrence tells me, eying my legs for a few seconds longer.

"As it is to see you Lawrence," I smile as I respond with my own greeting.

He claps his hands together and waves me toward him. "Come, let us not delay. I have a gift that is ready for you."

A gift? Sounds interesting. I follow Lawrence into the workspace and immediately the scent of something burning hits my nose. I frown. Hopefully, he didn't cook for me.

"Come, come, Rayne." He pulls me closer and points to the table.

There, lying on the table is a beautiful katana with a snake's tail carved expertly from the tip of the blade, seemingly wrapping itself around the entire katana until its deadly looking fangs reach near the hilt causing it to look as if it's coming out of the snake's mouth. The blade itself is white as snow reflecting back at me like a mirror. White steel? The hilt itself is wrapped with purple cloth making the diamond pattern that katana's have. The curve of the blade is perfect, the craftsmanship sharp. I gasp at the beauty of it, almost afraid to touch it. I look at Lawrence who seems confident in my reaction and his work.

"Go ahead and pick it up. It is yours."

I run a couple fingers lightly over this deadly tool before lifting it. It feels so much lighter than I expected and I half wonder if it will even do any damage.

Lawrence must have read my mind because he says, "In our realm, we have a special metal that I use when I forge my weapons. The metal is extremely light and incredibly strong. I also spelled it which gave it its white blade. Blood will run off of it easily. The katana isn't indestructible, but it can slice through much more than you'll ever be able to with a weapon made on your plane."

I decide to test his claim. I walk back out into the open. Then, I run full speed at the trees and swing down my blade diagonally with as much power as I can muster. The katana slices through four regular sized branches as if it were nothing more than warm butter. I nod in approval and turn back toward Lawrence who is grinning from ear to ear with his arms across his chest.

"Thank you Lawrence. You've been really good to me here. You found the demon that killed my family and you've helped make me into something I've never even dreamed of being. In the beginning, I wanted to kill you for all that you put me through. Now, you've given me this weapon. I appreciate it all," I say with a couple tears in my eyes. Who would have thought that girly me would get choked up about a weapon. I wonder what I'd look like with a sword strapped to my back and designer heels. Damn, I couldn't wait to wear some high boots.

"It has been nothing short of an adventure. I will not soon forget your strength and courage," Lawrence says honestly. We both smile, then, he's back to business.

"There are a couple things you need to know about your sword as it is no ordinary object. Your sword must have a name. It must feel as though it has a bond with you in order for it grow in power as you grow. Your sword was not only forged from our steel, but Diana herself put some magic inside the blade which materialized as the serpent that now winds itself within the steel. The snake is the symbol of Immortality. It also represents cunning, fierceness, and flexibility.

Thus, with the katana and a piece of our magic, you should be able to find victory in your battles. But remember, the sword will only be as strong as its master," Lawrence speaks like an instructor who is just as excited to be teaching as the student is to learn.

It doesn't take me long to come up with a name. Lawrence has already said it and it sounds fitting to me. "Well, this is a katana and I want to honor the culture of the blade itself. Do you know a Japanese name that means 'victory' Lawrence?" I ask.

He thinks for a minute, undoubtedly trying to recall all of the languages that he's learned over the years. Finally, he says, "Katsu. It roughly means, to win."

I say it in my head then finally aloud. "Katsu. I like it. That's my sword's name. Katsu." Just then, the tattoo on my chest comes alive with a warm tingling and a glow. I look down at the sword and realize that it's responding to its name through my mark. I smile and think that it must like its name. Naming things give them power in the world of the awakened.

"Good. The next thing you need to know is that you can glamour your sword so that it remains unseen. Since you have named your sword and it reacted through your bond, you should simply be able to think what you want your sword to do, such as be invisible, and it should. But know that it will only be hidden from normal humans and low level awakeneds. Those that are probably going to be your opponents will be aware of your blade's presence."

I nod again in understanding and once again look down at my sword as Lawrence hands me its sheath. Very soon this beautiful blade will run red with blood. I'd have to kill to get my justice, and I thought I was ready for that, but maybe I'm really not.

Oh hell, now is not the time to be having second thoughts. I've killed before, so what is the issue, why is this so real to me now? I almost have the urge to drop the sword and run, suddenly feeling sick. Lawrence catches my expression and gently takes the sword from my hands.

"Are you ill young warrior?" he asks.

I shake my head, trying to rid myself of the uncertainty I just felt and then I start to feel better. "No. I'm okay. I just think reality has begun to set in about what I'm getting ready to have to do," I admit.

"You have come so far in this time. Your heart has a fighter's rhythm. You will succeed in your quest as long as you stay clear headed. Do not let the hatred consume you."

"I will do my best."

"Good. Now, I have one last thing for you to do," Lawrence begins, but I cut him off.

"Wait. Before you tell me what it is, I have to warn you that today, Selene said that I'm all hers, or else."

Lawrence voice booms with laughter. "That witch of yours is truly something else. Fine, fine. Still, you will need your rest anyway, for tomorrow, you go hunting."

"For?" I ask, curious about what could I possibly be going after.

"You, young warrior, will be hunting down a lamia."

"Uh, what the hell is that?" I ask not remembering if I had learned about this.

"A lamia is a type of demon that devours children. They can take the form of an adult woman, but their lower half is actually that of a serpent. They are also very cunning. It will be a good challenge for you to prove if you are truly ready to hunt and fight on your own. However, I do understand that you are more than eager to track down the person responsible for the deaths of your kin. If you do not think it is necessary to go on this hunt, then I certainly will not stop you or object. Either way, tomorrow you will return home," Lawrence explains.

I think about my options for a few seconds then ask, "Is this lamia on the hunt now? And if so, how many deaths have been confirmed?"

"Well, when I first was hunting down your demon I learned about it and the death toll was at six. I decided to ask a source about it and the last count was about twenty three."

"What?!" I exclaim. "So, you knew about this thing killing many months ago? It has been killing children and you didn't even attempt to stop it?" I was incredulous.

"Human affairs in your world are not truly my concern Rayne. This is why we give you power; it is not our job to fight your battles," he says sternly.

My anger fumes. "But you were close. You could have saved about twenty children's lives. Dammit Lawrence does that even mean anything to you at all? Besides, I'm sure there hasn't been another like me in hundreds of years. There is no other but me. How many have died because there was no one to fight for them!"

Lawrence stares me deep in my eyes and for a second I see a hatred in his own beautiful green depths. "Humans kill and kill each other all the time, so what is the difference? There is no other race, not one, that murders their own the way you humans do. You who are short lived see no value in life at all. Yet, here you are with the audacity to try to preach to me about what I should have done!"

"Have we not done enough in our pledge to your kind? Have I not taken you in and given you the tools to do more than anyone of you kind had ever thought possible? You are young, and you are naïve, and I am not your enemy here today. You cannot and will not save everyone. You will destroy yourself in the process of attempting to do so. Now, you can take what I have given you and go on the hunt in the morning, or you can accept that this lamia will kill again, that there are other things out there that will kill again, and if you truly want to save your kind, then maybe you should turn Katsu upon mankind itself."

His words are harsh and the cut deep, leaving tiny stings within my heart.

We stare down each other for a few minutes, not speaking a word. My knuckles turn white from clinching the hilt of my sword too strongly. Finally, I turn and storm away from Lawrence, leaving him alone in the forest and calling after me.

"Surely, I have raised a fool!"

I honestly don't know how I ended back at our room with the red I was seeing, but somehow, I managed. Selene takes one look at my face, strides towards me, takes Katsu from my hand and pulls me into a warm, comforting embrace. I allow her scent to wash over me and then, I cry. After feeling the release of tears come to an end, I pull away from Selene and she stays silent as she waits for me to tell her what's going on. I start from the beginning and then describe how I exploded on Lawrence about the lamia.

Selene whispers a calming spell, and suddenly, I feel less tense. I smile my gratitude at her as she touches my hand.

"My Rayne. Don't you understand what's going on?" Selene says, sounding a lot like my mother.

"No, but I'm sure you're going to tell me. I haven't cried in so long, but I was just so angry at him for not saving those kids."

Selene smiles patiently at me. "Exactly. You were thinking of Jazzy, babe. That thing is killing children. You know what it felt like when you found your sister. You know the hurt, the pain, and the fear. You became angry because you know other parents and siblings had to go through that. You want it to stop, no more lost children. You are still angry inside. Maybe you always will be, I don't know."

I sit there, feeling more helpless than I have in such a long time. When I get back, the first thing I'll do is visit my family and explain to them that they had to wait on their justice, then, I'd keep other families from that pain. Lawrence is right, I can't save everyone, maybe I won't even try, but in this case, I will not ignore this.

"Fine. I will accept that," I tell her. "So, let us enjoy this night, because tomorrow, I'm going hunting."

"No, meu coração, we are going hunting."

Chapter Sixteen

At dawn, Selene and I enter Diana's chambers. Inside, it smells of lavender and sex and I force myself to pretend not to notice that Diana is naked in bed and one of her male lovers is standing before us in all his naked glory as well. He nearly glows with masculinity and fulfillment, but with my eyes betraying me out of curiosity, I notice that not all of him is completely satisfied yet. I'm sure if I were into that kind of thing, penis to be exact, then I'd be impressed at that package he was blessed with. Actually, even if I was into having sex with men, if all Immortals were packed like him, there'd be no way in hell I'd let him or any one of them put that beast inside of me.

Selene clears her throat and I realize that I've been staring. I give her a horrified look of embarrassment and she laughs. Great, there's no telling what she's thinking of me now. I try to put my game face back on and hope that I'm succeeding. Yet, the amusement on Diana's face tells me that I'm not being very triumphant.

"Leave us for a moment, but do not go too far," Diana commands to her man-horse.

"May I wait outside the door my lady?" he inquires.

"You may."

He nods and then bows to us before taking his leave not even bothering to cover himself up.

"Well," Diana begins as she stands up and reaches for her robe which is so incredibly sheer, that she might as well still be naked. "You are making quite a habit with interrupting me during my pleasure-letting. Next time, one of you will make it up to me."

I look at Selene and then back at Diana whose words seem to echo even more throughout this room, or maybe it's simply because of her words that have me thinking that way. I can't tell if she is being serious or not and I don't really want to know. Instead, I attempt to change the subject by getting down to business.

"I apologize, Diana, but I can assure you that it is important. I'm ready to go back home. Lawrence has informed me of a demon in my area that is killing children. I have the power now to stop it and I need to go," I explain.

"Foolish," Diana says.

"Excuse me," begins Selene, taking a step forward, but I stop her with an arm as Diana raises an eyebrow.

"What is your plan?" Diana asks.

"Well, I'm going to find out where it's been hunting, then track it down and kill it."

"Ha," Diana's voice booms all around me. "Have you done any research on what it is you're hunting? Who do you know that will have information on this demon? Have you even thought about how uncommon it is for not one but two demons to have been in the same area in recent months?"

"Well," I start.

Diana laughs, clearly annoyed. "I have allowed you to spend far too much time with my brother. He is not always a deep thinker. Still, I'd expect much more from you, after all, it was I who taught you to use your mind."

"I have contacts that we can use back home. They can find us information," Selene answers.

"You, little witch who has not even used the power of your name there? You, who has hidden from your kind and most of the supernatural community for years? You have not the informers that she needs."

I look at Selene and then remember that Diana can take information from the mind. Clearly, she's been inside Selene's head. I wonder what else she knows about my girlfriend that I don't. Then, I swear I see Diana give me a knowing look, but I shake it off. I don't need this right now.

"Okay, I get your point Diana. I'm sorry, I wasn't thinking like a protector and it's clear that I have a long way to go before becoming one. Luckily, I still have your guidance to show me the right way," I respond, hoping to gain points by sucking up.

"Good. Now, what you will need to do will be difficult, because you need to draw attention to yourself without drawing too much attention to yourself."

"Huh?"

She chuckles. "Let me explain." Diana motions for us to sit on the bed with her. I sink into the bed that feels softer than memory foam. "In a world of power and ruthlessness, you will need to prove yourself. However, if the wrong types of beings start to realize that there is a human with powers that humans normally don't possess, they will do everything they can to kill you. Also, whoever is behind the murder of your family is also still hiding in the shadows. Your name alone will turn his attention to you which could be a fatal mistake."

"Well, I'm not changing my name. Still, I understand what you're saying. Selene, are there places that I can go to be seen that are still fairly low key?"

Selene stands there thinking for a few moments then nods. "Yes, I think I have the perfect place."

"Good," Diana responds like a teacher who is finally proud of her slowest student. "Now, you have to figure out what is going on with the demon problem your city is facing. I have a feeling that this is the beginning of a larger scheme."

"If it gets too bad will you get involved."

"No. We Immortals do not involve ourselves with matters on your plane unless it deals with the oath that was made."

"If things get too bad for me personally?"

"No, my virago. I will not save your life if that is what you're asking. So please, don't expect it. I hope that you understand that we no longer interfere in that way. You now have strength and a purpose. Use your intellect to make good decisions to keep yourself alive at least until you have reached your goal. I will be keeping an eye on your progress, however, because I still think that one day you will be able to become a protector."

"I guess I can understand that. I am grateful for all that you have done."

"Don't worry, child. If you ever need my counsel or wish to come back, then you are welcome. This will always be your home," Diana smiles at me with open arms.

Okay, so I could come and go as I please, but I couldn't expect them to come help me, even though I'd done battle with them. How ridiculous. I try not to think too much about it though. I don't want her pulling that from my mind. In that case, I truly did need allies, and fast.

Selene stands up and grabs my hand firmly as if I need reassurance that she'll be by my side. I have no doubt about that. Keeping our hands locked, I hug Diana with my other. We both stand and then Diana nods.

"Shall I summon Lawrence to see you off?" Diana asks.

I think about our last conversation and how I stormed off. It's probably not a good idea to leave things the way that they are right now. Lawrence has always been there for me and even though I don't understand their way of thinking, I know that he is one of the good guys. He deserves to know that I appreciate him.

"Can you both meet us by the water in about ten minutes? I need to finish gathering my things."

"And I'd like to see Kaede too," Selene adds.

"Very well. I will summon both of them as well to see you off." With that, Diana simply disappears and the air around us becomes much colder, empty of her radiant glow. We turn to leave preparing to take our first steps back to our world.

◊◊◊

I walk slowly back to the room that I've been staying in for all this time, deeply inhaling the fresh air, soaking in the beauty, and the calm of it all. I haven't even so much as sneezed since being here. This land is truly amazing and rejuvenating. Still, I can't believe I've survived this long without internet, cell phones, cars, or hell, a microwave. I guess that's what happens when you go on a single minded mission of justice; other things that used to matter just don't anymore.

I'm ready though. Even my toes are beginning to tingle with excitement. I think I need some of that Earthly normalcy back and soon. I need the hustle and bustle of everyday life, the sounds of music playing in people's cars, children's laughter, and the sight of people simply enjoying life. Even though to the world I am long dead along with the rest of my family, I know Damien will be waiting for me, happy to pull me into a firm embrace with his chiseled dark arms. He's the only kin I have left, and that isn't even by blood.

I wonder what he's been doing all this time, if he's found the man responsible for ripping my life to shreds. My heart begins to pound in nervousness. I never thought of the possibility that he'd gone too deep in this and ended up getting killed himself. I am so cut off from my world that anything is possible. World War III could have broken out and I wouldn't have known. I wonder if the immortals would have even told me if they knew. Since I've been here, rarely have they traveled to our plane. I won't even know what day it is when I get back.

As I gather my few possessions, my hands become clumsy and shaky. Selene notices it and puts her arms protectively around my waist as I breathe in her earthy scent. Her long hair covers us both in a blanket of love. I start to feel grounded and I smile.

"Thanks. You always know when I'm losing my composure."

She turns me towards her. "I'm in tune with you Rayne, don't forget that. Diana and Lawrence may not be willing to break the rules to help you out if things get out of hand, but I'll be there, and I'm much more capable of handling things than you know," she says with conviction.

There's a flash of power in her eyes and I wonder just how much she's improved. Hell, I don't know how much power she had to begin with, so there'd be no way for me to gauge it. Though I'm sure she wouldn't have been marked as a high priestess of her people if she didn't have some serious magic inside of her. All I know is that it's clear that she's been running from something for a long time and I've always had this feeling that her meeting the Immortals was as much about her as it was about me.

Though I'm sure she had nothing to do with my family, it probably was a better opportunity than she could have ever imagined, being able to find a reason to summon them. After all, it seems that even among the supernatural community there is little knowledge of the Immortals or the pact that they made with my race; but Selene seemed to know much more than normal. She had been looking for a way in, of that, I'm sure.

That was a fact that I'd accepted a long time ago. After all, she stayed with me the whole time, supporting me, and healing me in more ways than one. Without her I would have never obtained this power, and if there was something extra in it for her, who am I to judge?

"I believe you," I tell her. "I'll keep a clear head and I won't just jump into situations that are impossible to win."

"Listen to your instinct on that. This is going to be more difficult that you can imagine. Trust me on this."

I listen to her words and let them sink in. I have no doubt that Selene is right about that. Quickly now, I gather the rest of my belongings.

When we get to the lake, our three Immortals are waiting for us, two smiling. The male of the group has his arms crossed, expressionless, shoulder-length blonde hair blowing freely. I give him a bright smile to let him know that I'm not upset with him anymore, and his body relaxes slightly. Selene and I both stop an arm's length away from the trio, but Kaede quickly embraces us in a long hug.

She may look like a young child with long hair dark as night, a round but otherworldly beautiful face, almond shaped steel grey eyes, and fair skin with that now familiar immortal glow, but she out-ages both of us by thousands of years. Still, she has this child-like demeanor about her that mirrors her outer shell. I'm sure that part of her personality never changes, no matter how old she looks.

Next, Lawrence puts one hand on my shoulder and nods, but I then pull him into a hug. He could never replace my own father, but in many ways, I could relate his own quiet strength and pushing to my own dad. For that familiarity, I am forever grateful. He returns the hug tighter and when we pull away from each other his smile is warm.

"You are a fool, but I believe that you have great things to accomplish in your future. You will become a Machaera and when you do, I'll give you my own blood for the ritual," Lawrence promises.

I smile at him, but don't respond. Being a protector, the immortal's sword, meant gaining immortality and that was something that I had yet to think about. Selene would age, I would stay young forever. Even if she and I didn't stay together for the rest of our lives, I have never been one of those people who thought living forever was cool.

"There are a couple things that you should know Rayne; lamia will not show their true self until she is ready to attack. They take human form and will often be beautiful, non- threatening, and appear to be someone trustworthy. Look for women hanging around parks alone or late at night on less frequented roads. They will rarely take children from anywhere other than poor neighborhoods or from areas where homeless people stay. With the rate of death this high, it is safe to say that there is a nest somewhere close to your hometown and that the hunting ground may be covering three states," Diana explains, and I imprint all that to memory.

"Also," Kaede continues, "You will need to cut the head off completely and then burn the bodies. Lamia may be low level demons, but they regenerate at a quick rate and can cause you a great deal of grief if they manage to get a good amount of venom inside you. It may not kill you, but it will paralyze whatever area it enters and too much poison can stop your motor functions and even cause you to suffocate."

"Thanks Kaede for those herbs as well. I know how to create that poison neutralizer too," Selene says proudly.

Kaede smiles at her like a teacher impressed by her student's progress.

"There is one more thing," I turn to Lawrence as he begins, his voice flowing all around me, deep and controlling. "This is just one of many Demon reportings that have been happening in a five state radius in the past couple years. There has not been this much demon activity since the Dark Days and even though there is no evidence that something bad is on the move, I want you to keep track of anything you may find out or uncover. Your world could be in danger, or it could simply be that Demon-kind is simply finding more ways to break through the gates, but I want to be sure."

Another thing that has been noticed, but that they've done nothing about. I try to hide my frown, but as always, Diana catches it, and probably my thoughts too. She doesn't say a word either, so I pretend to be oblivious to our exchange.

As we say our goodbyes, I think about where we are to go. Diana said to picture the place in my mind as she opens the gate for us to return. Since Damien is the only one I can trust, I immediately think of him. Still, I can't say that I'm not afraid that he won't be there, and if something has happened to him, it would break me so bad that I would not be able to put the pieces back together.

After this, I'd have to hardly ever see him again. He wouldn't become someone to be used against me, even if he argued with me about it. Because if the choice came over saving him and stopping the witch responsible for my family's death, I would let him die. That too would break me, but I knew what choice I'd make, and I didn't want to ever have to make it.

I decide on his front door instead of inside his house where who knows what could be inside, let alone give someone a heart attack. Diana takes the picture from my mind and with one more glance at the three of them, my tattoo begins to glow.

Together, Selene and I step through and begin walking, but within seconds, we're in front of Damien's door. His house was never as large as ours because he lives alone, but from the well kept condition of every single blade of grass to the trim around the door, you can tell that Damien is well off.

His neighborhood is full of old, upper middle class, retired persons and I hope none of them are nosey enough to be hanging out of their windows right now. I look at the dark blue door and I hesitate before knocking for a couple reasons, one, out of fear, and two, because my world now feels different and I need a second to allow my senses to adjust.

I look around me. It's almost evening, the sun making its trek back to bed. I can hear the slight vroom of cars rolling by and music in the distance, up-tempo, happy. I breathe deeply, taking in the different smells, smells that I haven't smelled for a long time like barbeque and gasoline. It's less clean, but it's home. I even feel lighter, not really ever thinking about the difference in gravity while I was there after the first night. That meant I'd be faster here, stronger.

Finally, Selene says patiently, "Are you ready Rayne, or should we come back."

I look at her smiling. "No, it's okay. I'm ready." There'd be time for sightseeing later. I need to see Damien now. I give the door three hard knocks and then stand back. About a minute later, a tall, dark, handsome man in need of a shave opens the door. At first, he looks confused. Then, I drop my luggage as he pulls me into a fierce hug and sobs a little. I return the force of the hug and shed my own tears.

"Dammit Ray Ray, I've missed you. I was so worried that something had happened and I'd never know."

"Me too, D. I thought that you wouldn't be here, that I'd never be able to find you."

Finally, Damien lets me go, and looks at Selene.

"You've kept her safe. Thank you," he says to her, voice shaky from the tears.

She just smiles at him and nods. Damien ushers us in his house and it's the first time I've felt at home in a long while. We all sit down in the kitchen and Damien pours us some juice. While I sip it, I watch him as he examines me from head to toe. He looks at my short red hair, so much like Jazzy's, my non manicured fingers, my newly muscled arms and legs, and more. Then, he lingers on my yellow milk maid dress and bites back a laugh.

I put the cup down and smile, taking in Damien's own uncharacteristic appearance. His growing beard, his weight loss, even his sad looking eyes. I don't know what battles he's had to face, but clearly, he hasn't been sleeping soundly for many nights. His eyes are beyond tired.

"You've changed so much Ray Ray. Not even your physical appearance, but the air around you is different. I don't know what it is, but I can tell that you're not the same," Damien tells me; uncertain on whether or not that's a good thing.

"I have changed, more than I thought possible, more than just losing my family. I am a warrior now," I explain.

"Ah, I see. But, what does that mean?"

I stand up, glance at Selene and tell Katsu to reveal herself to Damien. He leans back in surprise as my sword seems to appear out of thin air. "It means that I now have more strength than probably five or six of you, and that I have skills that will allow me to avenge my family."

He acknowledges my lack of explanation. I know he wants to know exactly what happened while I was gone, but I don't think it really matters, especially since this visit may possibly be one of the last.

"So, what is your plan Rayne?"

Selene begins before I can even respond, trying to save me from having to be the bad guy. "I'm sorry Damien, but the less you know, the better. What we are going to do next could endanger your life. I've convinced Rayne that it's better if we just keep you out of this. That may mean for a long, long time."

Damien looks at Selene in anger and clinches his fist, when he turns back to me, he unclenches it in defeat. I can see it in his eyes that whatever he's gone through in the time I've been gone hasn't been rainbows and sunshine. He's obviously had his share of threats.

"Please don't let me lose you too," I whisper.

"I can take care of myself Rayne. I've been doing it for this long. At least let me make my own choice," he says quietly.

"Can you Damien? Can you protect yourself from what could be coming? I mean sure you've known I was a witch, but what about a demon stronger than the one that killed her family? What happens when they use you to force Rayne's hand? You think humans are ruthless, you have no idea what my kind is capable of," Selene raises her voice as she stands, stepping closer to Damien.

She's pushing it, I know, but he needs to see the point. He stands up too, getting in her face. "I know how to protect myself. I have weapons. Jason and I, our company we've developed things..."

Suddenly, Damien is flying through the air and slamming against the far wall. Selene's hair is floating from the magic swirling through her. She's focused and I decide to let this play out. Damien is struggling against the push of her power to no avail. Then, a kitchen drawer opens and knives begin to fly out, towards Damien at disturbing speed. I have to force myself not to stop it, knowing Selene won't hurt him.

"Weapons will not mean a thing if you don't see the attack coming. You are human, you do not have the strength, speed, or skill to kill what could come for you. And now that Rayne has been un-made, she has become a different sort of target. Stay out of this or I will force you myself." Then, she drops him and the chill of her magic leaves the air as the knives drop to the floor.

Chapter Seventeen

He stands himself up again, but refuses to look me in my face, embarrassed and angry. "I will be here whenever you need me, but I won't force you to use my help. I've been waiting for you to return and have set you up with a new identity and place to stay as well as a vehicle. I just hope that's enough for now. The place is about forty-five minutes away from here."

"You know I appreciate any and everything you've done for me, D. I just want you safe. Please don't think that I think you're useless or weak."

"Then, why are you and your girlfriend trying to chop my balls off?"

Selene snorts and sits back down. "Appreciate our concern for your life Damien."

"I do. I just want to do my part."

"You have, and for now, your part is done. Let me do the rest now. Like I said, I will call you when I need you, believe me. Trust me. Trust in me, Damien," I plead.

"You are your father's daughter," he says and I smile and hug him, understanding all that he meant in those words, and appreciating the reminder that even though they were gone, all of them now live through me.

"I can do this. And I will have you to thank too. You have a job to do and that's running the business."

"Yeah yeah, the desk job."

We both laugh and the tension in the room eases slightly.

"Let me go get your information out of my safe." About five minutes later, he comes back with a bunch of paperwork. "Here. This should be all you need. Checking account information, new id's, social security cards, birth certificates, and more. Read up on it."

"Thanks D," I tell him.

"Oh, and one more thing," he begins, now with a smile on his face. "I've got a name for you. He may know the name of the witch who ordered the hit from the leads Selene gave me to check up on."

"Who is it?" I ask urgently.

"He's apparently an Alpha wolf, goes by the name Anubis," Damien says.

"How did you get to that name?" Selene asks before me. I wonder if she knows the name, but given her detachment from the supernatural community, I doubt it.

"Well, I've been using certain methods, asking questions, having sources ask around, and apparently, a couple years back, his wife or girlfriend was killed by a demon after a business conflict. One of your sources finally came back with the info. We put two and two together and figured it was probably too much of a coincidence for it not to be related to our situation here."

"You said a couple years? A couple being two or are you just saying a couple as a guess?"

"Well, I believe it was about two years, maybe three at the most, why?" Damien asks curiously.

"It's just something that we're looking into. So, where can we find this Anubis?" I ask.

"I think I know where to start," Selene tells me.

"Well, if her ideas don't pan out, there's another source we could possibly try."

"Okay. I'll contact you if it doesn't pan out."

We sit in silence for a few more seconds, then, I raise my hand like a student.

"Um, yes?" Damien asks, amused.

"Well, we're going to need a ride, but before that, can you do me a huge favor?" I ask.

"Sure, what is it?"

"Can you make me a burger? I am absolutely dying to have one."

With that we all laugh.

◊◊◊

Damien convinces us to stay the night before we get started on our day. When we get up the next morning, he takes me to see my family's graves, then to our new place. It's on the southside of town, quiet and peaceful. There's enough distance between the homes that we'll be able to keep a good level of privacy and if anyone comes snooping, you'd see them a mile away.

The home seems to have a large square footage, was recently built in the past five years, tan with a two car garage and a privacy fence in the back. There's nothing to make this home stick out and that's the point. We are to keep a low profile. Still, given that I am used to living in mansions, this will take some getting used to. But how can I even complain? Damien had set this up while I was gone to make sure I'd be safe.

He walks inside with us giving us a tour of the house and also the security code to the alarm system. I have to admit that Damien did an excellent job with the design and layout. The first area of the house is the living room and dining room. The dining room has a nice square mahogany table with a dark brown contemporary rug with red and yellow swirls under it. There is a large mirror covering the wall that is almost 3D in its design. The living room has a black leather sectional, ottoman, beautiful forest green throw pillows that are nearly the color of Selene's eyes, paintings with various greens and yellows, and a large glass table with a small silver statue of two women embracing on it. There are two silver lamps on either side of the sectional and an area rug that seems to pull it all together.

Next, is the kitchen tour. Selene practically has an orgasm when she steps into the fully equipped kitchen with a center island. All the appliances are stainless steel and ready for her use. I have always tried to steer clear of any kitchen and I don't foresee myself hanging out in here any time soon. The stove is gas and seems to have way too many knobs and buttons for me. Our sink even has a purple tiled backsplash wall. The counters are granite with multicolored flecks. The cabinets are mahogany as well as the pantry doors. There is no food in the house since he didn't know when we'd be coming, so luckily we'd grabbed a few groceries on the way.

Three steps down, lower than the area the kitchen, living room, and dining room sits is a den or family area. This room has a sixty inch flat screen mounted on the wall with speakers on each side. The cream suede couches in here are accompanied by a comfortable looking red chaise lounge. There's not much else to this room which is fine because Damien's done so much already.

Our bedroom is upstairs from the main level and as we trek down the hall, I am glad that our room at least has a walk in closet and a master bathroom. These are two things I just can't compromise on. The bed is a memory foam king with a black and gold comforter set and large headboard. I have to refrain from jumping in like a little kid. On each side of the bed are two nightstands with small bendy lamps.

We also have two spare rooms and a large finished basement with nothing inside of it, making it perfect for training.

Last, we go into the garage where there is not only a black Ducati parked, but a silver Jaguar. I give Damien a big hug.

"Hey, I can't let you just lose your love of nice things completely. Besides, most people have average looking houses but really nice cars or bikes. You won't stick out with these in the city," Damien tells me.

"You're right, but next time keep in mind that I like Lamborghinis too," Selene jokes.

"Well, once this shit is settled and Rayne stays safe, I'll buy you two of them," Damien promises.

"I'm gonna hold you to that then," Selene responds.

We all stand there for a few minutes without anymore words, letting reality finish sinking in. This will be the last time for a while that I'll be able to meet with Damien in person. This is the start of what I had fought so hard to do. I'm becoming that much closer to meeting my goal.

"Thank you D. I owe you more than I could ever repay. I love you," I tell him as tears threaten to blur my vision.

"Just do what you have to do so that we can all start over. I love you too, always have. One more thing I forgot. I need to run to my car." A few minutes later, he comes back in the house with a small box of things.

"What is it?" I ask standing on my tip toes, trying to peek.

"This was all the stuff in Jason's office that I kept for you. I know that we had to burn down your house so everything else was mainly lost, so I knew you'd want to have something."

"Thank you. This means so much," I tell him, my heart beating fast as I pull out a picture of the four of us. We had taken this picture on a vacation in Costa Rica four years ago. I can still feel the waves splashing on us just after the picture was snapped. My dad was holding my mom close and Jazzy was trying her best to give me bunny ears.

This is the first time in over a year that I have even seen a photo of my family. Suddenly, it becomes too much as I touch each smiling face. I clutch the picture to my chest, set the box on the counter and kiss Damien on the cheek before I turn away and leave the room. Neither he nor Selene calls out to me. They allow me my sorrow in peace.

When I come back out, Damien is gone and Selene is sitting on the couch with her legs crossed going through the papers and other items that he left for us. She looks up when I come into the room.

Hey meu amor, how are you feeling?" she asks, her accent like silk.

"I'm better. Can you show me what he left?"

"Sure. There are a lot of documents to go through, but the basics are that you are now Kennedy Hopkins, twenty three, from Chicago,

Illinois. You moved here two months ago and you were a ward of the state. No one knows who your parents were because you were left at a hospital when you were born. Apparently though, you have a pretty hefty bank account due to the fact that you were the victim of sexual harassment by a wealthy businessman at a company where you were interning that paid you off to keep you quiet."

I nod as I commit it to memory and also smirk at the background, surely he could have thought of something better, but I guess it's just enough to explain my lack of work history and the amount of money that I have. One good thing about being gone for so long though, is that as long as I changed up my style frequently, mannerisms, and wore a pair of sunglasses or something when I went out, people wouldn't really remember me. To the public, I'd just look familiar, they may ask my name, but then once I said I was Kennedy Hopkins from Chicago, they'd move on. We humans have a short attention span like that.

"There are also a couple credit cards, two secure cell phones, account numbers, our keys, and things like that. Basically anything that we might need immediately, we have."

I look through all the paperwork a few times before I grab what I need and put the rest in the safe that he had built into the wall. Next, it's time to go shopping and make plans for the rest of the night. I need to find that lamia, and to do that, I have to find out where it was hunting. I use my cell phone to browse the internet to see if I can find any hits on child disappearances in the immediate area, but there are none in the last week and I remember that Diana also said that I have to check other nearby cities and that if they are street kids, it may not get reported at all. Maybe I'd have to do it the Buffy way and go on nightly patrols.

It takes us about ten hours to do all the shopping that we need. Rebuilding a wardrobe is a difficult job, especially when I quickly regain my love of fashion and "must" buy myself sexy things, everyday things, and also clothes to fight in. A lot of those clothes to fight in are also sexy. Leather jackets, leather boots, half shirts, half jackets, sexy rompers, low cut tank tops, and more. Hey, I am still a woman after all. I can avenge my family and look good doing it.

Selene and I argued the whole time about what I needed right now and I ended up convincing her to let me pick out her clothes too. Let's just say we'll be the best dressed lesbian supernatural couple in town. I don't even know why she was even pretending to complain. She adores my taste in clothing.

Tonight, Selene is taking me to this club called Obsession and it is mainly all Wolf. If we wanted to find Anubis, he'd almost certainly be there. It is getting close to the full moon and wolves are looking for a mate to run with. That's what they call it when they change under the moon, hunt, run free, and then have sex afterward. Even though a black market pill was developed years ago to keep wolves from having to change, the urge still drives their nature and many still choose to turn anyway. It will be packed in there tonight she promised.

It does make me wonder just how many lesbian wolves are out there and how many she's hooked up with. I know that there are hardly any gay male wolves because the urge to mate and make pups is very strong in a male wolf. It just doesn't happen much.

I guess survival-wise, wolves probably have the shortest life span due to the high possibility of being killed by other packs, their own pack if they break pack rules, killing themselves when their mate dies, or if they lose control of the Wolf inside. It is almost imperative to find a mate and have children to keep their numbers. In countless places in Europe, the war between Vampires and Wolves wiped out their numbers so great that they have yet to recover. Thankfully, there isn't much bad blood between the races in America, or so I was told.

Werewolves, luna dasa, lycans, vrkolak, whatever you want to call them are interesting creatures. Their nature keeps their body temperature slightly higher than a normal human due to their crazy metabolism. They also seem to age very slowly, possibly because of their natural healing process. It seems to treat aging like a disease. A werewolf may not have the life span of a vampire, but beating the odds against them, they could very well live to be one hundred fifty years old.

I have just enough time to re-color my hair, then style it so that it's partially covering my eye and also framing my face. Then, I decide to throw on a white v-neck half shirt with some dark blue low rise denim jeans. I also throw on my white leather boots and a red leather jacket and a red belt to stand out. If the club is going to be as crowded as she claims then I want my auburn hair and red jacket to bring me some attention, but also keep me prepared for a fight. Since I'm human, there's no doubt I'll be getting tested tonight. But, I can't bring Katsu, my sword, with me. Not in a place like that, they'd never let me in the door.

When Selene's finally done, she ends up wearing a sexy ass black dress that hugs her round butt. I have to keep myself from slapping it one good time. Half of her long dark hair is up, with the other half falling in front of her breasts. When she pulls her hair out the way, I notice that the v-cut is so low that it's almost to her belly button. My eyebrows rise in surprise.

"I didn't buy this one," I say.

"I bought this one while you weren't looking," she tells me all innocent like.

"Sneaky, sneaky, you."

She does a slow twirl so that I can drink her all in with my eyes. "I wanted to surprise you. Do you think it's too much? I know I don't usually wear these kinds of clothes," she says, growing a little insecure.

"Baby, you look sexy as hell. If I wasn't going to get into a fight on my own, I most certainly will now, poking people's eyes out and ripping prying hands off of you," I tell her, trying to sound jealous and protective.

"Yeah, about that, we will have to go in separately. I don't want them to know we're together just yet. I want to see how they react to you first. I will go in, scope the place out, and then send you a text to let you know when it's safe. Feel like riding the Ducati alone tonight?"

"If you think that's best. You know more about this than me. I'm going to just follow your lead and hopefully find some information that's worth all the trouble," I tell her as I anticipate the worst. "And what if they don't even let me in?"

"Then you make them," Selene responds simply.

"Great." Just great.

"It's now or never Rayne. Welcome to my world."

"Yeah," I say. "Thanks for the invite."

Chapter Eighteen

It feels amazing to have the wind whipping against me on this beautiful night as I follow Selene to club Obsession. The ride is so smooth that I almost want to keep riding and put off what we are to do for another night. I know that isn't possible though, so I have to get my head in the game. After all, who really knows what I'll be walking into? I need to focus. This will be the first time I've really walked among supernaturals knowingly. I'll be a super-minority.

Once I see where Selene stops, I roll around the blocks for about five minutes before I check my phone. I get the okay to come in so I park my bike further down the street and make my way to the door. The street itself is empty of people but there are a lot of cars parked outside. The streetlights are on but they are shining low. I wonder if that was purposely done. Pop music is bumping faintly inside and I realize how much I miss going out.

The building itself is nothing spectacular to look at and it doesn't stand out in any way. There isn't even a sign that announces that it's a club. Before I even get about twenty feet away from the door, an overwhelming sense of wrongness hits me and I almost turn away. Then, I remember what Selene told me about the spells that almost all clubs for "other" races use to keep humans out.

The spells are supposed to unconsciously make people too afraid or uncomfortable to go inside. Sometimes people would get so afraid that they'd get sick and vomit she told me. So, I'd just have to ignore the feeling, and hopefully since I'm not a "normal" human anymore, it will break once I push through my initial hesitation.

Even though my mind is telling me to stop, I force my feet to move and a few seconds later, I can't feel the weight of the spell anymore. By the time I get to the door, it feels like I'm entering any other club. Before I can even pull open the door, a mountain of a man dressed in black slacks and a tight red t-shirt opens it for me smiling professionally.

He looks Native American, smells of pine and rain, his face average; slightly handsome, and showing proof of scars long healed. His nose is average sized with a tiny silver stud on the left side, his thin lips revealing white perfect teeth. His hair is cut into a short, stylish mohawk. I have no doubt that the rest of his body probably would have the same marks as his face.

He smiles at me at first, but as soon as I take two steps through the door, he takes a deep breath, frowns, and blocks my entrance with his bulky arm. I look up at his 6 and a half foot frame as if I don't understand why he's denying me admission.

"Whoa there. I think you're in the wrong place," he says, his voice as deep as he is big. There are two ways this could go: one, he would put me on my ass and I'll never get in, or two, he would put me on my ass but respect the fight in me and let me in. Either way doesn't look too promising for me.

I decide to throw out the charm. I bite my lip and give him a smile. "Oh, I think I'm exactly where I'm supposed to be."

I brush against him and he chuckles. "Trust me sweetheart, you don't want to do this, I don't know what you've heard or who put you up to this, but this club has a strict member's only policy."

"Well how do you know I'm not a member, you were about to let me in a few seconds ago," I respond, trying to sound slightly irritated.

"Look," he says growing more irritated himself. "You are not getting past me so don't even bother. I thought you looked like someone is all. Think of it as me doing you a huge favor. This is not your kind of place, now *leave*," he orders, trying to use the strength of his pack to put force behind the demand.

It hits me and then washes away. He looks confused and I smile.

Just then, another man walks up to the front, a lot smaller than my bouncer friend here. He decides he likes what he sees and gives me a slap on the ass, very hard. I see an opportunity. Before he can even walk past the man-mountain, I grab his arm in an iron grip. He turns to face me in surprise trying to pull away.

"Like I said, I think I'm exactly where I'm supposed to be."

The bouncer begins to reach for me himself but I slide away from his grasp quickly and give the touchy feely guy a roundhouse kick that sends him sliding across the floor and into the club. If people weren't watching our exchange before, they most certainly are now, I can feel it.

"What do you want?" The bouncer asks me, pulling me close to him, showing me that he could squeeze me to death if he wanted. He shakes his head in the direction of the other guy and I know he is pretty pissed for what I just did to him.

"I'm just looking for a good time is all," I lie.

"Blatant lies like that are easy for a wolf to smell. What do you want little human?" he asks, much more serious this time as his eyes begin to glow eerie yellow.

"I'm looking for a certain wolf. His name is Anubis," I tell him.

He lets me go but eyes me warily. "You couldn't possibly have business with him, but you interest me so I'll let you go. But know this, one wrong move here tonight and I'll kill you myself, do you understand."

"I get it. Thanks, uh," I say, trying to catch his name. I like the man mountain.

"It's Jaxson. Now, be smart in there."

"I will," I promise. I give him one last glance as he chuckles at me then crosses his tree stumps called arms as two more customers walk through the door.

The music is not too loud, but fast and electrifying. A club with wolves can't blast music without risking ear damage to all of their customers. I easily find myself sliding teasingly through bodies and notice that no one is really turning around and sniffing out the human. It must be from all the sweat and excitement in the air. My smell of humanity must be cancelling out. Good.

I look at the dance floor sitting on a level lower than where I'm at now and notice how closely all the bodies are pressing together. People are making out, dancing topless, and just having a grand old time. The upstairs level seems to be more laid back, with soundproof glass, pool tables, and a smaller bar. A few people are looking out at the dance floor from the top. The floor I'm on has a large bar in the middle of the room and comfortable looking tables and chairs throughout. Right now there's no sign of Selene, so I decide to just hit the dance floor for a few songs to release some of my tension.

I fit in easily; I loved to swim but dancing is my element, my release since I had been attending an arts school on a dance scholarship before my world went to shit. I let the beat fill me up and for a second allow myself to just feel the music pumping inside me. I dance with whoever is near me, simply enjoying. Either they still don't notice I'm human or they simply don't care, it's just as well though. I let the vibe and call of the moon that these wolves are feeling flow into me. Through my shirt, I can feel my tattoo glowing, like a battery recharging.

Once I have my fill of the dance floor, I order a drink, then find a table, my back against the wall so that I don't catch any surprises behind, hoping that either Selene will find me, or that someone will decide to come chat.

I sit alone for about three songs before I see a darker skinned wolf eying me from the top. I take another sip of my drink, pretending not to notice before I get up again and make my way towards the stairs, prepared to follow him. My watcher is coming down, however, and grabs my arm firmly, escorting me back down the steps and to my previous seat. He sits across from me after pulling out my chair. I look at him once he settles in his seat.

He may not be nearly as large as Jaxson, maybe 5'11" or so, but it is clear from the way his dark green dress shirt hugs his body that he is all muscle. I'm starting to get the feeling that this is a common trait among wolves. His hair is past his shoulders and in very well maintained dreds and a ponytail. His skin is like the brown of hot chocolate, darker than my own, and he has three piercings in his left ear, but none in the other. His nose is wide but not overly large and his lips are full. He appears to be in his late teens, but with the way wolves age, he's probably actually in his early thirties.

His dark brown eyes say that he has seen more than his share of stress. He is not strikingly handsome, but nonetheless, has a dangerous beauty about him. It's the kind that you'd have to look deeper, past the wall he'd so clearly built to see. But, I guess that is understandable, he'd lost his mate. When wolves lost their mate, they rarely mated again, if they even lived through it. He lost his clearly at a young age. I'll have to play that to my advantage, no matter how messed up it might be. Then, I zero in on the scar on his neck. A nasty one that starts from the bottom of his left ear to the right side of his collar bone. Someone had tried to slice him open. He is a survivor indeed.

I look into his dark eyes as he catches mine. I try to hold my gaze as long as I can, but the power behind his stare overtakes me. This man is clearly an Alpha and I stand no chance of dominance against him, not here, not when the full moon is this close. Even without that, I think his aura would have consumed mine regardless. I look away and try not to look into his eyes again. I dare not speak until he decides it's time.

After he finishes sizing me up, he smirks and says, "You really are a human. How interesting." His voice is quiet, almost timid, clearly deceptive. It's clear that he's confident in his own strength and has nothing to prove with his voice. He knows it will be heard and also listened to.

"I am, but I'm not like any of the others," I tell him.

"Hmm. Clearly. So, what is a young woman like you doing in a place like this?" he asks, obviously wanting to know more than just how I came to be here tonight. He wants to know who I am. I need to know if I can trust him before I say too much.

"Let's just say that I have friends in high places. Beyond that though, I heard that there was an Alpha wolf named Anubis that shared something in common with me. I was told that we could help each other out. I hope they were right."

He leans back in his chair and I see him do something with his hands. I glance around without being too obvious and notice that a few wolves in here are now paying attention to our table. They must be his pack. That means that I have to tread carefully. Finally, at the bar, I spot Selene. She's sitting next to some drunk guy laughing and talking, but I can tell that she's also eying the other wolves in here. Even though we are grossly outnumbered, I still feel much safer knowing she's close.

"I'm listening. Tell me why this is worth my time," he demands.

I slip him two hundreds out of my pocket just to peak his interest and keep him from walking away for a few minutes. "I understand that time is money, but what I'm asking for and willing to give is worth a whole lot more trust me."

"Who are you?"

He doesn't pocket the money, but I leave it there anyway.

"My name is Rayne Whitmore." I pause, waiting to see if the name creates a reaction, when it doesn't, I continue. "You may not know who I am exactly, but trust me, we have much more in common than you may know. Two years ago, my family was murdered."

His eyebrows rise slightly, but he attempts to show no interest.

"They were possibly murdered by the same man that murdered your mate. I know what it's like

Anubis to lose someone who means everything to you."

He interrupts me, "What do you want?" Anubis leans forward, still trying to give nothing away, but the ring around his iris begins to turn yellow, betraying the anger boiling up inside. I pretend not to notice his pack mates shifting in their chairs.

"I want his name. I want the protection of your pack so that I can do what I have to do without having to worry about any and everything coming at me trying to kill me before I can kill the son of a bitch who took away three people that I love," I tell him firmly, leaning forward in my seat and meeting his eyes briefly so that he can see the sincerity in them.

"What makes you think that you, a human, can do what I can't?" he asks humorously.

"I'm more than I appear Anubis, trust me on that. Besides, I have nothing to lose," I tell him.

"Oh?" he begins. "Is that so? What about your witch at the bar, is she so disposable?"

I glance up at the bar and frown. It's obviously one of Anubis's pack mates that is speaking with Selene. Then, I give my attention back to him. I know she can take care of herself. "How do you know that she is mine?" I ask.

"Your scent is all over her and vice versa. You smell of magic and human. Besides, what are the chances that a witch and a human appear here on the same night, a night that is usually all my kind. After I knew what to look for, I could smell you ten feet away." he tells me.

Interesting.

"Well, she is all that I have left in this world and she is certainly capable of protecting herself too. I have nothing to lose because she won't be going anywhere. She knows my aims and she understands that I will sacrifice myself to get my justice."

"You say that, but the question is will she let you?"

I consider his question for a few seconds before I respond. I know that he might be right. Selene wouldn't be quick to allow me to surrender my own life to kill the man who took my family's lives.

"I'll do my part, just give me his name. You are the only one who really understands me right now Anubis. You have no reason to trust me, no reason to extend the protection of your pack to me, but I can see it in your eyes that you want justice just as much, if not more than I do. I will be your answer," I nearly plead.

His eyes begin to return to its normal color and he blows out a long breath. It seems like hours before he answers. "I cannot."

It feels like a punch in the gut.

I stand up and slam my hands down on the table and say the hell with not staring him in the eyes. I meet his gaze with a fiery fury and hold it.

All around me I can feel his pack begin to stand up and walk towards our table. I also somehow feel the hum of Selene's magic wrapping around me, ready to protect me. The music even lowers slightly, an indication that a lot of people are now watching, waiting. I have no friends here. This could get ugly.

"How can you fucking protect this man after all that he's taken from you?" I hiss. My tattoo glows through my shirt as my power rises from my middle. Anubis notices the light through my shirt but doesn't comment.

"You know nothing about me or what I want," he growls. "You came to me demanding and expecting much more than you can even handle little girl. You play a dangerous game and you don't even realize it. The man you seek will destroy you in seconds." The force of his pack lending him strength through the magic of their bond finally forces me to look away again.

"Then tell me his name, who he is, and let me decide for myself." I wipe my hair from my face and realize that I'm beginning to sweat. "I've changed who I am completely to find this man. You have no idea what I've been through either."

"Sit down," he commands, voice like a cold snap brushing against my skin.

"No," I tell him defiantly, chin up. He's not my fucking boss.

"If you don't sit down, I will consider this a challenge and you will not walk away this night, believe that, human," he commands again, quieter, more focused, deadly.

I sigh and find my seat once more. Slowly, the room goes back to normal and the sound of laughter and the thump of bass begin to fill the air. "I apologize. You are not my enemy."

"Nor do you want to make me. Let me tell you about how I got this scar on my neck," Anubis says. I look at him impatiently before I decide that it's best to just listen and hope he gives me what I need.

"Ok. I'm listening."

"It was the night of the Wolf Moon, about fourteen years ago, and it was freezing cold out, even for my kind who naturally are resistant to cold temperatures. I was with my pack at the time, my father was the Alpha. We all ran together in the forest, hunting. I felt alive, free, wild. I was sixteen and it was my first hunt with the whole pack together."

I watch Anubis's eyes as they remember better days, a deep longing in their depths. His silky voice is easy to listen to.

"It was amazing. When it was over and we had run until our feet were sore, the pack headed back to their cars. Yet, I wasn't ready to leave, so my father told the rest of the pack to go without us, that we would have one more run, just the two of us. When we finished, we headed to our car, but there was someone there waiting for us. My father ordered me to hide amongst the trees and I did. I waited and listened. He spoke with a hooded man about pack territory, experiments, and me. My father didn't agree with whatever he was saying. But, it didn't matter because whatever happened next changed everything."

I lean forward, struggling to hear as the music seems to blast even louder now, the tempo speeding up and the lust of the crowd increasing.

"My father was an Alpha. He was strong and always in control. Yet, whatever the hooded man spoke next forced my father into a change. Alphas are the only wolves that can force another wolf into change and for a non-wolf to do so is unheard of. Then, he just disappeared, leaving a hint of his scent behind, blowing in the wind. Not only did the man compel my father into change, but somehow he became feral, no humanity left, it was the moon rage. I left the safety of the trees to go to my father and that's when he attacked me." Anubis leans back in his chair, folding his calloused, ringed hands on the table.

"His teeth shattered my shoulder as his paws sliced through my neck. I've never felt pain like that in my life. It was indescribable. The hurt mixed with fear must have triggered something within me. I myself blacked out, thinking for sure that I was going to die. When I awoke however, it was my father who lay lifeless beside me, and I, covered in his blood, half alive. If my own body didn't trigger the change, I would have died. It took me three days to heal."

I frown at his story. There was no way that he should have survived that. Not when his father was already attacking him while he was still in human form.

He knows what I'm thinking and continues to explain, "I like that think that my father regained enough of his senses to allow me to change and protect myself. What's more likely is that the man who did that to him killed my father before he could finish me off. Yet, my brain will not allow me to remember. I searched for the man he talked to that night for years, all the while being challenged over and over by pack mates that wanted to best the former Alpha's son. I learned how to be a deadly fighter as I fought for my life every day. Ruthless and cunning. I became Alpha at a young age, probably one of the youngest in the U.S."

"Then, I found the man again. Or rather, he found me. Once I started running my father's business, he came to me with the same proposition that he had given my father. Use my pack to conduct his experiments, be loyal to him, murder his opposition, and anything else he might need. In return, he claimed we would live like the kings of old with more power and more terrortory. Unlike my father, I didn't refuse, all the while gathering information on the man, biding my time. I did small things for him to gain his trust. Then, he had another proposition; he wanted me to be one of his lieutenants in the organization he was building. He knew I was special. I thought it was a good opportunity to get close to him, to make my move."

"The bastard knew my plan all along; he had no intention of letting me get close. He let me get close enough to let me see why I wouldn't be able to kill him, then, he had my mate murdered. I was restrained by his powerful magic that smelled of death and rot, fighting to reach her. My mate was pregnant with my unborn child and all I could do was watch as he had one of his demons destroy her."

Demon? It was definitely the same man.

"When I asked him why he didn't just kill me he said that he was going to kill me one day, but that my suffering would be like the sweetest wine he's ever tasted. He said he'd make me fear him, use me, then take my life. The man is too skilled, too well guarded, and absolutely insane. For the first year, he had me followed by a demon. I was constantly looking over my shoulder, going crazy over how to protect my pack from any fallout. There's a reason why he chose my father and then me, but I've never been able to figure it out. What I do know is that I can't get close and it's been a quiet year. I want it to stay that way. I'm not in a hurry to cut my life short," Anubis finishes, sounding slightly shaken.

"Well, this man thinks that I died along with my family. I can get close to him," I explain.

"Is that so? Do you honestly think he's not watching you? He always finishes his job. Unless you've fallen off the face of the earth, then he knows where you are."

"What if I told you I haven't been on Earth?" I smile.

"Then I'd say that you have some explaining to do," he responds, interested, hands folded on the table.

The song changes to a slow number.

"I will, but first, I need his name."

"You just won't give up will you?"

I just stare at him with my arms crossed, determined.

"He's a witch. His name is Namen Young," he tells me, not defeated, but seemingly believing in me.

I don't know how to feel right now. I've been trying to get a name for so long, to be able to speak the name of the man responsible and now that I have it, I don't even know how I feel. I say his name softly to myself, letting it roll off of my tongue. It's such a nonthreatening name, but I know the truth. I reach in my pocket and pull out one thousand more dollars. I would have paid a million for it, but since he didn't ask, I figured he'd be happy with what he got. At least he knows that I'm serious about the information.

"Thank you Anubis. You've done more than you know tonight," I tell him gratefully.

"If you were truly grateful, then you'd value your own life and listen to what I just told you. When he comes for me I won't be able to stop him. If you are free of him, then why even make yourself a target?"

"Because I have been un-made. I wear the mark of the Immortals and I have thought of nothing else for nearly two years but finding this man. He murdered my mother, father, and my little sister.

They deserve justice. Your family deserves justice and I will be the one to deliver it," I answer.

"Well, those are beautiful words, but I'm telling you the reality. Namen Young is a force. He has powers that are greater than any witch in this time. He has aligned himself with demons and may even be stealing powers from other awakeneds somehow. He also has people protecting him at all times. I think he is up to something that is far greater than we could know. You are just one human. I am just one wolf. I could offer you the protection of my pack, but it would only go so far. Namen will find you first and when he does, your protection is out the window. I will not put my family in any more danger where he's concerned," he advises me, eyes tinting yellow again before blinking it away.

"Then, that is all the more reason to stop him. You just said it. This is greater than the two of us Anubis. I will at the very least find out just what it is that he is up to and then I will take it from there. Can I at least ask this of you? If you hear word of any of his dealings, let me know?"

"You are asking a lot of me human. What will I get from you?"

"The truth is, I don't know what to offer. I may not have anything that you want," I say honestly.

"Oh, don't worry. I'm sure I will come up with something," Anubis answers. "Here, take my card. I hesitate to give this to you, but my curiosity about you has gotten the better of me. Call me if you need anything else." Without another word, Anubis leaves me at my table, alone, with much to consider.

Selene finally comes over to me looking slightly wary. I stand up and meet her before she comes completely to the table. "What's wrong?" I ask her, concerned.

"I don't know for sure, but I think it's time for us to leave. We'll talk about what we learned when we get back home. Don't go straight to your bike if you think you're being followed. Loop around to the car and wait. I'll be right behind you after I handle something." Before I can ask her what she needs to handle, she walks away, her dress hugging her like a lover's embrace.

I look around and try to see if someone is watching me, but with this many people, I can no longer tell as the crowd seems to close in on me. I get to the door and Jaxson tries to whisper something to me, but he's clocked hard in his head and hits the ground with a thud. Before I can react, there is a rush of magic and I am knocked through the door, skidding to a stop on the hard pavement. Not even a second after I hit the ground, numerous hands grab me and soon the same blow that caused Jaxson to be knocked out hits me too.

They couldn't have gotten far because once the world stops spinning and my vision returns, I can still hear the music from club Obsession in the distance. From the smell, they've dragged me in an alley. Gee, how cliché; bad guys and alleys.

Whoever it is that's dragging me hasn't even realized that I've woken up. Clearly they didn't think that I'd be conscious so quickly. They're probably trying to take me to a car so they can drive to a second location. Not going to happen. I slam my feet hard into the dirt and cause my kidnappers to stumble. It's just enough for me to pull my arms free and roll away. It doesn't take them long to recover from the shock and come after me. I pretend to take a step back as if I'm prepared to run, but I come at them full speed, much quicker than they expected from a human. I use this surprise to my advantage as well.

I clothesline the guy closest to me and his head slams against the ground hard, but not hard enough to keep him down. He's bald with a thick brown goatee and white skin. The other one is a pale vamp that smiles at me with deadly teeth, poised to strike. His hair is cut short. In this dark alley, he'll have the advantage of the shadows.

Vampires are able to become one with the shadows for a short period of time which was why they are the greatest hunters the night has to offer. Right now, he's probably listening to the thump of my heart. Then, I hear footsteps behind me and curse my luck. This one is wearing a bandana on his head and on his arm giving him the look of an old school biker.

They have me pretty much surrounded; all of them are dressed in black from head to toe. I don't know if I can count on Selene to back me up. Still, I'm not too worried that I'll lose this fight; I'm just worried about what they want with me.

Chapter Nineteen

So, is there a reason that you needed me out cold to come with you? Don't you know the proper way to ask for a date?" I wipe the dirt from my leather jacket and try to look as though I'm the one in control of the situation. While doing that, I try to turn my body so that I can see every single one of their moves.

No response, great I'm not among the talkative group. Then, I look at the one that I knocked down. He's pointing at his mouth. When he opens it, there's no tongue. Shit. None of them could speak even if they wanted to. Who would want that kind of job? Psychos, that's who. That means that they were chosen specifically for jobs like this. I wasn't even back two whole days yet. How in the world am I already a target?

"Well, let's just move this along then," I say.

As the one behind me shifts to his left, I track his movement right before I'm hit with an electric shock from the one I knocked down. Baldy. It brings me to my knees as the surge courses through my body. He's a witch, just great. I need to take him out first.

It isn't hard to analyze their plan. He will attack from a distance and while I'm trying to dodge those, the other two will come for me. I still don't know what biker dude is, so I'll have to watch him closely. I can't wait for Selene. The chances are that there is some type of commotion in the club that caused her to not be able to get back to me. That, or they are spelling this area making it hard to follow my trail.

He shifts again and another blow of magic hits me. They're communicating. The third time, they will attack. I'm right. Once the witch shoots again, I use the wall for leverage and deliver a swift kick to the vampire's head. I don't hesitate since the bandana wearing one has come into the fray with hands that are on fire. I try to dodge all his blows, but one connects, causing a hole to be burned through my clothes. The heat coming off of him is unreal and I sweat drips from my brow into my eyes. Quickly, I wipe it away.

He's a half fire demon and I'm unarmed. I can't block his blows with my hands or feet and I definitely can't keep much distance between us because every time I do, the witch attempts an attack. As I long as I stay close to these two, the witch won't risk it.

The demon's job is to create enough fear of him to cause me to keep that distance where the witch would incapacitate me and if need be, if I become too much trouble, the vamp will finish me off by draining enough of my blood that I can't fight back. It's in my best interest to not let that happen either. Once a vamp locks onto you and starts pumping pheromones into your body, it can sometimes be damn near impossible to force them to break from a feeding alone.

It wasn't hard for me to figure out their plans and see through it. I was praised for my vision in battle from Diana and Lawrence. It was apparently one of the things that I inherited when I'd been un-made. My analytical skills had increased tremendously since it had been one of my strong points before. Now, what I need is a way to draw the witch's fire to hit one of his own. I have to let the demon think that I am afraid of him. I have to let him get close. It hurts my heart profoundly to know that I'll have to sacrifice my beautiful red jacket.

The vampire isn't that strong. It is obvious that he's a young vamp that had been turned recently. Thank God he isn't a pureblood. I know I can end him at anytime, but before I do that, I need the witch to play into my plan. The demon's next punch comes uncomfortably close to my face. The heat beats against my skin, scorching it. I feign fear and the half demon's face reveals smugness. He thinks he has me beat.

Good.

I keep backing up, closer and closer to the witch. The vampire is standing down, also assuming that they can handle me on their own. If he would have been paying attention to his instincts, then he would have heard the calmness in the beat of my heart. Instead he's watching my eyes and the fictional fear that I put in them.

The half demon's hands begin to glow even brighter. I allow one more brush against my clothes as he picks up the speed on his attacks. Still, in reality, his attacks are too slow, too easy to read. They're not professionals this bunch. They are a test. I understand that now. Now, I'm tired of playing the game.

I pretend to stumble, and the demon reaches for my throat. I use his momentum to pull him forward by his arm, straight into the neck of the witch. It takes too long for the half blood to realize what has happened. By that time, the smell of burning flesh and the attempted scream of the witch hit him with full force. He turns to me, but I'm already behind him, snapping his neck, quickly and efficiently. I have no time to think about my kill. The vamp is enraged and sprinting towards me like a freight train.

Before I can react, his head is removed from his neck and his flesh begins to crumble away like all vampires that meet their final death. I'm sure my own surprise echoed his. I never saw it coming, so I know he didn't either. Just as quickly as it had happened, the deliverer of the strike is back in the shadows. I stand as if I'm frozen to the ground, afraid to budge because I don't know if they are friend or foe. I don't even know if they are still there.

"Hello?" I ask warily, suddenly feeling like the next victim in a scary movie.

"He knows what you are. You will need more than the protection of that wolf. I know who you are as well and I will give you my protection too. He's building up an army and you need to be prepared. I will help you get stronger. This is just the beginning Rayne Whitmore." Her voice is determined, prepared, but somehow familiar.

"Help me how?" I ask, but there's no response other than the wind. I turn and walk back out of the alley. This time I know that I'm alone. No matter what Selene said, I wouldn't be going anywhere without Katsu, not when Namen Young knew about me clearly well before I even knew his name. Anubis was right. He was dangerous. He'd sent three people to test me. Maybe he'd sent them to watch Anubis, but they figured out who I was. Maybe I just put him in more danger.

Shit!

I run back in the direction of the music and fling open the door. Jaxson is sitting there with Selene holding an ice pack against his head.

"What do you mean you didn't see who took her!" she screams at him before looking up at me, relief evident in her dark green eyes. "Jesus Rayne. I hadn't even left you for five minutes. What the hell happened?" she asks frantically.

"Namen Young happened. That's the bastard's name who took my family. He knew I wasn't dead Selene. He's been waiting for me to show my face," I tell her.

Selene and Jaxson both give me a look. Jaxson stands up and pulls out his cell.

"I have to call Anubis. He could be in danger." Jaxson dials his number then looks at me as he waits for the call to go through. "I can't believe he told you. I'm his second, his enforcer and if his helping you brings any harm to him or my pack. I will hunt you down."

"Well, right now, I'm under your protection, so don't ruin our treaty just yet," I tell him.

Jaxson walks away and when he returns he breathes a sigh of relief.

"You won't be attacked this close to the full moon and you know it. Do not threaten my girlfriend again," Selene warns calmly, but with a deadly and promising look in her eyes.

I smile at her protectiveness and so does Jaxson. Clearly, he appreciates a spirited woman. "Packs will protect their own. You can't blame me for doing my job."

"And if you lay a finger on her, I will do mine," she reiterates.

"Well, from what I've learned tonight, Anubis is allowing Namen to destroy him with fear. If you truly cared about your pack, you would do all you could to help me put an end to this man," I tell him.

Jaxson considers my words for a second, then says, "Come back here tomorrow night and we will talk. If you can't make it, then call this number." He gives me his number and Selene suggests that we leave now.

"Did you get what else you came for?" I ask.

"No. I think I was mistaken," she responds quietly.

Selene takes me to the Ducati and waits until I pull off before driving down the street. On the ride back, I think about how easy it was for me to snap the half-demon's neck, how I did it without a moment's hesitation. Maybe it would always be that easy. I think about how I felt that day when my father had beat that man. How I was hurt by how my father handled his business, how I grappled with the morality of it. Now, I am a killer. Did I think I was wrong? No. Would I do it again? Yes. Amazing how life can turn.

We get home and I fill Selene in on all that Anubis had explained to me. I tell her about the fact that Namen had said that he knew Anubis was "special" when he was trying to recruit him and what that meant. I wonder if it is something more to this wolf than he is letting on. There has to be another reason that Namen has kept him alive for so long. Anubis probably doesn't give himself enough credit. Once I handle this lamia problem, I would find out. I need to find out what Anubis really is if I'm going to use him.

Next, I ask Selene if she knows anything about Namen Young. She tells me that she's never heard of the name and that I need to also remember that she hasn't been here for that many years, not to mention the fact that she's kept a low profile, hiding from her own past. It really doesn't make any difference though. I have his name now and I will find him. Even if he attacks first, I'll be ready.

"So what happened when they took you? What did they say to you?" she asks.

"Well, it happened so fast. I saw Jaxson go down, and then they had me. Honestly, I don't know if they were all in the club or outside the door waiting. They knocked me out for all of maybe two minutes. As I came to as they were dragging me in an alley," I begin.

"They couldn't have followed us. They were probably watching Anubis." She agreed with me on that.

"Yeah, then they came after me. It was like Namen wanted to verify who or what I am. It was three of them, but they weren't very strong. They knew how to coordinate their attacks on a basic level, but they had no real skills. One was a half-fire demon which is why my lovely jacket looks like I'd been in a barbecue. There was also a vamp and a witch."

"A witch? What did this witch look like?"

"Well, he looked dead now. I tricked the demon into burning his throat."

For a second there's a glimpse of fear on Selene's face, I swear it.

"Are you okay Selene?" I ask. "Is there something wrong?"

"No, just tell me what he looked like."

"Shit, I don't know. He was average looking. Average height, average build, bald with a brown goatee. Oh, and none of them had any tongues. It was pretty creepy actually."

"No tongues? Interesting. I wonder what's the point of that, if it's forced or whatnot."

"Me too. They seemed far too willing to do his bidding, but that still didn't mean much. There was something else," I say, thinking about the mysterious stranger in the shadows who'd finished off the vamp with so much skill that I never even realized she was there.

"What is it?" Selene asks as she puts on something more comfortable, obviously hearing my hesitation at my thoughts.

"There was someone else in the alley with us. I don't know where she came from, if she was there the whole time or what. Hell, I never even got a look at her," I admit.

"Did she try to attack you? What happened Rayne? Did she do or say anything to you?" Selene clearly didn't like the fact that I hadn't been aware. Shit, I didn't like it. Maybe it was because I was still new to this.

"No, she didn't try to hurt me. It was the opposite. She helped me by taking the vamp's head off. Neither one of us ever saw it coming, and lucky for me, it was him she was after because there was no way I'd have been able to stop that attack," I say honestly. If she'd been my enemy, I'd be dead right now, period. Suddenly realizing that, my hands start to tremble slightly. I need to pay more attention. I had gotten cocky about beating those three that I never even thought that they could have very well been bait to the true attack. Then, I know the truth.

"I knew that it was a test once I started fighting, but now I understand a little better," I begin as I start stripping off my clothes, tired of feeling constricted in them.

Once I am down to my bra and panties, I continue. "Namen was learning my weaknesses, and I could have just given him a big one. He could have had someone much more efficient waiting for the right moment to strike. That's basically what those three were teaching me, that's what they were doing by the vampire and half breed fighting me and the witch targeting me from a distance."

"Still, that wasn't the lesson, the lesson was to pay attention to what had been hiding in the shadows even farther away. Whomever that stranger was Selene, they may have very well saved my life tonight," I explain. It did seem odd to me that she'd intervened when I obviously had a handle on the battle. Maybe I never did. Maybe she made her move so that whatever else had been out there would back off. As soon as I thought it, I knew it to be truth. Damn.

"You'll have to be much more careful then. I know you wanted to find this lamia, but maybe it's not the best idea. We don't even know what we're up against right now, and this whole lamia thing could end up being a trap or at least an opportunity to kill you. From what you've told me, Namen apparently doesn't like loose ends."

"I can't Selene and you know it, so you might as well drop it. I'm not changing my mind on it. Once I have the information I need, I'll end it quickly okay, so don't trip."

"Well, I won't stop you, you know that. Did this person say anything to you?"

"Yeah, she seemed to know exactly who I was which means that Namen isn't the only one keeping tabs on me. She said that he, presumably Namen, knew who I was and that I needed to become stronger. She also said that I was under her protection too."

"She never said who she was or why? This is not making any damn sense. I don't like it Rayne. There is something else going on here. It seems like too much too damn fast. Merda! Eu não gosto deste." Great. When Selene started to worry in Portuguese that meant she was really troubled.

Maybe I should be too.

"Ok, well first things first. We know I can't handle all these things at once, and it was my decision to add the lamia to the plate, but I'll handle it. Having Anubis put me under his protection won't help with Namen, but maybe it'd help with other supernaturals. This woman though, her words carry some weight, I can feel it. I have time to at least learn more about Anubis, Namen, and kill the lamia before anything major goes down. That woman will find me, she said she'd help me."

"And you will go nowhere with her alone right?" she asks.

I pause before I answer, knowing I couldn't promise that. If she could help me and Selene wasn't around, I'm positive I won't wait.

"Really Rayne?" Selene says, not so much in a question. "It shouldn't be much to think about on this. You don't know her. All I'm asking is that you wait for me, can you do that?"

"I will try Selene," I tell her.

"That's not fucking good enough. This is not a game."

"It wasn't a fucking game when I was almost taken tonight too, and I handled myself anyway," I snap, realizing that I was kind of angry with her for not following me out and not telling me what was so urgent inside.

"So, you being mad at me, blaming me, is going to make it alright for you to run off and train with some strange cadela? Wow. I can't believe you right now."

"Do you not trust me?" I ask.

"This isn't about trust, Rayne, are you serious right now? This is about your safety. Where is this coming from? We don't argue about things like this. If I wanted to argue with you about trust, I would have said something when we were with the Immortals and Diana tried to seduce you every other day, not to mention Lawrence. You are attracted to her and I never complained, never threw a fit because it's okay to appreciate a beautiful woman without acting on it. But, don't pull this trust crap on me right now."

Selene shakes her head at me in disappointment. "That is the most immature thing you've said to me in a long time and you're very close to pissing me off. I'm not trying to boss you; I just want to be there," Selene raises her voice, before lowering it at the end. Her beautiful features are framed with irritation and I can feel the magic rising within her. She was half ready to knock me on my ass.

I don't even know why I said that.

Maybe it was because I felt that she herself was hiding something that I couldn't yet place, nor ask about. Selene was looking for something and I think tonight she left me alone because she thought she'd found it. I'm not stupid. I obviously said some stupid things, but I have good instincts. I could probably wait for her to tell me what was going on. Besides, I probably don't need any more surprises in my life right now. I should just apologize and finish this conversation.

"That was childish of me. I know you trust me and I apologize. I never have liked to feel bossed around and thought maybe it was just because it was another girl that had saved me. I have to remember that I'm not dealing with humans anymore," I respond to her, reaching out for her hand, hoping she'll let me pull her close.

She looks into my hazel eyes with her dark green ones, kisses my forehead, then my lips gently with her soft, full ones. I respond to her kiss with a teasing tongue caressing her lips before she slowly pulls away from me. It's obvious that she'd like the kiss to go deeper, but there are other matters to attend to first.

"I forgive you, but don't ever think that's the case. I trust you, just like you trust me. Now, if you're really hell bent on stopping these lamia, I found out where they've been hunting the last two days," Selene informs me.

"Good, let's do this tomorrow night then," I say excitedly.

"Wait, there's also some bad news."

"And…"

"There's a nest of about twelve of them."

"Twelve? Is that a normal nest size? I'm going to assume that it's not."

"Hell no it's not normal on our plane. They have been hunting for an extremely long period of time without one of their group being killed or spotted, until now. Or so I was told."

"Then all the more reason to take them out. Let's come up with a plan. I think our biggest disadvantage and mistake we made when we were with the Immortals was not learning to fight together enough. We need to be able to fill in for each other's weaknesses and watch each other's backs. I say we do that now. There's no point in waiting."

"And what do you propose we do?"

"Let's start with sparring each other. No holding back either. That way we can gauge each other's weaknesses," I tell her.

"Alright, if you insist. I don't think you'll be able to handle me," Selene warns jokingly.

"Well, bring it. I think you might want to tie that pretty hair of yours up. I wouldn't want you to use that as an excuse if it gets in the way."

She laughs and pulls it back. Before we head to the basement to train, I grab Katsu and ask my sword nicely to not cut my girlfriend. She reacts with a wave of magic. When I feel her sleek white blade, I'm glad that it feels dull and unable to cut.

"Thank you Katsu," I say to my magical katana.

"So, you're not going to put on any clothes?" Selene asks me.

"Naw, I'm hoping this will be a distraction technique."

"Fine." Selene proceeds to strip down too. "Let's see who gets distracted first."

◊◊◊

We stand about five feet away from each other, face to face, and I smile appreciatively at her fantastic body. "Maybe I should keep my sword sheathed until we're sure we're at the same level," I suggest, changing my mind slightly. Even though Katsu won't cut, it will still hurt like hell when I strike.

"You said no holding back, you pussy," Selene teases dangerously before blasting me with some kind of orb of energy.

I shuffle to the side at the last second, but it still catches me and it burns my arm before flickering out. "Pussy huh? Such language, tsk tsk." I respond, ignoring the tingling from the graze. "So you really don't have to use incantations for your spells?"

"Oh, I'm beyond that when it comes to many middle class and some high class spells. I'm a high priestess remember? There is deeper magic inside me and I'm not limited to what other witches may have to do. Now, I've got it figured out thanks to Kaede. So, are we going to talk or spar?"

I unsheathe my sword and get into my fighting stance, but before Selene can adjust, I shift my foot and run straight at Selene, swinging my blade down with fury. Still, she doesn't seem fazed by my speed or willingness to rush at her like this, she just stops Katsu, my katana, with her hand, which causes a jarring motion in my body.

I don't have time to be surprised. Selene uppercuts me hard in the chin and almost sends me to my knees. Okay, now I am acting like a pussy. She gives me a smirk and a raised eyebrow as if to ask me when am I going to stop holding back. Oh, she's in for a shock.

I drop down quickly and trip Selene before rolling on top of her to send a blow to her face, but she manages to throw me off in time. I roll away, grabbing Katsu off the ground, before slicing through the air, and then feinting a swing of the blade, before landing a leg strike into Selene's midsection.

Before I give her a chance to react with a spell, I toss her across the room and into the wall, putting some distance between us. Selene will expect me to try to actually attack at as close a range as possible, knowing what I know about witches, but since she clearly knows a spell that lent her some kind of strength, it's more obvious to me that I'll have to wear her out until her chakra level becomes low before I can attack close.

Still, Selene isn't the type to attack unnecessarily, so I have to figure something else out. I take a deep breath as I feel the strength given to me through my un-making course through me. My tattoo begins to hum through my body, then glow, and I feel Katsu become surer in my hands, more a part of me. Selene seems to breathe in the air as if she feels it too. We lock eyes and smile before both of us poise for attack. I almost miss it, her tell, the slightest twitch of her brow, before another blast of energy seeks me.

All witches have a tell that gives them away, some are just better at masking theirs. This time, I'm too fast though, too prepared. I'm on her before she realizes it. Or, so I thought. A blinding light hits my eyes just before I get ready to make contact. I see nothing and for a split second before I regain my composure, I have to trust my other senses. A searing pain hits my back. I hiss and duck under the next assault that I hear before my eyes start to work again.

I remember all that Lawrence taught me about the battle turning at any minute, to be prepared for anything. It helps me clear my head and I spin to the left, landing a fierce kick to Selene's leg, even without my vision. I hear her grunt in pain and I can't help the satisfied smirk that paints my face. I slide back and put some distance between us as my vision comes back into focus, with only tiny little lights dancing in front of my eyes. Selene stands up, dusts herself off, and wipes some loose hair from her face. Her bra is falling off her shoulders and her eyes are shining with magic, making her green eyes brighter, and more exotic looking.

I lick my lips and motion Selene to make a move as I get back into my fighting stance. Katsu's stretched out before me, my feet firmly rooted to the ground. Selene is much more skilled than I thought and even though we both agreed not to hold back, we both know that there was no way we'd attack each other the way we would a true enemy. I can feel her love for me through her magic as we come to blows. I know she can feel my heart as well. Still, we will have to do this dance much more seriously each time if we are to truly protect each other.

She speaks something this time, something musical that I don't understand, two fingers held to her mouth, her lips pressed against her pointer finger. The lights begin to flicker. I force myself not to move, to remain in my stance, until I feel that it's time to strike. Suddenly, Selene is no longer in front of me. The air shifts, and I can feel her magic behind me. But when I turn and swing, all I slash is air.

The lights flicker again, and I turn my head to the side trying to feel the surge of power I've come to recognize as Selene's magic. It doesn't take long before I feel it and even though I can't see her, I trust my instincts as I let Katsu fly through the air. Selene gasps as she drops her glamour and stares at my sword sticking out of the basement wall a foot from her head.

Then, there's a tap on my back and I spin around to see Selene standing with her arms crossed. I spin back around to see what I thought was my witch disappearing from sight, no actually, becoming Selene's shadow, creepily sliding across the floor to connect with her. "You lose," she tells me smugly.

"I see." I had gotten cocky again. Damn, that would be my downfall.

"It's called a shadow puppet. The spell is a very difficult one and very draining, but as you can see, it's very effective because it mimics the feel of the users magic as well as the person itself. It's as if my shadow itself had become real. Mix that with a glamour to disappear and that is what I did."

I look at her up and down, the sweat on her brow, the slight shaking of her hand. Yes, very draining indeed. She almost looks pale. "Let's get some food in your stomach and we can talk about each other's assessments."

"Sounds good, but now you're starting to sound like a teacher."

"Hmm, now there's some role play we haven't tried yet," I respond.

"Indeed."

Chapter Twenty

After filling our stomachs and then taking nice, long, hot showers, we discuss each other's opinions on our skills and how to best work together. We both come to the conclusion that I get overconfident when I feel that I'm winning and end up letting my guard down. Even though I'm excellent at evaluating situations during battle, I need to learn to maintain that focus, keep my training at the front of my mind. I also need to train with not only Katsu, but other weapons as well, just in case. I told Selene what I felt with Katsu and how she was supposed to get stronger as I did. So, it would benefit us all for me to keep her by my side.

Selene on the other hand needs to first work on her tell which let me know when she was ready to attack with her magic, then, she needs to learn more martial arts skills so that she won't have to rely solely on spells that will dry her chakra up too quick. Although, when training with the Immortals, Kaede was able to assist Selene in increasing her levels much more than before. In fighting, Selene isn't adequate at paying attention to how much magic she is using at the same time as hand to hand combat. Because of this, she could potentially misread situations and use a more powerful spell when there was no need and actually put her in danger if she had no power left.

For now, our strategy is simple: Selene will attack first as a distraction while I get a feel for the situation, then we'd go from there. If there's a group of them, I'd engage the strongest one while Selene played clean-up with the others until she could help me from a distance. We'd tweak it as needed. When it came time to take out Namen Young, we'd have to have a plan a,b,c,d,e... well, you get the point. We need much more intel on him. I wanted to kill these damn lamia quickly and focus on Namen. I want him dead like yesterday. But for now, the best thing to do is rest.

◊◊◊

I wake up to Selene doing stretches, her long legs spread out in front of her, her back towards me. "Good morning," she says without turning around.

"Hey, how long have you been up?"

"Maybe thirty minutes. Do you want to grab something to eat? We could go out before we get down to business."

"Sure, let's go downtown for a bit."

As usual, downtown is full of people in a hurry to get places in expensive business suits and briefcases, chatting away on their phones, cars honking bumper to bumper, and people fighting for parking spaces close to their destination. The air is filled with delicious scents of fresh food like bagels, bacon, eggs, fruits, and coffee. I absorb the sights, sounds, smells and smile at the people who really have no clue about the real world who only have to worry about their next business meeting or their son's next ball game.

Our city loves its football and I see many people sporting our team's jerseys. My dad had season tickets and he made sure that at an early age I understood and loved the game. A frown threatens to form on my face, but then I force myself to be grateful for the memories that I do have, and I smile instead.

We go to a small coffee shop called Pete's and grab a seat near the window so that I can feel the sun on my face. I feel normal for about forty five minutes, talking and laughing with Selene, flirting, commenting on people's outfits, but it doesn't last. Sirens pierce through my false bubble of normalcy, police cars zoom down the streets, zig zagging through traffic, and I remember that I will only have these small pockets of peace until I finish my goal, and even then...

This is why supernaturals sometimes used to term awakened to describe themselves. How can I go back to what I used to be when I've already seen so much?

I have a different purpose now. I am needed to be a hero to my kind. Is it heroic of me to try to kill a man for his crimes against me and others? No, I don't really think so, but I also know that true heroes are those among us who would do what other's dared not. At the end of the day, I would not do this for the approval of others; instead I'd be doing this so that they can continue to live in their bubble of happy ignorance.

"Can we shop for a few more things? I just want to feel normal for a little while longer," I say to Selene. I can simulate blissful ignorance for a few more minutes.

She looks at me and smiles, her gaze filled with love. "Yes, baby."

In the end, I managed to buy many unnecessary clothes and shoes that I wouldn't get the chance of wearing for a while, but I didn't care, it's what people did, it's what Jazzy would have wanted to do with me. It's what she deserved to be doing, living, enjoying life. Damn, why is this so hard for me? I just still can't accept their deaths, even if I try with all my might, I just can't accept it. Maybe I need therapy.

Chapter Twenty One

Night falls and Selene and I go back to Obsession to talk to Jaxson. This time, I have Katsu firmly strapped to my back and I'll be damned if she didn't stay there. When we pull up, the music is low but vibrating against the windows and doors just like before, but this time there's a line. I also don't feel the pull of wrongness that I had felt when I first tried to enter. Maybe it wouldn't affect me anymore since I had broken through once. We wait in line patiently with more than a few glares directed our way. I give them a couple winks and a finger in return. Probably not the smartest thing, but oh well. They leave us alone.

Jaxson is working the door again dressed in a grey polo and black jeans. When he sees us, he says something over the radio in his back pocket and tells us to wait as another wolf, medium height with blond hair takes over for him with a smile. Apparently, he has no issues with me being human, or having a sword.

"Follow me," Jaxson tells us, as we weave through the crowd of people who are body to body, grinding to the slow r&b music. I don't recognize the song and I'm slightly irritated about having to catch up on all my favorite artists songs that I missed. We head upstairs as the music switches tempo and then becomes quieter when we walk through one set of steel doors, then Jaxson unlocks another until it's all but a hum.

Jaxson pulls out a couple chairs for us in a small, but comfortable office with no pictures on the desk or wall. Only a laptop and paperwork sit on the table. Selene and I take our seats, me crossing my legs, letting my heels catch his eye. Hey, I want some compliments, at least notice of my excellent taste.

"So, Jaxson, what is it that you plan to do for us?" Selene asks straightforward.

"As I said, I am Anubis's second. I answer only to him, for he is where my loyalty lies. If he gave you Namen Young's name, then he must see something in you that he's willing to bet on. I love my Alpha and I will do what it takes to keep him safe, so it is not what I plan to do for you witch, but what I will do for him."

"Ah, my mistake," Selene apologizes humorously. Clearly we are grasping straws, even if none of us say so, we all know it.

Then, I understand. "When your Alpha gives an order, it is absolute is it not? So, Anubis must have told you not to help us unless he gives the word."

There is a cleverness in his dark eyes that I appreciate. "You could be on to something there, but as I said, I am not helping you, I am helping Anubis."

We all nod in understanding and I smile and look towards Selene. I let her take the lead on this. "Jaxson, if you want to help Anubis be rid of Namen, why has it taken so long? Surely, there are other resources at your disposal."

"True, but there has not been an opportunity before. There also doesn't seem to be many here who either know what Namen is doing or who are willing to oppose the man. And for all he is, Anubis may have one major fault, he cares for his pack more than his own life."

"One would not find that a fault among wolves, especially not an Alpha."

Jaxson obviously doesn't seem to be fearful of telling us something that could be seen as a weakness to Anubis's enemies. Obviously Jaxson would protect his Alpha to the death, even from us.

"Perhaps, but there is a difference when there is a threat and you'd die to protect your pack from the threat and allowing the threat to slowly destroy you rather than risk your pack. Either way, you'll lose, but Anubis doesn't seem to understand that he is losing much more doing this his way. He is still young yet, and doesn't always see the bigger picture. He has over twenty wolves that are willing to die for him, yet he doesn't make one move. The pack is starting to sense his fear and they will turn against him and look for a new leader and he will lose it all anyway. An Alpha that is frozen with fear is as good as dead."

"I think I understand. But there is something else to this. How is he controlling a pack this large anyway? Packs are usually no more than fifteen, eighteen at the most?" Selene asks, leaning forward, adjusting the collar on her black v-neck.

"First, she must tell me her story. Then, I will decide if knowing about our pack will help you help Anubis." Jaxson turns towards me, waiting for me to begin. His dark eyes seek my own, testing me. I give him ten good seconds, studying his scars on his face, his short mohawk, his slightly large nose, and then change my vision, satisfying him. He may be second in the pack but he doesn't have the aura of his Alpha. Still, it would be rude to drag this out any longer. Then, he looks at my back as if just noticing my sword and raises an eyebrow out of curiosity.

I tell him as much as I feel that he needs to know of my family's murder, my un-making, and how I came here today. I leave Damien completely out of it as well as what my father's business was. He didn't need to know that my father was making weapons against supernaturals, not yet at least. Though I had never made it a habit to do so anyway, I still had to remember that werewolves could smell lies easily when it came to things that I was telling him. He needed to trust me, he wanted to trust me. I needed Jaxson to know that he could.

"I'd heard rumors when I was young that humans used to have strength like a wolf, brains like a fox, and could hunt our kind down single-handedly, but never thought I'd meet one. I just thought that you were another kind of super that I didn't know about, even if you smelled human. Interesting. Not only that, but the Immortals do exist. It just goes to show that there was still a lot that even our kind does not know."

"Well, Jaxson, imagine how I felt, finding a demon about to eat my dead sister," I say rudely, then apologize. There was no need to snap on him, it's not his fault that I grew up in the world that I did.

Oblivious. Especially when my father knew and could have told me a long time ago.

"It's okay. I can understand your anger. When we luna dasa, the moon's servants, as some of us wolves call ourselves, first hit puberty, we begin our change as well. Imagine the challenges of becoming a teenager, mixed with rage, indescribable pain of those first turns, thinking of yourself as a monster, afraid that you might snap and kill your loved ones, and the need to hunt, taste blood. We all have different crosses to bear and trust me, imagine how I feel when I have to kill my own because they can't handle the change; the young ones, when they become feral. You wouldn't switch places with me for a second." The seriousness of his tone makes me feel sorry that he has to do such a job.

I nod in respect. I had forgotten that not all wolves survived the change, or should I say were allowed to survive the change.

"This is part of the reason why our pack numbers are so strong. Thanks to Anubis, we do not lose hardly any more of our young. We are thriving. We take care of our own and we've learned something that not many other packs have. This is the real reason why Namen will not kill Anubis. It is because he is special and he wants to break him until he can use him. Anubis has conquered his Wolf and taught him how to shift as well," Jaxson says, excitement evident in his voice.

"I do not understand what you mean Jaxson. Please explain," Selene requests looking at me with the same look I give her.

He smiles. "When man shifts he becomes Wolf, but when wolf shifts, what does he become? Man, of course, or at least partially so. For us, we once thought that the shift was to wolf and wolf alone, that you could not stop the change once it began or that if you were caught in the middle of the change that you would die like that. This is not true however. Anubis discovered this when he had been caught in the middle of a change and panicked. He was able to stop the shift and come back."

"He practiced with this, over and over, forcing the change on his hands, his feet, his face. Do you know how painful it is to change? How much skill and resolve you'd need to focus enough on one part of the body while fighting back the pain? He did it, and he did it alone. And he meditated and spoke to his Wolf, understanding, learning, until he realized something else. He could have the look of a wolf, with the body of a man, one that had more strength than a wolf, sacrificing the speed of four legs, but gaining so much more. It is the ultimate form for our kind to fight in. Somewhere along the way, we had lost that skill as the world developed, but Anubis, he, brought it back to us."

I can understand the advantages, and it is actually slightly terrifying to think about. Weres were already extra large in size in their wolf form, I couldn't imagine how this mountain of a man sitting in front of me would be in wolf-man form slashing at me with razor claws and teeth. Hell no, I didn't want them as enemies and I bet Namen didn't really want them as enemies either, he wanted them fearful and complacent.

"Scary," I say truthfully.

"Oh, it is. Anubis and I can even use weapons in that form," Jaxson says, eyeing Katsu. "For some though, it takes too much focus just to maintain the shift. For now, at least."

"But, to what end? The world has changed."

"Our kind is becoming scarce. We are not naturally urban creatures, but cities are popping up everywhere and in rural areas, there's just too much suspicion for our kind to have large packs. Because of this, many of us are hesitant to mate or breed, and for the last ten years, we've had to kill many of our own kind because they've snapped and gone rogue. If humans were to find out about us, we'd need to have better skills to protect ourselves. Our packs must get stronger because that day when our numbers reach a low is when they'll find us out, and they'll come for us. I say, let them fear what we could do to them so that they'd leave us alone."

"So how do you cope with the issues of the cities then?" I ask.

"Well, most of us join the police, firefighters, or even the military. We have a drug that almost all of us take that keeps us from having to change during the full moon, but because of that, we have a lot of pent up aggression inside, most of us choose dangerous, adrenaline filled jobs that help us blow off steam. I'm actually a volunteer firefighter myself."

"Hmm, I'd have to keep that in mind. Don't piss off the wolf behind the counter."

Jaxson laughs and grabs my shoulder firmly. I take it as a sign of friendship.

"We need to find a way to learn Namen's end game. Maybe if we cut off his plans, it will bring him out of the woodwork, or at least cause him to make a mistake that will allow us to get close," Selene suggests, bringing us back to the point.

"You then need to take out some of his lieutenants, and his minions. There's also a rumor going around that he has been having a group of demon's kidnap young children for him to experiment on. It is said that he has been trying to turn them into supernaturals through DNA manipulation. The ones that don't make it, he allows the demons to eat."

"What the hell! You can't be serious. It's the lamia isn't it?" I ask, already knowing the answer.

"How'd you?" Jaxson begins.

"We were just going to ask you if you knew anything about that. We heard rumors that kids had gone missing and were going to take care of it ASAP, but this is different. If Namen actually is involved, we really have to be careful," Selene says.

"But it still needs to be done," I say, with finality. We weren't going to argue this anymore. The lamia are going to be handled. By me.

"Then, I guess that is not up for discussion. Tell me what you know then and I will see if I can add to it," Jaxson offers.

Selene gives him the information she learned and he adds to it by telling us that he knows the town where the lamia is keeping the children. But, since he's been ordered by Anubis to stay away, he can give us no more than that.

"I will do my best to convince Anubis that we need to take action now. Namen Young is a threat and I think that it's time to do something about it. I'm ready to stand with you on this," Jaxson promises as there's a knock at the door.

"You may enter," he permits.

"Mr. Kellog, you're needed at the front," says a short haired female employee. She gives us a friendly smile and then leaves.

"Well, duty calls, I'm afraid. But you are welcome here if you wish to stay, if not, then be careful and do not make a move until I give you a call. I want to see if I can talk to Anubis first, then I will come with you. If the lamia's numbers are that great, there may be something else there that he's hiding. You just might need a nose like mine," Jaxson tells us.

"You might be right, but I really don't want to have to wait any more nights than one or two. Children are dying," I explain.

"I understand that missy, but sometimes patience can give you a whole lot more than rushing in blindly. You don't want any mistakes when it comes to that witch."

"Alright, now you're sounding like Selene. I get it, just don't keep me waiting too long okay," I tell him, trying not to sound too much like a demand.

"I will handle my end human. Now, if you'll excuse me, I need to see what the issue is downstairs." With that, he leaves us to converse among ourselves.

Selene busts out in a cute, school girl giggle, covering her mouth as I look at her sideways.

"What is it?" I inquire.

"Mr. Kellog. This whole time I thought his last name was Jaxson."

We stand there silently, staring at each other for a few seconds before we burst out laughing, louder this time. "Hell, I thought so too," I admit.

After that, we decide to have a couple drinks just to see if Jaxson will come back to speak with us. He never does, so we take our leave for the night.

Chapter Twenty Two

The night air brushes against my bare neck and a chill courses through my body like an electric pulse. When we got here, the street was fairly quiet, but now, it seems even emptier of life. I try to shake off the feeling.

"What now?" I ask Selene as we head down the street to our car.

"Pay attention Rayne, what do you sense?" Selene snaps at me quietly. I start to slow up, but she snaps at me again. "No, don't slow your pace, just pay attention. What do you sense?"

I take deep breaths as we continue our pace and that's when I feel it, harmful intent. They're surrounding us. There is at least six of them, but there's something else, someone that I couldn't sense last time, but now feel her a clearly as if she is standing two feet in front of me. Maybe it's because she's allowed me to. I find her presence weirdly comforting when I know nothing about her. To make sure I'm right, I glance up to see a hooded figure crouching on the roof a few buildings down. For some reason, I don't think Selene can detect her presence.

"Are they wolves?" I whisper, hoping that they can't hear me if they are.

"I think so, and clearly not of Anubis's pack, which is dangerous in itself for them, since this doesn't seem to be their territory to be trying to hunt or kill. My only guess is that Namen put them up to this," Selene responds.

"Your guess is probably right, which means, not only is it a day from the full moon, but we're going to have to deal with at least six of them when they're nearly at their strongest. We may have help though."

"Yes, if someone hears the commotion and Jaxson and his pack come to help," Selene agrees with me, at least thinking that it's our werewolf allies that I'm talking about. I was referring to my mysterious watcher above.

How did she even know I was here? There's no time to think about it now. We have to do something before they figure out that we are on to them.

I pretend to find some money on the ground as I laugh real loud, as if I'm continuing a conversation. Then, I whisper, "Selene, do something about these street lights, then try to make as much noise with these cars as you can. Maybe it will cause them to hesitate and even back off; if not, then at least it will get someone to notice." I speak quickly as I hear the grunts of the change come over some of the wolves. I lift my head back up and say, "Now." I pull Katsu from my back as the pop of the street lights fill the air.

One by one, they go out in sparks, just before a chorus of car alarms slice through the peace of the night. One stupid wolf moves forward anyway, seemingly now unsure of his task. I'm not unsure of mine, however. I launch myself one handed over a car and slice through his stomach as he tries to leap at me, me up under him. Then, I spin back around to face him as he howls in pain. I flick his blood off my sword as he attacks me again, this time, not alone as another wolf leaps at me from behind. Selene knocks the second one away, mid leap, shaking on the ground as if electrocuted as I take the leg of the first wolf.

I get shivers at the feel of the lost limb as Katsu slices through it, but I force myself not to think about it. He too drops to the ground, the pain causing him to change back to human, unconscious and bleeding. Werewolves heal better in wolf form. It isn't looking good for stumpy. I try to figure out which one is the strongest of the group as I count my enemies.

Howls come from the direction of the club and then the thunder of powerful paws on the pavement fills my ears. Seconds later, I recognize Jaxson even in his half-wolf form as he stops in front of me, growling at the shadows.

Jaxson has the face and ears of a wolf as well as the lupine structure of back legs. His feet are even those of a wolf's, but his arms, hands, and torso is that of man covered in light fur. Razor sharp claws and massive teeth complete his killer form. He is a chestnut color with a long black streak going down his chest. His glowing yellow eyes make him look deadly and alien.

He is just as massive as I imagined in his wolf-man form. At least seven feet tall and pretty damn wide. Other pack members fall in line flanking Jaxson, me, and even Selene who is still a distance away, fingertips glowing, next spell at the ready.

There are eight of them and they are all different shades of color from red to black and even multicolored. A few of the stronger wolves are in their half-wolf form, but the rest are in their full werewolf shift. Amazing. Beautiful and lethal.

"Our territory. Our pack. Leave," he orders the other group, his voice sounding incredibly animal like and almost too hard to understand. That's probably why he only used a few words. It was something else he'd forgot to mention though, that they could still speak in that form. Other weres couldn't.

They refuse to budge, but try to decide what they are going to do. I guess they take too long to make a decision for Jaxson, because the next word he snaps is, "KILL," and his wolves don't hesitate. They move with all the precision of a trained military squad. The enemy wolves that never shifted don't even stand a chance. It's actually horrifying as I watch the wolves tear apart the other pack. Bones crunch, screams are muffled under bloody snarls. I'm completely frozen in place as my eyes digest the carnage.

Before long, there's silence. Even the two wolves in front of me are torn apart. I try my best not to vomit every part of my insides, knowing that if I seem frightened or vulnerable, these wolves may not even be able to stop themselves from making me their next prey. Instead, I just back up, find Selene's hand and squeeze it tightly, hoping that I'm not shaking too much.

When Jaxson finally changes back, he's standing naked and bloodied, eyes still yellow from the change and far too wild for my liking. I almost take a step back, but Selene holds me firm. A couple of his men and one woman start to collect what's left of the bodies after they finish their Change back to human. The rest take to the streets, probably searching for any other threats. I don't even want to know what happens next. I force myself to turn away from the scene and back to Jaxson.

"This is the life of the luna dasa, human. If you are to walk among us, you must not turn away, you must accept what is. They were given a chance to leave our territory. They all knew the penalty for breaking pack law and attacking one under our protection," Jaxson says simply as fact, not for understanding.

"Thank you for coming to our aide," Selene says. "It would have gotten really ugly without you."

"Agreed," I tell him.

"If Anubis said protect you, then we shall. I said to be careful, now can you do that this time?" he asks, almost amused. His eyes slowly return to their normal dark color.

"I think we can manage it from here now. Although, Namen is really trying to stop me isn't he?"

"Maybe he's threatened. Good. But that also means that Anubis too will have to be careful. It is definitely time to make a move."

"How will you clean up, this, uh mess?" I ask, slightly afraid to know the answer.

"We've been doing this a long long time, Rayne, don't you worry about it. We have our ways," Jaxson assures me. "Now, get outta here before something else goes wrong."

I nod, then look up at the building where my watcher had been. She's no longer there just as I suspected she wouldn't be. I have no doubts that I'd be seeing her really soon.

It turns out soon will be tonight. We get to the car without incident, but there is a note on the front window of the driver's side. Selene picks up the note, reads it quietly, and hands it to me.

You will come alone. 3375 Turner Ln. One Hour.

"The hell you will! Cadela louca," Selene practically yells into the night as I put the note into my pocket. "And don't think for one second that you can convince me otherwise Rayne; I'm warning you."

I put my hands up in defeat. "Hey, hey. I think we should play it how you want to okay. We'll both go and you can watch my back from the outside."

Selene gives me the death stare, then sighs long and hard. "You'll have five minutes Rayne to figure out who the hell she is and what she wants before I come in after you. I'm not playing around on this. This could be a setup from Namen."

"It's not Selene. I saw her on the rooftop earlier, she was watching, waiting to help if we needed it. I don't know why, but I know that's the truth," I argue.

"I said this already, but I will say it again. I. do. not. like. this. Still, I will allow you to use your judgment. But if this stalker bitch turns out to be bad news, I will say I told you so a million times," Selene promises, clearly perturbed.

I kiss her on the cheek. "We make a good team baby, if anything happens, you'll have my back."

"Let's just hope it doesn't come to that, okay," Selene replies, rolling her eyes at me as we file in the Jag.

Chapter Twenty Three

I punch in the address into my phone's GPS and we get there with about fifteen minutes to spare, not even having to fight traffic. The streets were fairly empty and we barely got caught by any lights. Selene pulls up into the driveway of the house which looks pretty much in shambles. Actually, the entire neighborhood looks that way. Abandoned, run down. There are some porches that aren't even together anymore, windows broken out or boarded, steps that are completely missing, and plenty of overgrowth in every yard. Hell, even homeless people had to have more pride than to live somewhere like this.

Selene and I give each other a look that is something along the lines of "you've got to be kidding me," before I almost find myself trying to lock the doors as if we are in danger of being mugged. Then, I feel ashamed that I even think that way. Living a privileged life has given me some prejudices. But how could an entire neighborhood look this shitty? What is the city doing about this?

I take off my jacket and Selene asks, "What are you doing?"

I raise one eyebrow at her and respond, "Ain't no way I'm gonna get spider webs and dust all in my new jacket after I just ruined one last night." The jacket in question is black leather with gobs of zippers.

"You have a point there diva," she answers. "Now, what's the plan again Rayne?"

This time I'm the one who rolls my eyes. "I have five minutes. I know, I know. Shit, I don't know if I even want to be in there five minutes."

"Good." We start to get out of the car when Selene grabs my arm. "Wait."

I pause and look at her. She gives me a firm but caring look. "Pay attention."

"I will. I promise."

We get out of the car and Selene starts to look around as if feeling the air. "Do you sense anything?" I ask cautiously.

"No, not yet at least. It's very quiet though. I don't even really hear any animals around. I don't think this person is witch born. There's no spark of magic anywhere."

That was something at least. It means that Namen is nowhere around for the time being. Hopefully that's a good sign that my instincts were right. We take a look around the back of the house together before Selene goes back to stand near the car so that she can see if anyone is coming or going. She also sets some kind of trigger spell around the back so that she'd know if anything was coming from that way. It helps her relax a lot more and allows me to be able to come and do what I need.

I have to know who this woman is and what she can do for me. I take the three steps up to the front door as my stride causes the raggedy floorboards to creak under my feet. I knock at the white, cracked door even though I don't expect an answer. With one more glance at Selene, I pull Katsu from my back and step through the door, into darkness and cobwebs.

She'll know I'm here, so I don't call out; I just look around as my eyes adjust to the darkness of the house, and try to watch my step as I glide over broken floorboards and shattered glass. The dust coats my tongue and I wrinkle my nose at the stuffy, moldy smell of everything around me. I almost sneeze as I walk into a wall of cobwebs and swat them away. Good thing I left my jacket in the car. Freaking ew.

There's old furniture placed throughout the first room, chairs, a dining table, and a couple dirty couches, one overturned. A railing overlook above me is missing most of its wood. When I reach the middle of the room, I stop. That's when I think I feel something behind me. Slowly, I turn and face the woman. Even though she's still covered in shadows, I can clearly see the burning red eyes that she possesses.

Vampire.

Before I can speak, she chastises me, "I had thought better of you, but I guess you do not follow rules well. You will pay for that. Or maybe, your witch should pay instead." Her voice is quiet and silky, almost in the same way as Anubis, but there was much more power and confidence in her tone than his. She cocks her head to the side studying me. She's one who knows her power and won't hesitate to use it if tested.

"You won't touch her," I challenge, although I know it's not the best thing to do.

"Oh?" she asks, teasingly, seductively, taking a step forward. My eyes follow her flow and her gait is so graceful, her feet barely seem to kiss the ground. "I will not touch her again, then? I have already handled her. You may go see for yourself if you wish, but you will not find her." She points back towards the front door with all the grace of a noble.

"You said that you could help me," I begin, hoping to reason with her, hoping that she wasn't a psycho vamp even though that's the vibe I'm getting from her.

"I also said to come alone, did I not!" she roars as her aura hits me, bringing me to my knees as surely as a physical blow. Then, she's in my face, touching it, lifting my chin, examining me and I can't help but shiver. In fear and in excitement. She's forcing her aura on me and I can't do a damn thing about it.

When someone forces their aura on you, they are attempting to make you submissive. It's a power pull. Sometimes the aura can be so powerful that one can't even move under the force. I'm very close to that point as my body wants to bend to her will. Satisfied, she releases me.

I stand up and get a good look at her face as I wipe the dirt from my low cut blue jeans. She's probably only a hint darker than me but still caramel complected, and she's stunning. She has deeply set, alluring eyes, small round nose, and perfectly shaped, full lips, even as she bites down on the right side showing her fang.

The danger, the power, and dominance that she represents make my breath stop. Selene is absolutely gorgeous, but this one in front of me has something else, not necessarily something more, but it's different. And I fear it. Her eyes are like lava, burning straight through me, leaving me exposed. Her black hair is shoulder length and braided in an intricate cornrow design and layers. She has to only be about 5'4" or 5'5", but that doesn't matter, her presence will easily fill a room.

Even her smell makes me want to be closer, breathe her in. It's like clean linen out of the dryer, fresh, crisp. I know it's the vamp pheromones, but I find myself breathing deeper. She's still feeding me her aura and I can't fight it; all I can do was ride the waves.

By the time I even manage to speak, my voice is cracky and unsure. She smiles triumphantly. "What do you want?"

"Your blood," she tells me, stepping away and turning her back on me, as if I could be easily dismissed. Her graphic tee catching the moonlight. Skulls.

It causes me to grip Katsu tighter. Irritation rolls through me. "Say again," I demand.

"Are you slow Rayne? I do not like to repeat myself. I want your blood," she repeats slowly, clearly amused.

"This has to be some kind of joke right? First, you help me, and then you stalk me, now you want my blood. Stop wasting my time vampire. Tell me what you did to Selene and then leave me alone," I order, my voice becoming more confident. I touch my intricate tribal looking tattoo in reassurance.

"With an attitude like that, you will not be long for this world. Shall I help you along?"

"Fuck you."

She laughs dangerously, the sound piercing my ears like a poisonous arrow. Even as her voice echoes from where she just stood, her iron hands grip my neck, squeezing the life out of me, my eyes bulging. Mercifully, she flings me across the room with all the exertion of tossing a pillow. I smash through an old table feeling it buckle under my weight.

Somehow, my katana manages to remain in my possession. I stand up, coughing as my throat burns from the pain of being choked, searching the darkness for this psycho vampire. I should have listened to Selene; my instincts need to be fine tuned.

She's on me again before I even hear her, see her, or smell her. One second she's nowhere around, then the next, she's in front of me, kicking me with so much power that I destroy the wall as my body catapults through it. The dust flies furiously around me. I cough up blood, surely having internal bleeding from the punt she just gave me.

This time, I have no idea where Katsu is. Trying to ignore the sensational pain the kick caused is not helping my ability to quickly search for her either. Despite wobbly legs, I manage to stand as I call for more strength, more focus from deep within me. I see a blur, quick, to my right, then behind me. I spin just in time to x block a tornado of punches storming at me. She attacks with such fury and power that I feel my bones threaten to break under her assault.

I panic as I pitifully attempt to exchange blows with her, but find no openings. She head butts me hard on my nose and I drop to the ground, nose broken and bloody. Another kick to my face and I fall backwards rolling a few feet like a log rolling down a hill. As I try to force myself up, the pain reminding me of the days when Lawrence tortured me, healed me, and tortured me again, I touch steel and begin to gain more hope.

She laughs again, this time not in amusement, but in incredulousness. "You thought that you'd be able to kill that witch?! The man who knows over 1000 spells and has raised demon after demon. You think you can stop Namen Young, the soul stealer? You are a fool and you will die a fool who couldn't even stop me or save her witch. You are standing near death's door and yet you still make no effort to live, to fight back. You are a waste and I will put you out of your misery. I'm here to finish the job for him. There's no need for him to waste his time with the likes of a pathetic human." She spits the last words out in disgust and somehow manages to look even more wildly beautiful.

I attack first, initially swinging wildly, panicking as the vampire simply dodges each blow, laughing, not even trying to attack. Then, I just get angry again. Angry at my overconfidence, angry that I didn't listen to Selene or Anubis, angry at the Immortals for not pushing me harder, angry at this vampire for mocking me, and angry at my family for dying in the first place!

Then, I explode.

My tattoo burns so hot that I scream. It's almost as if I can feel my blood boil as my temperature rises and I see red. I can't die here, not in this dirty ass house and not before I land at least on blow on this smug son of a bitch's face.

"I am someone! I am strong and I'm not done yet. If that's all you've got then it won't work, you won't break me." All my limbs are tingling now, the power growing inside me. My katana feels almost weightless in my hand and I can feel her telling me that she's ready to do damage, to live up to her name.

We clash again. Either her movements have become slower or my power boost wasn't imagined. I stop feeling the pains she inflicted on my body as my adrenaline goes into hyper drive. She tries to grab my arm, but I shuffle away and counter with an upward slice. She reacts a fraction slower than before and her red v-neck graphic t-shirt comes away with a nice foot long cut in it. I don't let up though, ramming an elbow right into her bottom lip. She doesn't go down, however, and I'm forced to push her away in order to create some distance. By this time, my body is drenched in sweat from the exertion. I've never had a fight like this before, and I certainly don't want this to be my last. If I don't win, it will be.

I don't know how long the fight proceeds, how many times our fists meet, or how many times I have to force myself back up again. We crash through another wall and the ceiling begins to crumble around us in warning that this old house can't take much more of this battle. I fight with all the heart I have, truly giving my all with every slice of my blade, every kick, every strike. She has taken some damage but with her vamp healing and exceptional skill, I've barely made a dent in her defenses.

My limit has been reached. I'm not skilled enough to win against her. Maybe if I had more time to learn I would have been able to. At least, I was finally able to land a few. I still have some pride left. As I accept this truth, this knowledge that I am simply outclassed, she lands one final blow to my midsection, causing more blood to come pouring out of my mouth. I fall forward, vision going black. Before I can hit the ground, she catches me with her other arm. This is it, the final strike. My body is finished, unable to push itself anymore. Katsu falls from my weak and shaky hands and my eyes begin to close.

I want to at least beg for Selene's life with the last of my strength, but I can't form the words.

"It's okay Rayne, you can rest now. I've seen all that I needed. When you awake, I will tell you what you need to know. I'm sorry that I hurt you so bad." her voice is now sweet, protective, and calm as if the psycho vampire she just was never even existed. I can't reply, don't really attempt to comprehend; all I can do is allow myself to slip into unconsciousness.

Chapter Twenty Four

My head feels as if a college drum line has made it its practice field. I groan loudly as I try to turn on my side, trying to figure out just where the hell I'm at. Prying one eye open, I make an attempt to figure out my surroundings. I'm in a bed and Selene isn't with me. The room has some light peeking through the window blinds. There is a mirror on the wall across from me and the walls are painted a cream color. The closet door is closed. There is a brown dresser with a few items sitting on top of it. The room smells like bleach and I wonder if my blood had to be cleaned off the hardwood floor.

"What the hell happened?" I ask myself quietly with my scratchy voice. Then, I remember and reach for my nose to check the damage. Tender, but not broken. I also don't feel nearly as bad as I should have. Hell, I shouldn't even be alive.

The door opens and a dark shadow appears there, leaning nonchalantly against the frame. "I gave you my blood to help you heal," she explains gently, her voice sparking memories of our battle and how I was utterly throttled.

Before I can respond, Selene pushes past her and plops on the bed, jarring my aching muscles. She doesn't notice however, but instead squeezes me tight. "I thought you weren't going to make it. You were in bad shape."

"Sorry about that, but it needed to be done," the vampire says.

Selene lets me go and turns toward her. "The hell it did! You didn't have to put her through that. And I'm sorry Rayne. I guess I was the one that should have been paying attention. Asshole over here knocked me out before I even knew what hit me."

"Oh, suck it up, I didn't even hit you that hard and she's not a baby. Stop treating her like one if you want her to live. She needs to be pushed. The situation has changed since you've been gone. Namen has gotten even stronger and she will die slowly and painfully if I don't help her gain her true strength."

I look at the vampire's face and notice that her eyes are no longer blood red, but simply dark and caring. But why is the question. "Why do you care so much about me? How do you even know who I am?" I ask, forcing myself up to turn on the lights so that I could get a good look at her.

She's dressed in another v-neck, this time dark green, with loose black jeans, a long silver necklace and about six piercings in each ear. I wondered what else is pierced, but quickly shove that thought away. It had to be the after effects of her blood. She has a full sleeve going down her left arm. The designs are too intricate to see without studying closely. Other than that, her skin is flawless, not like the immortals but as if she's never been hurt in her life.

She's definitely a stud, as most of us in the black gay community call dominant females who dress similar to a man. Still, there's a feminine air about her that I'm finding attractive. It's obvious to me that she prefers females because my gaydar is on high alert.

This time, she turns towards me and gives me a sly smile. No vamp fangs sticking out though just straight, white teeth. She's obviously under control, as cool as a cucumber. We could be fast friends, I know it. "I saved your life once, a long long time ago."

"I don't remember that," I say.

"And I don't believe you," Selene adds.

She just chuckles and takes a step towards me, hands stretching out. I slap them away, but she gives me an exasperated look and proceeds anyway. The vampire touches my face softly and moves my hair out of the way of my left temple. "You have a scar right here from when you hit your head from falling down the stairs."

I tilt my head sideways and slowly remove her hand from my face not liking the feeling I was getting from her touch. How would she know that? "Yes."

"That's what I told Jason that I made you think. That's not what happened though."

"Jason? You knew my father?"

"Well, we had a slight business partnership," she begins then raises her hand when I get ready to interrupt. "And yes, I'm aware that he was not fond of our kind at the best of times, but still, he respected me. He also needed me that day. I don't think you realize how deep into unsavory business your father used to dive, but it almost cost him his oldest child." I search her eyes to find the truth in her words and when I nod, she continues.

"There was a car accident. He picked you up from daycare and was t-boned on the driver side and trapped. They took you from the car. The bottom line is, I found out who took you for him because they said that if he went to the police that they would kill you. They had you guarded by some traps and vicious dogs, which is a shame because I'm a dog lover and it crushed my heart to have to kill them. The kidnappers, I had no sympathy for them though. I handled them all, except for the one I saw slapping you around when you were crying. He gave you that scar and I had to give you some of my blood that time too so that you could heal. Him, I saved for your father. After it all was done, Jason asked me to make you forget, so I glamoured you and told you to never let anything scare you again. Once it was all over, you seemed so happy and carefree. After that, Jason was in my debt, but I never collected on it."

"So, you're here to collect on that debt now then?" Selene asks, perturbed. It's clear that she doesn't like this vamp.

"I won't deny that my motives are not simple, but I will say that through my blood that I shared with that little girl that day became a desire to help protect her. Both of your parents loved you and I want their legacy to live on. If you do not believe my story, you can even ask that friend of

Jason's, his business partner. He will verify that I saved you," she shrugs.

"I lost something once too and a little girl's smile gave me hope again. As I said, I knew your father and I think that he was a good man. You Rayne, have more potential than you know. It's unusual for one that I've given blood to to have a bond with me after so many years. When I felt your power that night, I was confused. Then, I heard Namen Young's name and knew that you were in danger. I've been slowly infiltrating his people for years now, trying to stop him, but I need more help. There are others in other states where he is planning other things that I have allied with working on the inside opposing him. You can't even begin to know what he's planning to do and it could ruin us all. Even though he deserves justice for what he's done to your family, if I help you get stronger, this can no longer be a quest for revenge. Priestess, I will need your assistance too."

"So what is it that makes him so unstoppable? What is he trying to do?" I ask.

"From what I've learned, Namen has been working his plan for over fifteen years. He has been building up an army, so that he can overthrow the government."

"To what end?" Selene asks. "I mean, we've all heard it before, the bad guys want to rule the world, but what's his end game?"

"Maybe his end game is the world, but right now, he just wants America, the strongest country militarily and technologically. He wants all of our kind to reveal themselves, to start a new government with us at the top."

"And what about normal humans?"

"They'd have the choice to turn or become slaves."

"To turn? I don't get it."

"He has been doing experiments on children, trying to change their DNA. Apparently, he's had one or two successes."

"Okay, stop. Let me get this straight. Namen wants to be high ruler of the U.S. and take over the government so that all supernaturals can come out of the woodwork, which in itself may or may not be a bad thing. The problem is he wants to force every human to make a decision on becoming awakened or becoming slaves. He probably found out about my father's weapons and thought they'd be a threat to his plans, when my dad wouldn't deal, he had my family murdered. If that's the case, if my dad had dealt, he probably would have had them killed anyway because once he realized what Namen's true goals were, he could have just made more weapons. Namen's also been taking the kids, via the lamia, and testing on them, the failures he's been using as demon food," I summarize as I sit down due to my headache becoming worse.

"There are a million things wrong with this plan of his," Selene speaks up.

"Exactly. Everyone cannot be awakened; it is just not the natural order of things. We vampires for one depend on humans for life and companionship. I've been ordered by my family to end him and it's going to be harder even for a vampire like me if he keeps getting all these power boosts and alliances."

"What kind of power boosts are we talking about? While Rayne was asleep, you called Namen the soul stealer. Please don't tell me that it means what I think it does," Selene says, worried, now pacing.

"You're damn right. He's using dark, no, demon magic in order to steal souls of other witches. When he does that, he gains a fraction of their power. It allows his to increase. He is a necromancer by birth but with his ambition and willingness to deal with demons, he has become a witch that can use earth magic, elemental magic, healing, and many other gifts that should not be his to claim. "

Selene stops in her tracks and covers her mouth. "Oh my God."

"What is it?" I ask, leaning forward.

"Then, you're wrong on your timeline. He hasn't been doing this for fifteen years. He's probably been doing it for hundreds."

"Shit," the vampire says, now pacing back and forth, rubbing her braids.

"What are you saying Selene?" I ask, feeling as though I got lost somewhere in the conversation.

"I'm saying that if he's this proficient at demon magic or even forbidden witch magic, then, he's probably been transferring his own soul into other witches in order to sustain his own life. He could be at least 500 years old then. It's because demon magic has a deadly cost and the user usually doesn't live longer than a couple years because demons come to collect their souls after being used for an extended amount of time." Selene bites her lip and then snaps her fingers as if having an epiphany.

"I bet that he's been feeding these demons other's souls as payment to keep himself alive. He has probably gone through thousands of trial and errors when learning how to control his new powers and keeping himself able bodied enough to do something with them. If you said that he's gotten stronger exponentially over the past couple years, then it must be due to something on the witch's calendar. He's aiming for a specific date isn't he?" Selene guesses.

"Dies sol solis cado ex divum," the vampire says grimly.

"Meaning?" I ask.

"Roughly: The day the sun falls from the sky. It is prophesized that an eclipse will black out the sun and that the boundary between our world and the other planes will be at its weakest. He will be able to move his armies and if he is truly in league with demon kind, they will break the plane and walk the earth in numbers not seen in thousands of years. Once they're here, I don't think they're going back."

Selene lets out a big breath and plops down next to me. "You need to contact Diana."

"What's going on?" I ask.

"We need to find out just how much time we have, and see if they'll be of any help."

"The Immortals? Don't waste your time. They won't help." The vampire barks a laugh.

"How can you be so sure?" I ask.

"I just know. Anyway, if you do, contact them away from here. I am not allowed in their presence."

"What do you mean? And just who are you anyway? You seem to know so much about me, but you haven't even told us your name."

"It doesn't matter why, it's unimportant to what's going on right now... My name is Zara Drake." She bows with one arm across her chest, upper body perfectly parallel to the ground.

"You can't be serious right now," Selene interrupts, putting her hands over her face. "You are a Drake?"

"I am. So you must know what that means then priestess."

"Well I sure as hell don't, so why don't the two of you stop talking above me and fill me in," I say, snapping on the both of them. My heart begins to pound wildly and Zara gives me a look that says cool it. I forgot that we have a blood link now and that she'd be able to feel my heart beating, my emotions changing.

"I apologize, Rayne. Allow me to continue. My family is pureblood. I was born a vampire over three hundred years ago and am the youngest in my line. Each line of purebloods possess special gifts. My family is known especially for our extraordinary talents," Zara tells me, clearly trying to explain without explaining.

She doesn't want to tell me what her 'talents' are, that much is clear. "I myself am an Enforcer for the Nine. The Nine are the original pureblood families that all who are of the blood originate from. They call me the Blade of the Night."

"Yes, or the Crimson Princess. No wonder why you had no chance Rayne. This one was a trained killer before she could even speak," Selene jabs.

"Do not pretend that you come from an innocent upbringing witch. We all do what we must to protect our own. I do not kill on order unless it is necessary, and I have done more to protect each of your kind than you will ever be able to accomplish. The last thing you want is to make me angry. I haven't fed in a week," Zara warns, and as if to prove her point, her eyes become redder.

Purebloods didn't have to feed the way that turned vamps had to, so if her need to feed was threatening her, it must be because of stress. They could even eat normal food on a regular basis. It didn't sustain like blood, but it helped them keep up the human charade and push blood cravings away. They could also walk under the sun with no restrictions unlike made vamps that can't manage durations of sunlight longer than forty five minutes and that is during times when the sun isn't high in the sky. It weakened them and could also mean death if they weren't careful. Summertime must be hell.

"Would it help if you fed just a little from me then?" I ask, the words fumbling out of my mouth before I even realize it.

Selene smacks her lips and rolls her eyes, clearly not liking this one bit either, but knowing that my offer is a practical one. Our blood link may become more profound, but that would also mean she'd know when I was in danger, and that could help save my life.

"Don't worry Selene, even though Rayne here has grown incredibly attractive, I can feel the love between you two. I will behave myself," Zara promises.

"That means you won't glamour her or me ever."

"If I see you as friends or allies, you have my word on that. I will not force my will upon you." Then, she continues, "Rayne, a feeding can be a very sexual experience, but I don't want it to be something uncomfortable for you. Open your mind up and do not try to struggle because then, you may trigger my need to kill. Priestess, why don't you hold her hand," Zara suggests.

Selene scoots on the bed next to me, while Zara crouches down before me. We lock eyes for a second before I blink and turn away. For her to be over three hundred years old, she doesn't look a day over twenty three. I wonder when she stopped aging.

"Thank you Rayne for your blood. Now, are you ready?" I nod slowly and grip Selene's hand tighter as Zara gently grabs my wrist and turns it up towards her. Her fangs elongate, sharp and intimidating. I swallow hard. With one last glance at me, she unhurriedly brings my wrist up towards her mouth and licks a small x as if to signal to me where the bite will occur, then, my skin breaks and she catches the runoff with her quick tongue.

My breath catches as tiny surges of pleasure ripple through my body from the pheromones in her saliva. As she sucks my life force from my vein, I try to force a moan back down my throat, but as my head falls back, the sound escapes my body and I find myself not caring how much blood she takes from me. With each suck of her lips, pulses of pleasure ripple through me. How can feeding feel so much like great sex?

As my mind goes cloudy, somehow I find Selene's lips. At first, she's hesitant, obviously not comfortable with the circumstances, but sure enough, her lips press harder against mine as I open my mouth to let her sweet tongue in. My tongue roams, enjoying the feel of her soft lips. I bite gently down on her lower lip as Selene presses closer to me, rubbing her hand through my hair. Zara slowly, purposefully continues to feed from me as the feeding sparks the flames of my growing desire. Then, far, far too soon, it's over.

Chapter Twenty Five

Zara closes my wound with her saliva and smiles at both of us, who are now breathing heavily.

"I didn't take much, but you'll need to eat and drink something just in case since it was your first time." Then, she looks at Selene slyly. "You know, a feeding mixed with magic and sex is absolutely the best feeling in the world." She winks then leaves the room, searching for food for us.

"Oh my, now that was something," Selene says, surprising me.

"Yeah, it was," I agree, pulse pounding down low.

"I think she pushed her aura on me while feeding from you. Behave herself my ass," Selene says trying to sound incredulous, but not succeeding.

"I think she was just teasing you for being so uptight," I tell her, already seeming to know her personality.

"You may be right, but I know vampires, and they're always up to something. Don't get too sucked in by her charm. She's comes from a powerful line and we are absolutely disposable," Selene warns.

I remain silent as I think about what I just learned and how Zara had apparently saved my life when I was a young child. Did I really have that much impact on her way of thinking? Did her glamour on me help me to be as fearless as I am today? Maybe I owed much more to her than I knew. Whatever the case, I need to know more about this tattooed vampire.

After a short while, Zara comes back to the room and tells us that the food she prepared is ready. I have to travel down the stairs and around to a hallway to get to the kitchen. She has some expensive Moscato on the glass table with three filled glasses. I take a seat in a black cushioned chair under dim lights and look at the food as Zara sets it in front of me. Selene takes the seat next to me and Zara serves her as well.

She baked some tilapia with baked potatoes and broccoli. I thank her for the food and hesitantly dig in as I feel her watchful eyes on me. It isn't anything like my cook at home used to make, but it isn't what I expected either. I find myself eating faster than normal, realizing how drained I feel. Then, I top it off with the wine before I look at Zara once more.

"So, can you tell me what the point was in almost killing me, instead of just telling me what was going on?"

She sets her own drink on the table after taking a long sip, then grabbing the bottle and topping it back off. "I needed to know where your skills were. If you knew that I was not going to really kill you, then you wouldn't have fought me seriously. I needed you desperate so that you could reach for more of that power inside of you. And it's just like I suspected, the Immortals taught you how to fight, how to survive most situations, but they didn't teach you how to truly use your power, they didn't teach you how to call for it or what sets you off. You are expected to learn that on your own."

"And how do you know so much about the Immortals, Zara Drake?" Selene asks curiously. Hell, I'm curious too, but I already know that I won't be getting a real answer from her.

"We purebloods have long known the Immortals. After all, we both share a common bond: extreme longevity. You could say that we are cut from the same cloth," she simply says, sounding as if she's open to this conversation, but truly isn't. I'll have to watch what she doesn't say more than what she actually reveals.

"So, have you ever met them? What about someone like Rayne?"

"Ah, I have much that I could tell you, but I am not ready to share my entire background with people I have just officially met. When the need arises, I will tell you what's important. The only thing that is important right now is that we need each other or else we will both not only fail in our personal goals, but we will fail most of the world too," Zara says with a sense of finality that I'm not about to argue with.

"I've already made my decision to go after Namen, that hasn't changed. Just remember that trust is earned vampire and even though I want to like you, I not let my guard down so that you can screw us over," I tell her.

"You will learn to trust me Rayne. Both of you will," Zara promises. "And I will keep you safe; you have my word on that."

We shall see.

◊◊◊

Finally, we drive home. Altogether, the whole ordeal lasted about fourteen hours, so it is about four p.m. when we get back. I am still a little sore so my shower lasts a lot longer than usual as I let the hot water pound me. When I get out though, the water isn't the only thing that wants to batter my body. Selene ends up giving me a rough session of lovemaking that concludes in both of us having to shower again. It is nice to know that even when the world is going to shit, I can still find time for an orgasm or two, or four.

Sleepily, we lay next to each other, my head on her chest, enjoying the rhythm of her beating heart. "I need to call Anubis," I yawn.

"Not now. Thirty minute nap," Selene mumbles, rubbing my scalp, nearly making me purr.

"Mm, okay, but just thirty."

"Okay."

Three hours later, I finally reach Anubis.

"I assumed you would call me sooner."

"I was busy."

"Jaxson told me what happened. I'm not happy about it."

"Not my fault Anubis. Besides, Jaxson said they were being hostile on your territory anyway."

"Not that. The fact that he skirted my orders and met with you. I'm not a child that needs protection, or my second sneaking behind my back."

I laugh. He may pretend not to like it, but he clearly appreciated the fact that his pack would go out of their way to try to protect him.

"What's so funny?" he asks.

"It doesn't matter. Look, the reason why I called is because I have some information that might change your mind about Namen Young. Are you familiar with the name Zara Drake?"

He's silent for a second. "The first name, no, but if you're talking about the Drake vampire clan, then yes, I've had some dealings with them."

"Good or bad?" I ask, not wanting bad blood between potential allies.

"They are a vicious bunch, but only if you cross them. I have no quarrel with them."

Good. I proceed to explain the situation to him.

"So, he had been trying to use my father in the same way that he used yours. Now that he knows that I'm special, he wants to control me so he can control my pack. Rayne, if that happens…"

"You don't even have to say it. I saw what your pack did to the others, remember." I shiver thinking about it.

He grunts and mumbles something to someone in the background. Then, he rattles off an address and I commit it to memory.

"I think that you should stay with us until this is all settled. I have a large plot of land since I bought up most of the neighborhood and tore down the houses so that our pack could have privacy. I need to speak with the pack's elders and then, I will send out my trackers with the information that we have to see if they can spot the lamia so that we can start to put a dent in his plans. Who knows how many altered humans he has at his disposal. We can try to make a move by tomorrow."

"Okay, I'll let Selene know, but I think that we should have Zara hunt with your trackers just in case something goes down."

"My wolves are more than capable."

"Anubis I mean no disrespect to the skills of your wolves, it's just that she knows what to look for."

"No. I have a better idea for Zara," Selene tells me, forcing me to turn around.

Anubis gets quiet as he listens as well. Wolf hearing and all.

"She's going to stay and help both of us train with the rest of the wolves on this full moon."

"Sounds interesting. I think I'll join you. After all, the moon is calling to me," Anubis replies.

"I guess we will see you soon then," I respond.

"I am counting the minutes," Anubis replies. I can practically see the smile he's sure to be wearing.

Chapter Twenty Six

Soon, I'm alone in the forest behind Anubis's giant house with Katsu strapped to my back. Selene, Anubis, Jaxson, Zara, and some other pack members are out here too. But tonight, it is everyone for themselves, a test of skills against many types of opponents.

A human, werewolf, vampire, and witch walk into a bar. Ha ha.

Anubis has purchased every house on this side of the street, combining two homes for his main house and also creating a compound of sorts. High walls and intelligently placed trees create a perimeter and a means to keep nosey onlookers from seeing daily activities. Many of his pack choose to live here, Jaxson not being one of them. The woods behind the houses create a perfect place to hunt and test skill.

Someone at the house will give the signal any minute. Each of us have three black flags tied to our bodies and we have to attempt not to lose any. If we are knocked down by an opponent we have to give up a flag. They also can be taken from us by skill. Once we lose all three, we will be disqualified. The main objective along with that is to find and retrieve the white flag that has been hidden in the woods. I just feel as if I'm in the Hunger Games. I'm not going to be counted out easily though.

As the cold caress of the wind reaches through my leather jacket, I hear the signal, a car horn honking three times. With that, I take off as I fast as I can through the trees, dodging branches and shrubbery, suddenly feeling as if I am back with the Immortals, running with Lawrence.

That thought helps calm my nerves and makes it easier for me to believe in myself. Yes, they were born with their gifts and yes, they had been at this longer. Zara had kicked my ass already, Selene had outsmarted me, but I'm persistent and special. I have to remember that I have to first believe in myself. I need to keep in mind that I haven't come into all my powers yet. I won't allow a few mishaps to shake my confidence.

Suddenly, I stop and listen. With the breeze comes the taste of excitement. I can feel him, barreling towards me, the man mountain as I like to call him. Jaxson is in his true wolf form, hoping to use his speed to ambush me. It isn't going to work though; I feel his intent, even from this distance.

I call for my power to rise within me, breathing deeply and picturing it building up inside my core like a slow flame. Then, it explodes, zipping through all of my synapses and I feel very much alive. I think having Zara's blood inside me also makes it easier for me to accomplish this power surge. Jaxson doesn't feel the change in me however, because he's jetting towards me with the same speed.

I turn just as he's flying through the air with jaws open wide, his teeth as sharp and as powerful as any great white shark. But, I stop him, my head tilting out of the way of his bite and my hands on both of his shoulders. My feet slide about ten feet from the force of his attack, but I manage to root myself and push him back. With a leaping kick, I send him flying through the air.

As expected, he lands on his feet with a growl and then does part two of his change.

It's intriguing to watch his body tremble, distort, then grow into another beast. One that's now standing on his hind legs, torso all muscle with defined abs like a man, smaller muzzle, and arms that are shaped like a human. His body is still covered in his chestnut colored fur. The black streak of fur looks like an unnatural bolt of lightning down his chest, eyes glowing yellow under the moon. His moon, full and giving him even more power. On this night, he is truly one of the luna dasa as he called it, the moon's servant.

"C'mon Jaxson, all this for lil old me?" I joke.

He laughs, the sound coming out like a bark. "I want to win."

"In that case…" I draw my katana and grip it firmly in front of me with two hands. I'm not worried about slicing him up a little because weres tend to heal as quickly as vampires as long as they're in their wolf form and the wound's not too serious.

He gives me something that's probably a smile, before ripping off a huge branch and hurling it at me. Instead of wasting time dodging it like he expects, I rush to meet the tree limb, slice through it and slash down on Jaxson's thigh before landing an elbow into his chest. Jaxson then manages to knock Katsu from my hand before breaking through my attempted block and landing a blow to the side of my face.

I'm surprised that bones didn't crunch, but not amazed at the blood coming from me from his razor claws. He leaps through the air, clinging on to a tree, hopping from one to the other at blinding speed, before making like a missile targeting me from behind. This is when my dance background kicks in and I flip out the way, twisting just in time to dodge another strike before countering with my own takedown. I grab one of his flags that are tied to his waist in triumph.

Swiftly, I reach for Katsu, my sword with the name that means victory, just in time to block a hard attack from Zara who has now joined the fray with a double bladed staff.

My body vibrates under the blow, but I manage to make her unbalanced and land a kick to her inner leg. She pretends to allow the fall to take her and handsprings backwards out of the way just in time to miss getting stepped on by Jaxson. Then, it's all three of us in a brawl, acting on an opening that the other created, exchanging blows with one another. I can't believe that I'm keeping up with them, but I don't question it, don't lose my focus. I allow my clarity that I possess at the moment to allow me to think two steps ahead. My mind begins to create a counter for ever counter, and soon, I am the one making Zara lose her weapon.

She gives me a look of approval and tosses me one of her flags before taking off into the night. She's just enjoying the game, trying to test everyone's skill level. Maybe I needed to do the same.

Once Zara disappears, I put my hands on top of my head, catching my breath as Jaxson sniffs the air before taking off at ten o'clock.

"Shit," I say to myself as I see sparks, then a burst of light from the direction that Jaxson just took off in. I wonder who Selene is going at it with. I run through the trees, jumping over fallen branches and weaving like a football player, doing my best to keep up with the wolf in front of me who is using him human-like arms and sharp claws to jump quickly through the more dense trees in this area. After getting smacked in the face with a couple branches, I slow my pace down until I reach the outer area of the battlefield. There, Selene is standing over one of the other wolves in Anubis's pack, a white wolf I recognized as the female from the fight near the club.

Selene is also looking very pissed off. Her hair seems to be floating from her use of magic and the left sleeve of her dark blue shirt is torn. What a waste.

Before anyone can attack, she says, "Anubis took the flag from me while I was fighting her. He's probably already back now, sneaky bastard."

The female gets off the ground and huffs, shaking her body like a wet dog, before going into the trees and changing back to human form. We all listen to her painful grunts followed by heavy breathing as she completes her change and then comes back into the clearing fully clothed.

"Um, how come last time you guys were all naked and now you have clothes on? Because, I'm sure you didn't just pull those out of the bushes," I ask, very interested in her response.

"It's the wolf magic inside of us. If we are more focused when we change, we can help the magic keep out clothes intact, but if we shift in a hurry or in a rage, it's not likely that we'll be focused enough to guide the magic into concealing our clothes, and we destroy them," she answers, her voice sounding like she just woke up from a long nap.

The signal that someone has brought the flag back to the house goes off. I look at the two flags that I earned tonight with satisfaction. We all walk back slowly, with Jaxson lagging behind in order to shift back. Up ahead, Selene and the female wolf are talking about their fight. There seems to be a mutual respect between them, which is good. When we reach the light yellow house, Anubis is sitting on top of the roof, shirt off, legs dangling, waving the flag mockingly at us.

"Did you even fight?" Jaxson asks him, clearly irritated.

Anubis laughs. "Don't be such a cry baby. I won and you lost. Deal with it."

"Whatever," Jaxson mumbles.

"Hey, where's that vamp?" Anubis asks, looking around, making it obvious that he doesn't want her lurking around alone.

"She left the premises, said that she had to look into something real quick, but she'd be back in about an hour," another one of his wolves responds.

Interesting. An hour is when Anubis's tracker wolves are due back. What is she up to?

"Well, I can't say that I like her disappearing like that, but she's going to be a valuable asset. Let's fill our bellies and talk strategy while we wait," Anubis declares. We all nod and join him as he jumps from the roof, landing perfectly balanced and silent, and walks into the house.

◊◊◊

A little over an hour later, the other wolves return and give us the long-awaited details on the lamia and their whereabouts. They are on the outskirts of town in an old university research building. The place was supposed to be closed by the government which meant that someone in the local government had to be working with Namen. I guess it makes sense if children were really coming up missing in such high numbers, then someone had to be covering it up. If I find out who it is, I'd pay them a visit too after this was all said and done. Bastard.

It's awesome to finally know where we are headed, but there's also bad news as well. First, they had to allow the lamia to take another child. She, the lamia, had been dressed up like a woman begging for money. When one of the street kids tried to chat her up, she bit him to immobilize him then disappeared. Second, the wolves said that they actually smelled more along the lines of twenty of them. This means that there are enough of them to make a horde, which is what a large group of demons is called. There's probably a gate that needs to be closed before more demons discover it and make their way through.

Namen is gaining quite a following. He must be feeding them well, meaning that there are many failures with his experiments. This could be interpreted as a good thing or bad. Next, there is pretty strong magic guarding the place. Namen will probably know immediately once we are inside. We have to be prepared if he does come.

Chapter Twenty Seven

Zara stalks in with hair freshly braided into singles, looks at our little group, and smiles, her fangs out and deadly looking. She throws me a bottle of something. "Here, you drink some of this and give the rest to Selene. It has my blood in it and it'll help boost your strengths."

"Hell no, you won't be creating a bond with me," Selene says, reaching to snatch the bottle from my hand to examine it. I pull away from her.

"What's in it anyway?" I ask, slightly disgusted at the thought of drinking her blood like this. At least the other two times, I had been unaware.

"It's an herbal compound designed to lengthen the amount of time that the blood is effective. I'd offer it to everyone but it only works with humans and witches since they are the only two groups that can be turned into vampire," Zara tells us matter-of-factly, crossing her arms in that nonchalant signature way. Her black sleeveless hoodie makes her look like a dangerous thug. I kind of like it. Her tattoo sleeve making her ten times more attractive.

"Just swallow the shit and be done with it. We have work to do," Anubis says in his Alpha voice. Meaning, this is final, let's move on.

It is actually a wonder that Anubis and Zara could stay in the same room together for too long since both of them are clearly Alphas in their own respects. One or both of them are showing a lot of composure. Zara must also be keeping her power suppressed as much as possible allowing Anubis to be in charge in his own home.

I look at the drink one more time then shrug my shoulders as I open it and take three big gulps, leaving some for Selene. It doesn't taste like anything at first, then, the flavor, or should I say power, hits my senses. It tastes like liquid fire. It scorches my insides, but also warms me in ring of safety as if nothing can get past it.

"That's our bond becoming complete, Rayne," Zara tells me, her voice spinning through my mind.

I give her a look, but she is already focused somewhere else. I sit quietly as the power of her blood cushions me. Then, I hand the bottle to Selene and give her a look that says, 'drink.' She huffs and obeys.

"Good. Now, what's next?" the female wolf asks. She pulls back her blonde hair and I watch her dark blue eyes settle obediently on Anubis. She's about the same height as me, but much smaller. Tiny breasts, tiny waist, small lips. Her boyish body makes her look like a young teen.

I glance at everyone, studying them. Their aura is much easier to feel now. All my synapses seem to be firing from the mixture I just consumed. I want to run, jump, and swim. I force my body to stay seated. Is this how I'll always feel with vampire blood in my system? I hear Anubis speaking and Jaxson muttering a reply, but I'm too intrigued by what I'm feeling to give it much attention. Okay, time to focus.

For the next hour, we come up with a plan. Then, we come up with another two in case those fail. By the time we finish, we are all set on tomorrow night. It is time. I can't deal with any more innocents getting taken. We all know however that this is only the first step. We'd have to locate his lieutenants if we wanted to do some serious damage. I'd have to get in contact with Damien as much as I hated to admit it. He had resources up his sleeve and it would make our job a whole lot easier.

"So, let's go over the plans again," Anubis tells us as we finish up our discussion.

Selene will start off with a perimeter spell that will keep the lamia from getting away. It would force them to stay in the building. However, since the building is so large, she can only hold it for five minutes, if that. Therefore, Zara will stay with her to protect her and eliminate any of the ones that happen to get free if she is unable to hold the spell or if she becomes weakened. Using our newly formed bond that Selene is also not too happy about, I will tell Zara to let Selene know when to start the incantation once we are closer inside. We then are to attack in three waves.

Jaxson and I are the first wave. Anubis and the female wolf, who I now know is named Taryn will try to circle around and catch them from behind. Last, two more of Anubis's best hunters would take advantage of the confusion of battle and finish it all up. They will also stay behind to burn the bodies.

We are hoping to be quick and precise enough that we'll be able to rescue the children afterward. If there are any children to rescue.

If the children are being directly guarded by the lamia, which Zara doesn't think they will be, Jaxson will give a signal through his pack bond and the last three will meet up with us and create a path for me to get to the kids while they take out as many lamia as possible. Anubis and Taryn would then decide what to do based on how many children there are.

The trackers had also informed us that there are plenty of cameras around and that we'll need to destroy as many as we can. Zara said that she'd be fast enough to take out the ones around the building before we were set up, then we'd have to move quickly inside to handle the rest. The strategies are based upon our individual strengths and weaknesses and in the end we all seemed satisfied with who will be watching our back.

I have to remind everyone about the potentially deadly venom of the lamia as well as the fact that they can regenerate. Last, we'd have to find that damn gate that Namen opened for the demons. Needless to say, there is a helluva lot of work that needs to be done.

When we finish, I stand and walk towards Selene to ask her what her next move will be, but Zara has already beat me to it.

"Hey," she says to Selene, slightly touching her arm in as friendly a way as possible. I notice Selene flinch, but make an effort not to pull away. "I need you to come with me. I have a spell that's going to be able to close that bridge that the demons are getting through, but it's blood magic. That's part of why I needed to have you drink my blood. You're going to need the strength to practice this," Zara tells her gently, making an effort to seem non-threatening. Selene doesn't care for vampires, that much is obvious. That in itself is weird to me because Selene never seemed like the prejudiced type. Maybe I'm wrong; maybe she just doesn't like Zara.

Selene turns her beautiful green eyes towards me and asks, "Are you going to come with us?"

I think for a second, wondering how Selene would feel about being left alone with Zara for such a dangerous spell, but I know that she'll definitely have to rely on her tomorrow, so the sooner she gets used to it, the better. "No. I think I'm going to take Anubis in the forest with me and see if I can contact Diana. Maybe she will have some ideas about that day we talked about and how much time we have before the eclipse hits."

She nods in agreement, even though there's a small frown on her beautiful face. That's happening more and more lately and I don't like it. We need this done with so there can be more smiles in our lives.

"I understand. Now, come here." I obey and wrap my arms around her waist as she pulls me in close. I inhale her scent and smile. I'll never get tired of her touch. We kiss lightly and then she brushes a few strands of hair from my eyes. "I love you Rayne."

"I love you too. Now, get going okay," I say as I pat her soft round ass.

"That's not going to make me want to leave," she whispers, even though everyone in here can still probably hear.

I laugh. "We'll finish that later then. For now, we have work to do."

"If we must. Let's go vamp lady." Selene waves Zara towards her indifferently and much like a noble would a servant.

Playing along, Zara gives her a sarcastic bow with one arm across her chest. "As you wish priestess." Then, we lock eyes and she winks at me, mischievously.

There was something in that look that made me shiver. She's up to something alright.

"Anubis," I call out. Not too loud though, knowing he wouldn't be too far away. He comes back into the room and gives me a look that says that as an Alpha he's not used to people beckoning him.

"What is it Rayne?" he asks, slightly amused with himself it seems for coming so swiftly.

"Would you like to take a walk with me through the forest? I'd like you to meet someone."

Chapter Twenty Eight

We walk for fifteen minutes before we find a nice clearing. In that time, I get Anubis to tell me about his mate.

"She was stunning. She could walk into a crowd and change the entire mood on a bad day, but she also had a mouth, which got her into a lot of trouble at times. The first time I met her she told me off actually. I think that's what made me desire her even more." He laughs a laugh full of happiness and I'm glad that I got him to open up.

"I was running late for a business meeting and I walked through the doors of the office so quickly that I didn't even hold the door for her while she was walking out. Her hands were full of bags and I guess when the door hit her she dropped them. Well, she left those bags right there, stomped to me as I was getting on the elevator, pulled me by my suit jacket back out of the elevator and gave me a piece of her mind. I ended up picking up all her bags, carrying them, and walking her to the car. Then, she told me that I owed her dinner for all the trouble that I put her through." His voice is full of so much love that it almost brings me to tears.

"Can you believe it? I ended up being over twenty minutes late for the meeting and losing that client, but it didn't matter. After that, I couldn't get the girl off my mind." When Anubis talked about her, his entire aura shifted. That woman was his soul mate, no doubt.

"How did you know?" I ask. "How did you know that she was the one?"

Anubis stops and looks me square in the eyes until I am forced by his Alpha nature added with the pull of the moon to look away. "The first time we kissed, there was an explosion. It was like every fiber of me had been destroyed then reborn. It's not the same for everyone, but that's how it was for me. There was no doubt."

I consider his words and smile. "I know that it may not feel like it, hell it may never feel like this, but I think you're lucky Anubis."

He looks at me to continue.

"Even though she was taken from you and it was so unfair, I think that you are so lucky that you had a chance to meet someone who loved you so completely," I tell him honestly.

Anubis freezes and considers my words, then does something completely unexpected. He pulls me into a fierce embrace. I return it happily. Then, he finally lets me go.

"Thank you Rayne. Thank you for helping me remember."

I reply by putting one hand on his shoulder and squeezing gently. Then, we reach the spot where I'm going to call on Diana.

It takes me about five minutes for me to clear my head enough to reach for my power to call on her. Then, about two minutes for her to respond. The air shifts and becomes colder. I hear her voice swirling all around me like a surround sound system before she appears.

"Child, are you well?" Diana's melodic voice fills my ears.

"I am Diana, but I need your advice," I tell her as she blooms into existence.

She appears before me in an aqua dress, cut short in the front and long in the back, one strap draped over her right shoulder, glowing and fierce. Her silky blonde hair flows in a non-existent wind. Her beauty is otherworldly from her impossibly light blue eyes to her model-like height made possible by her perfectly toned legs. Behind me, I hear Anubis's breath catch. Diana hears it too and tilts her head towards Anubis. I turn and watch as he is unable to hold her gaze the same way I wasn't able to. Diana's eyes twinkle with curiosity.

"Who is your handsome wolf?" Diana asks me, still eyeing Anubis, flirtatiously.

"Diana, this is Anubis. He has allied with me to take down the man known as Namen Young. Namen not only killed my family but his as well. Not only that, but it seems that Namen may be over two hundred years old. They call him the soul stealer and he's more powerful than I imagined."

"The witch is a taker of souls? Do you know what he hopes to accomplish?"

"He wants to take over our country and then force humans to take drugs that will alter their DNA to make them supernatural. If they refuse, they'll be enslaved. There's going to be war Diana if this happens, not only in our country but supernaturals will either have to come out of the woodwork everywhere else, or humans will go after them," I explain. Then, it dawns on me. That's his entire plan. "He wants to move swiftly taking over here, but he wants the rest of the world in chaos, so that he will be in the best position for control. It's a gamble. He's forcing the hands of everyone in the whole world. If supernaturals in other countries win he wins, but if they don't, he can offer them sanctuary, he'll own them, even if they hate him."

Anubis grunts at this perspective and I know I'm right.

"I have never heard of this man. But if what you say is true, then, the repercussions of this will be dire. Is he behind the lamia as well?" Diana asks, although I'm sure she's already guessed.

"Yes. Selene is going to try to shut the gate down that he's using."

"With blood magic? Kaede did not teach her such things."

"We have more help. She's showing her how to do it now."

"Who is this person Rayne?" Diana asks suspiciously.

"Her name is Zara Drake... She's a vampire," I hesitate in saying, remembering what Zara said about the Immortals, but stop abruptly when I see the fury in Diana's eyes.

"Surely, you are mistaken, that vampire wouldn't dare come near one of mine. Take me to her at once," Diana demands coldly.

I hesitate and exchange glances with Anubis. He doesn't know that Zara is familiar with the Immortals or that Zara has something against them.

"Um, well," I start.

"Now!" Diana erupts. I stumble back a few paces. The rage is burning off of her like a furnace and I wonder just what it is about this vampire that could bring out such fury. Not only that, but I do not want to see a battle between them. Especially not when I need us to be strong and intact.

She won't fight me Rayne, it's alright. Zara tells me through our mind-link. There's a sense of danger in her thoughts as well as excitement and I don't know if I like it.

How did you know what was going on? I ask, not understanding the power or limits to this link.

Your thoughts called to me. Is all she says, then, there's silence that I understand as her closing the bond. I'll have to learn how to do that quickly.

Together, we walk back to where Selene is working with Zara. There's tenseness in Anubis's step and the silence is super awkward.

Finally, Anubis speaks up, "I respect the fact that you are here, but please remember that this is my home and I need you to respect that as well." There's a warning in his words as well as a request. I wonder if it will fall on deaf ears.

"Don't make threats towards me mortal. I will do as I please. However, I will do my best to take into account that you are helping Rayne."

Anubis growls under his breath. His eyes glow a goldish-yellow as he turns to face Diana. She inclines her head towards him in the same way one would look at an unruly child. I start to reach for Anubis' arm, but I don't want it bitten off, so I decide to let them settle this.

"This is my territory old one. I don't care about your power, longevity, or position. You will not disrespect me on my lands." There is ice in every single syllable and his defiance sends chills down my spine.

Diana studies Anubis for a few seconds before tilting her head back in laughter. "Rayne has picked a fine ally. There is fire inside of your wolf's blood. But, make no mistake, with or without the guidance of the full moon, I could end you here. However, you are correct. I am a guest on your lands and my manners have escaped me. I will do my best to keep your land from tasting any blood tonight."

Anubis huffs and stalks ahead of us, clearly unhappy. He'll probably let me have it later for bringing her here.

When we reach the front of the main house, Zara and Selene are already outside waiting. Selene gives me a look of confusion and then looks

Alanna J. Faison   The Unmaking

at Diana. Diana gives her a nod in acknowledgement, then, turns her deadly gaze upon Zara. Zara pretends not to even notice as she turns her back towards Diana and sets her weapon down. It's as if not only does she not respect her, Zara doesn't even see Diana as a threat. I can't tell if she's a fool or if that makes her that much more dangerous. I guess only time will tell.

"What is your game vampire?" Diana asks, her voice sounding like poison. I step away from her and join the rest of the group in the huddle they've formed as we watch the next events unfold, unsure of what will transpire.

"I have no dark motives Diana. Actually, I've known Rayne for a long time. I've come to see her through her battle and I will do her no harm," Zara says smoothly. There's an undercurrent of rage there too. I can feel it through our bond.

Diana looks at me quickly before turning away. They stare each other down, an unspoken conversation flowing between them.

Then, Zara warns, "You will not turn her against me with your lies. We are blood-linked now and she will feel the truth of my words when it is time. I will get what's mine, even if I have to wait one hundred more years."

"What have you done Rayne?" Diana asks me.

"She's done nothing!" Zara snaps, her aura threatening to blow me over. I wonder if it's just because of our link. "The question is what have you done? You, with so much power, but what have you to show for it? I am the one who pushed Rayne into more of her power and I did it in one night. Were you just playing games with her in your world? Do you even believe in their kind anymore?"

Diana almost attacks, her weight shifting as she changes her stance, but something in Zara's face calls her to hesitate.

Zara continues pretending not to notice, "When the time comes, I will make my move, but until then, rest assured, you have nothing to fear. My duty now is to her, the one who was marked. You will help her Diana. This entire world depends on it." With that, Zara turns her back on Diana once more and goes silently back into the house while saying. "When you are finished here Selene, I will be waiting."

Then, the air shifts again and Diana is in front of me, grabbing me harshly and pulling me back into her world.

◊◊◊

Vertigo takes over as I'm not prepared for the speed at which I'm brought here. I fall to the ground on all fours and almost puke, but Diana is hastily grabbing me by my arm and pulling me back up to her. I'm not nearly as tall as her six foot frame, so she forces me to look up at her as she squeezes my cheeks much more painfully than necessary, especially since I still have no clue what's going on.

"What…the hell Diana?" I sputter, still trying to keep my food down.

"She is dangerous! That vampire, you cannot trust her. She doesn't want to help you. She just wants to use you to get to me Rayne. She seeks to ruin us," Diana wails angrily, her British-like accent even more pronounced. I've never seen her lose her composure before now. It's unnerving watching her pace back and forth full of rage and hate.

"I don't understand Diana. She's told me nothing and you're not telling me anything either. What's going on? I need to know exactly why I can't trust her."

"What you need to know is what I wish to tell you."

"Fuck that. That doesn't fly with me. I'm not a child that you can just keep in the dark and expect to behave. You should know me better than that."

Then, her icy blue eyes turn on me, the power behind them piercing me to my core. My tattoo reacts to her as if telling me that nothing good will come of this. She attempts to raid my thoughts after knocking me to the ground with a blow that I never saw coming. I try to push up from the ground, but she puts her foot on my back with the force of a ton of bricks and holds me in place. My own anger builds up inside at the invasion of my thoughts like an overflowing tub. Finally, she lets me up, seemingly satisfied.

I dust myself off and look her square in the eyes, them watering in the process. Part of it due to the pain of the violation and the other from standing up to her. "How can you expect me to trust you over her when you do things like that! If you want to know something all you have to do is ask me Diana. You don't have to take my thoughts from me. That's no better than a molester or a rapist taking what they want. I can't fucking believe you right now! Where's Lawrence? Maybe he'll give me some answers," I snap on her, fighting back angry tears. Then, I start to call out Lawrence's name loudly, hoping that he'll be around and can sort this out.

Diana looks at me in false apology, then in determination as she grabs my arm again. I try to pull away, but she won't let me. She only releases me when I stop calling for him.

"I'm sorry Rayne. It is only a matter of time I suppose before she tells you her side of the story. Maybe it's best that you hear me out first," Diana says, looking uncharacteristically defeated.

I cross my arms and wait.

"Come. Let's walk to the lake while I tell you this story." I follow Diana hesitantly as we stroll to the place where I would often go for reflection. The place of peace.

I take off my shoes as we settle into our favorite spot and dip my feet into the cool water. I don't look at Diana as I wait for her to speak.

After what seems like an eternity, Diana speaks, choosing her words carefully. "Child, we may be Immortal, but we are not infallible. We make poor choices and sometimes it's much harder for someone as long lived as we to live with those choices. Somewhere along the way, we may have lost sight of what was important and gave up on your kind when you stopped believing in us. Because of that anger, we took it out on another. She was like you, but was incredibly gifted even before she had been unmade over two hundred years ago. I marked her myself, amazed at the promise she displayed. She once stopped an entire pack of wolves from massacring a village. We were proud of her. There was no one ever made stronger than her. Then, a certain vampire was ordered to assassinate her; she was becoming too dangerous for their liking. They fought, but the vampire couldn't do it."

Diana's voice changes as if she's watching the story unfold before her eyes.

"The vampire watched her from afar, studying her habits, seeking to gain knowledge on the best way to defeat a prodigy much like herself. I'm sure that vampire never truly imagined that she could meet someone who could truly best her and she became intrigued by the human. When our warrior touched blades with her, they fell in love. It was said that their souls sang to each other through their swords."

"They would play a dangerous game, fighting and letting each other go, never truly putting any malice into their battles. They finally saw the futility in trying to be enemies. Somehow, the vampire convinced her family that she'd be no threat to them as long as they kept their own in check. So, Zara volunteered to police her own so that our human would not have to worry about it. What your vampire didn't know is that the other families had gotten permission to assassinate them both because together they had much more power than some of the rival vampire families combined."

"She's that powerful?" I ask quietly. Clearly, I have a long way to go in terms of strength if I ever hoped to be Zara's or even this other woman's equal.

"Yes. Zara's own cousin Apollo begged us to take them in to let them live with the Immortals until things had blown over. We agreed, but we also warned them that if they chose to go back to their realm that we would not intervene in any of punishment if they were caught."

"For ten years, they lived here together, happily. But then, the Dark Days came and a plague swept across Asia. The plague only affected the supernaturals and made them feral, unable to control their urges. They were like zombies, ferocious and deadly, but mindless killers. To this day, no one knows how the plague started, because one day, it just stopped. But, when that human heard about what was unfolding, she knew she had to help. It was her nature, too many humans had been slaughtered already and too many supernaturals had succumbed to the madness."

That must have been horrible. How did such an event get covered up from history? I listen more intently now, completely enthralled in hearing this revelation.

"She and your vampire went there. They did their best to clean up the mess, but it was just too much. They had fought too many battles without stopping and a simple mistake cost the human dearly. The human became mortally wounded and something inside Zara exploded. That is the day that she came into her own gifts and became known as the Crimson Princess. It is said that she massacred every single supernatural in the area, whether affected by the plague or not. She was bathed in so much blood that there was no speck of her caramel skin showing. When it was all over, the vampire was forced to turn the human into one of her kind in order to save her life."

If I wasn't watching Diana so closely, I might have missed it. Her fingers begin to tremble slightly and it isn't from the light breeze kissing us.

"Yet, as you know, those who are turned cannot stand daylight the way that one pure of the blood can, so they were frequently forced in the shadows. Then as if fate was the cruelest being to exist, the plague touched the newly turned vampire as well and Zara's heart broke even more. She called to us hoping that our blood would heal her. We refused. Our blood is sacred; no vampire is ever allowed to drink from it, for it is blasphemy."

Her voice becomes lower, more passionate. It fills my ears in a deep echo. "The one who answered the vampire's call that day was not me, it was my brother. Not Lawrence, but Blake. Blake refused her pleas and her requests for the blood and Zara did the unthinkable. She… murdered my brother, blood raped him and let her newly turned vampire drink from him as well. I don't know what his blood did for Zara, but the new vampire was saved, the effects of the plague reversed and she was able to withstand the sun as if she were pure of the blood."

Her anger at the act reaches me and causes my eyes to water. Without realizing it, Diana is calling to her own power. "Please calm down a little bit Diana, you're hurting me," I ask, reaching out to her. She tones it down, continuing as if I hadn't spoken.

"But, my brother was dead and retribution was in order. Zara begged to be punished for the crime, but it wasn't enough, she wouldn't suffer properly that way. We took her lover, punished her and locked her away," she finally finishes quietly and I sit there dumbstruck, the entire story painted in my head.

"I honestly don't know what to say. I mean, do you still have her imprisoned or is she dead? What's her name?"

"She is still in our tombs, in chains and put in a magical sleep. Her name is Sage. She was born of a Japanese mother and a European father with fair skin, white hair and grey eyes. She always looked like a fallen angel to me."

Now, she is sleeping beauty, waiting for her crimson princess to rescue her.

So, she's been in chains for nearly two hundred something years because Zara killed their brother. Because the same Immortals who unmade her refused to save her. Would they do the same to me, just ignore me if I needed to be saved? Is that why Zara so fiercely wanted to protect me too? Did she really have to kill him?

There are far too many questions that I have no time for. I think I understand more now what Zara wants. She'll try to use me to get Sage back. The question is, will I let her?

"How long, how long do you plan on holding her like that?" I ask quietly, afraid to hear the answer.

"Blake was one thousand years old when he was murdered. She will stay as she is for every year of his life," Diana says as if it's no big deal.

I shake my head in disbelief. "That's too cruel of a punishment." Plus the fact that time was slower on this realm, it would be thousands upon thousands of years before she was released.

Diana laughs. "You know nothing of our pain. We will never get our brother back, so why should she get her lover back?"

I frown. There has to be a limit to punishment right? Especially if the actions were done out of love, even if it were wrong. Maybe Zara didn't have to kill him, but who could say what I wouldn't do to save Selene, how crazy I'd be if something happened to her. "What about Zara's pain? Why are they both being punished for her actions?"

"It is our way," Diana snaps still looking so uncharacteristically frazzled.

"Diana, I think that it's time to let go now before Zara ends up killing someone else," I begin.

"That is not just up to me. Lawrence has a say in it as well as our elders. And trust me, Lawrence's hate for that vampire runs much deeper than mine. Lawrence loved Blake more than anything else in this world."

I sigh and stand up, brushing myself off. "Then, let's get to the reason why I summoned you in the first place. Zara has determined that Namen is planning on making his move on a day of an eclipse. It deals with the sun falling from the sky. I was hoping you could lend your mind to tell us anything you may know that will help."

Diana gazes at the gently flowing water, thoughtful. "Hmm. It sounds familiar and if I am thinking of the same event, it is not the eclipse that will be the main concern, it is what can be done under the power of this eclipse. What I can deduce is that the witch you seek is going to capitalize on the fact that every couple hundred years an eclipse lends the awakened enormous strength. Witches can perform such powerful spells alone that you'd better pray to the creator that a group of them do not attempt any such thing in numbers."

"You will not be able to stand against him if he is to get his way. The human government will surely tumble child. The best I can do is alert any of my Machaera to seek out any unusual behavior that may be related and eliminate it in their regions that they are protecting. It will be top priority. I hope that this small deed will lend you some relief Rayne." Diana sounds nearly apologetic this time. I nod to my immortal, still not understanding why they will not intervene when they could potentially save millions, and ask to be returned to my world.

With my newfound knowledge like a ton of bricks on my shoulders, I step through the circle of blinding light wondering how in the hell did the fate of my country come to rest in my hands.

Chapter Twenty Nine

*I*t's a couple hours later when I get back due to the time difference in each world, and unsurprisingly, no one is outside waiting for me. I knock on the door and one of Anubis's own answers. Then, I set off to look for Selene and Zara, hoping they've made progress and needing to speak with the vampire. Soon, I discover them in one of the larger guest rooms where Selene is sitting cross-legged on the floor, sweating from the difficult task. Zara is behind her, coaxing her to push harder. Neither one of them look up when I come in the room.

"Do not let the magic consume you priestess. Do not let the blood become tainted. Zara's eyes are rimmed in red and with the smell of blood and the feel of Selene's fear in the air, I know that she is working hard to keep her composure.

Finally, Selene falls over and Zara catches her before her head hits the ground. I rush to her side and take over for Zara, bringing Selene in close.

"Is she going to be alright?" I ask.

Zara stands up from her crouch and looks at the blood that's now on her fingers with hunger. Then, she looks at me and wipes it on her pant leg with a look of regret at letting good blood go to waste. "She's been at it since you were taken. It's just exhaustion setting in. Her chakra level is just low. But, she did the spell correctly."

I smile down at my beautiful girlfriend and brush her hair and sweat from her face. Her soft features make her look like a sleeping angel and at this moment I really wish she had wings and could take us away from all of this. Finally, I look up at Zara.

"She told me about Sage," I say quietly, releasing Selene and pulling Zara into the hallway.

"Did she? Hmm."

"What does that mean?"

"I just wonder if she told the truth."

"You mean if she told her truth. Zara, you've lived long enough that you know people are blinded by their own circumstances. You had a chance to tell me first, but you didn't. Now I only have one side of the story. So, what is your truth?" I ask calmly. I lean against the wall with my arms crossed, frankly growing tired of the mind games and round-about ways that these people operate.

"My truth is that I had a choice Rayne. I could have followed orders blindly and killed Sage without a second thought, but I didn't. I let my heart lead me. Those Immortals believe themselves to be gods, better than any other race. If they are not worshipped then they begin to hate those who they feel should worship them. They have no sense of love for anyone but themselves. They wanted revenge on the human race for not believing in them, so they abandoned her the way that they felt abandoned by mankind."

We lock eyes as she lets the weight of her words hit me. She definitely doesn't want me to trust the very people that made me what I am.

"When Blake came to us, he laughed at her weakness. He spit on her and told me that she was nothing but a 'thing' now. The fact that she was now vampire meant that there was no obligation to save her, that she was beneath him. I went berserk. I was fueled with a rage that I've never known before and I killed him, no I slaughtered him, drank from him, and shared his blood with her to save her life. When it was all done, I brought Blake's body back to the Immortals for proper funeral rituals and then I was ready to receive my punishment. Instead, she was the one they punished," Zara laughs bitterly.

"They took me first because I was compliant and bound me to a stone wall with their magics. I never knew they had intended for her to be the bearer of the retribution. Once I was magically bound and unable to fight back, they tortured her for days upon days until she begged for a final death. I was forced to watch every aching second, crying out for mercy that never came. It was horrible. She was a newly turned vampire that barely had any blood to sustain her and they did that to her. Then, they bound her in chains, and put her to sleep. I tried to save her, but they sent me back and locked me out of their realm." I feel the pain of her words, her sorrow for her lover through our bond and I can't help but reach out for her hand, to offer her some small comfort.

She looks at me and smiles, gripping my hand firmly, but I still manage to feel its slight tremble. "For years I wandered the Earth, unfeeling, uncaring. I've taken other lovers of course out of necessity. Blood and sex often go hand in hand, but the hole in my heart remained. I found out years later that members of the nine had gotten permission from the Immortals to kill Sage should she become too much of a nuisance. Those members I killed, brutally, and since then, no one in the family has ever stood against me. I tried and tried to get her back, to find a way back to their plane, but there was no hope."

Zara touches my face in such an intimate way that I feel guilty and remove her hand slowly. She smiles a sad smile and says, "Then, I met you Rayne. You, a small child, somehow filled my soul with hope again. When I told you never to fear, it was like I was telling myself that as well. I started to believe again that day. I feel like our paths crossing was not a mistake. There is a reason that we were brought back together as well. This is destiny. There is a bond between us Rayne and you may not completely trust it or understand it yet, but we are the keys to each other's goals."

The intensity in her gaze is overwhelming and I realize that I've now begun to sweat. Zara lets down the walls of our bond and a hurricane of emotions threaten to topple me. Her rage at the Immortals tastes bitter on my tongue, her love for Sage is like a tsunami, a desire to taste me is like a pin prick, her honesty strikes me like lightning, her ambition like a blaze, burning my skin. I find myself shivering from all the sensations. She let me see it all and because of that, I don't think I will be able to deny her.

"Let me decide once Namen is taken care of what I will do," I tell her.

"You, young protector will make the right choice. Of that I'm sure. I will not bring it up again until you are ready." Then, she lifts my hand to her lips and kisses me gently before walking away, hood pulled up. It feels like her kiss burned straight through me, the feeling still lingering.

I sigh deeply as I lean back against the wall. What a freaking life I have.

After I finally get Selene undressed and in bed, I end up falling into a deep sleep. However, there is nothing peaceful about this slumber. My first dream is of my family getting murdered. I have that nightmare three times and each instance, I try to save them, but am either too late or just too weak. My last dream, I'm chained and beaten by the Immortals while Selene looks on, helpless. They laugh and mock me, spit on me and leave me to die.

Selene ends up having to shake me awake from the nightmare, saying that I am calling for her in my sleep. I end up grabbing her by the neck before I realize what I'm doing. Then, she pulls me in close while I sob on her shoulder. Eventually, I'm able to tell her about my dreams and about what I learned from Diana and Zara. Selene seems just as surprised at the news as I was. Then, there's something else in her eyes, reflection. But, when I ask her what's wrong, she doesn't tell me. After that, we drift back off into sleep, me praying that this time, my sleep is sound.

Chapter Thirty

At long last, nightfall comes like a curtain falling on our final act. We begin our last preparations for our hunt; all of us ready for part one of our plan to slow Namen down. We all move with silent intensity as we grab our items, a quick drink of water, or a quick glance at the plans. During the preparations the excitement is obvious. Even I can taste it in the air. The night has a sharp chill to it, colder than usual for this time of year. I tug my black leather closer and zip it before strapping my weapon to my back.

I'd always hated watching movies where preternaturals were fighting with guns and such, but since nearly all guns had become illegal or just absolutely way too expensive to afford, it didn't matter.

It took one final mass shooting at a large church to finally get legislation passed about four years ago. There were four shooters. Three had gone through the building through separate doors, and one waited outside to catch those who might have gotten away. They ended up killing fifty people, men, women, and children alike. Despite that, I wonder how easy it would be to just put one damn bullet into Namen's sorry head.

I shake the thought away, because there is no way he'd deserve to go that quick or easy. No, I want to slice him open. I could do it too. That is a big difference in our crime rates now as well. People, especially gang members for all their talk simply don't have to balls to stab someone or slit their throat in a turf war that had to be fought up close. Most people just can't stomach the feeling of piercing hard into someone's flesh. Lawrence had once said that guns were the tools of cowards. I understood what he meant. Still, law enforcement and military carried them. For a year, there was uproar and protests daily because normal citizens felt like that government just wanted to be able to keep us under their boot easier.

"Does everyone know what their job is?" Anubis asks, for the second time tonight. We all nod and finally he seems assured. Anubis is dressed in a forest green tank top and black basketball shorts, probably knowing that he may very well destroy them in the fight. He looks every bit of a professional athlete in them too. Even if it was ten degrees out rather than the fifty or so it is now, he is Wolf, he won't feel the bite of the cold. His long dreds are pulled back again into a ponytail and his scar on his neck that is a testament of his survival makes him look that much more deadly.

This time, Zara has on a plum colored sleeveless hoodie with a black shirt showing underneath and black pants. She still has all of her jewelry on and looks as if she is going to a concert and not a fight. That is, until she equips herself with throwing knives and a blade.

Selene has on a lightweight, brown pea coat with dark jeans. Her silky black hair is done up in a neat bun leaving the brown of her ombre showing. Her brown leather boots with double straps click clack quietly on the bamboo floor. I laugh quietly at how fashion conscious our group is.

Jaxson is wearing something that looks like black Under Armour and I have to admit that it hugs his muscles deliciously. I appreciate good looking forms and he's built like a brick wall. Taryn even looks decent in her royal blue half shirt and jeans. I don't pay much attention to the other wolves with us.

After a quick look around at each other followed by a longer stretch of silence, Anubis gives the nod and we all head out. Once we are five minutes away from our destination, we all get out of our respective vehicles and begin our silent trek to the labs. Zara takes one more look at us and then vanishes into the shadows of the night, ready to take out as many cameras as she can. We have to follow quickly behind, so we break off into our groups to go our separate ways with Selene coming with Jaxson and me until she meets up with Zara again.

Excitement plows through my body, head to toe, filling me up with a high I'm sure no drug can match. My intricate tribal looking tattoo magically given to me through Diana's blood also begins to tingle, revealing itself with a glow and I have to breathe slowly to settle my power. Jaxson's eyes are now rimmed with yellow as he feeds off of my own enthusiasm. Selene too looks as if she's eager to test her power. When we reach the outer edge of the property, awareness surges, then I feel Zara next to me. It catches the other two by surprise and I smile.

"Are you ready," she asks all of us, looking back and forth. Her eyes are still a dark brown, but the influence of her aura in the air tells me that she's seconds away from becoming a deadly assassin if needed. I have no doubt that Selene will be perfectly safe in her care.

"Let's finish this quickly. I'm ready." Selene's magic jumps off her body to send sparks through the air as the electricity makes her hair nearly glow. She's ready to use her power alright.

"Good," Zara smiles, her fangs dropping. Then, she looks at Jaxson and me. "I can feel heartbeats in there, some are fainter than others. You need to go, now."

We don't say anything else, but Selene slightly caresses my hand and I hesitate for the briefest of seconds to let her know that I love her. At last, Jaxson and I take off to make our move. Our footsteps are light and just as we reach the front, he expertly breaks the lock on the door with one hand.

Jaxson is planning to stay in his human form since we need to get in there quickly and catch them by surprise. He still has the strength superior of a normal human and also has equipped himself with two claw blades, one for each hand, as well as a dagger hidden in his boot. He can't carry much else if he indeed needs to change because a large weapon could slice him up.

I check the first set of doors that we hit as he looks around for any hidden cameras. Inside, there's only a set of computers and a couple desks. The room itself has one large window and a few encouraging educational posters still left on the wall. There are no clues here that will help us find what we need. We move on in tandem, silently scoping for cameras or other traps. The next hallway up ahead is silent as well except for the noise of the broken blinking lights on the ceiling.

This hallway forks off into two different areas. We decide to check them separately, but only until they begin to run off into another zone. After that, we go through each zone together. There are more computers, some of them still plugged in, but there is nothing on them that is important. My guess is that they are in the process of getting ready to be used. Jaxson and I decide to destroy them. We repeat the same thing three more times going through three silent floors and still coming up empty.

We're losing too much time and I grow more frustrated with each room that we hit. My search again comes up empty so I head back towards Jaxson. I'm about ready to tell him we need to change our strategy. When I get beside him, I notice that he's sniffing the air followed by a low rumble in his throat.

"What is it?" I whisper.

"We're getting close and something's not right," he informs me, his head tilted to the side as if hearing something that my ears will never pick up.

"Okay, let's get there then," I respond just as I mentally tell Zara to have Selene begin the spell. It should take her at least two minutes to activate it correctly, and by that time, we should be where we need to be.

I push the next door open slightly and that's when I see the camera in the corner. It's not a fixed one, so we just time our movements with the movement of the camera and slide through undetected. There are more fixed cameras up ahead and those, we break.

Then, it strikes me like bolt of lightning. The smell of death and decay. Of fear and urine and feces.

The foul smell assaults my nose. Jaxson growls again and I put a hand on his shoulder to quiet him. The lamia are feeding right now, on a child. Maybe more than one; I don't know. What I do know is that I'm ready to kill them. These things will get no mercy tonight.

In that moment I think about all the children who won't be coming home tonight and all the parents who can never know what happened to their babies. I feel their terror and their cries for help as none came and I hate the cruelty that Namen represents. It is my duty to end him, even at the cost of my own life. Namen Young is too much of a threat to humanity itself and I won't stand for it. There is no rush of anger inside me at this fact. There is only a deadly resolve built up, fortifying my intentions. I pull Katsu, my beautiful white blade, from her sheath and I swear I can feel her cry for justice, for blood, for victory. Yes, she will bathe in red tonight.

Jaxson pushes through the door first, ripping it from the hinges, and leaping left into the huddle of demon filth as they feed on a young boy, his face twisted in utter terror, insides torn apart. The lamia are covered in blood and other body parts. Their human-like female faces all share the same look of surprise as he attacks with the rage of a bull.

It is easy to see how they could pass for normal women aside from the fact that right now they have shark-like teeth. Their hair color ranges from blonde to brunette, styled in bobs and flat irons. There are also bits of flesh and blood in their hair and face from their meal. I look on in disgust. Some of them with their snake-like bodies manage to slither out the way, hissing. I wait one more second and sprint through the door, slicing low at the ones whose backs are now turned towards me. I cut two in half before I end up back to back with Jaxson.

We fight in sync, me ducking under with a slice as he leaps over me with a kick. We're slashing sending blood flying and creating a slippery mess of fluid and guts all over the white tile. Out the corner of my eye I see some of the lamia attempt to get away as the others try to surround us. I don't know how many actually slip through because, through the other door, Anubis and Taryn push them back inside, both of them in their man-beast form, standing on hind legs, grabbing and slashing with powerful paws.

I do my best to break free of one as it grabs me, trying to give me a paralytic bite. Taryn rips it free of my shoulder, just as its teeth graze me and breaks its neck. Then, I slash my katana, detaching its head. Without hesitation, we turn back around and continue our assault just as the other two wolves all in wolf form attack like the hunters they are. The attack is so choreographed and precise that it can't be anything but pack instinct taking over these wolves. I don't have long to appreciate the beauty in the battle because two more lamia attack me at once.

The lamia are surprisingly fast as they slither at me, striking out with their tails as well as their claws. I dodge, but trip over the dead boy and find myself on the ground covered in all kinds of bodily fluids. Bile rises up in my throat and I have to push it back down as one of the lamia manages to bite my leg. I hiss as I kick the thing right in her mouth, shattering teeth. That gives me enough time to roll away as Taryn again saves my ass by pulling me up. She gives me a look as if telling me to get it together. I nod and then slice the lamia in half that's trying to sneak up behind her. She then gives me an amused smile at the favor returned.

A tiny bit of numbness rises up in my leg from where I was bitten, the venom trying to make its way through my body. One bite isn't enough to stop me, but it's irritating as hell. I try to shake it off as we try to finish off the rest of them. It doesn't take long and by the time it's all over, every single one of us looks like we've been in a massacre. Well, that's exactly what it was. Dutifully, the wolves pile up the dead lamia parts for disposal.

Anubis orders his other two wolves to finish disposal of the bodies and then leaves the room. He changes into a wolf, sniffing the air prepared to search for the children. The rest of us split our group in half and search the building. After ten minutes all we find to save is three kids. My heart nearly breaks and I do all I can to keep the tears from flowing at the sense of failure at not being able to do more for the others, wherever they may be.

"Three is better than none baby. We did well tonight," Selene assures me.

"She's right. Now, I'll glamour them and then someone can take them near a hospital or police station," Zara says, wiping off her blade in the grass, a dead lamia at her feet.

"I'll do it," Taryn volunteers. "I have a change of clothes in my car so I'll wipe myself off and then go. Someone can help me carry them there." Two of the other wolves follow her, carrying the kids once Zara finishes up her mind control.

"Now, Selene do you have enough energy to find and then shut down that gate?" Anubis asks after turning back into human form.

"Yes, I'm fine. Let's do this." Selene sits crosslegged on the ground, taking deep cleansing breaths.

Suddenly, Anubis doubles over in pain. Before Jaxson can run to him, he falls over too, the other wolves following suit.

"What the fuck?" Zara begins, drawing her sword once more.

"My pack!" Anubis growls. "They're dying."

"Zara! Go after Taryn," I command and without hesitation, she takes off into the night like a faithful soldier following orders.

"No," Anubis hisses, holding his head, still on his knees in the dirt. This is bad, the pack felt the loss of a pack mate, but this means that there are many if it is affecting Anubis as well as the others this much. "No, the pack left at the house. Something's happening."

A whine escapes Jaxson's lips and I feel completely helpless as I reach for him.

Chapter Thirty One

𝒜 surge of magic whips through the air unlike anything I've ever felt before, wrong, evil. It happens so quickly that I almost believe I imagined it. That is, until I'm hit so hard in the chest that I fly through the air and into the brick wall of the building, unable to breathe for a few seconds. The back of my head is bleeding. When I do catch my breath, I look up to see a man standing over me, eyes grey and as cold as death itself, and a look of utter satisfaction on his face.

He is a man who loves delivering pain and suffering. He has a goatee that is graying in some places and his brown and grey hair is slightly curly and styled uncharacteristicly for the aura he's putting out. His nose is sharp, his lips a thin line. He is dangerous. Standing at about 5'11" and dressed in all white as if he were a god himself, his magic shimmering off of him making his body seem to be bathed in darkness.

Namen.

The man that ripped my life apart. The man that stole the life of three people that I held dear. The man I need to kill.

I try to stand, but the force of his magic pushes me right back to my hands and knees as if I weigh a ton. My face begins to burn and as I look up, there's a thick wall of flame surrounding us and I'm sure it's to keep everyone out. In the distance, I can hear Selene call out my name in fear and urgency, but I can't respond. I'm too fixated on this figure in front of me. I finally have a face to put with my dreams.

I jump up, forcing my power to break the bonds on the magic, Katsu in my left hand, slicing at the man in front of me. But I'm too slow and he hits me again with something. Then, I see nothing.

◊◊◊

I awake in coldness. I'm naked, exposed, unbound by physical chains, but somehow magically restrained. I don't have to look up to know that I'm here with Namen. I can feel the sense of death in the air and the utter insanity in his power. He slaps me hard and I nearly fall out the chair. I take it without comment, not giving him the satisfaction of hearing my pain. He laughs. It's deep and uncaring. Evil.

He has worse planned for me, that much is obvious. I just need to find a way to get out of here, even if I have to bite him to death. Selene and Zara have to be looking for me right now, and I try to open our bond to call out to the vampire, but there's nothing but silence.

Namen whispers something and it feels wrong, demonic almost. Where Selene's magic sounds musical, his sounds like nails on a chalkboard. Then, he touches me and my whole body seems to be on fire. This time, I can't help but to scream out in sheer agony at the feeling of being burned alive. When my throat is raw from my cries, the pain finally stops. I finally look up at him, tears in my eyes, rage in my heart, and he returns my stare head on.

"Kill me now, because if you let me go, I will come back and find you. Whatever you do to me here, now, won't make me fear you." I tell him, my voice coming out harsh but determined.

He doesn't reply, simply whispers something else. He steps closer to me and I can smell the burn of magic all on him. It's not fresh and herbal like Selene, but like sulfur and rot. I turn my head and try to prepare myself for what's to come next. But, it's something I never expect.

There's the tear of flesh and muscle from bone and then my right arm is removed from the rest of my body. The shock of looking at my limb on the floor, the blood pouring from my arm, the helplessness I feel all sinks in. The pain is indescribable. He forces me to hold his gaze as he reaches into my flesh where my arm once was. I scream hysterically but he silences he with a spell and even numbs my pain. My hate grows as it really sinks in that my arm is missing. Fear penetrates my heart like a bullet.

"I could slice you apart right here and now, but I won't. I have one message for you, human. Now that I have your attention, listen well." His voice is just as dark and as cold as his eyes. I force myself not to move, not to feel anything as he whispers to me, carefully and slowly. My eyes widen in surprise and anger as he pulls back away from me. Last, he laughs one more time and I finally pass out as he releases the spell and my pain increases dramatically.

"Rayne! Get up!" Selene cries, pulling me off the ground. "We have to get out of here now."

I reach for my armless stump, attempting to stop the bleeding, but there's no bleeding to stop. My arm is still attached, healthy. I cough a couple times and then look up at Selene despite the blurriness in my vision. Then, I look at my surroundings and silently curse. What in the hell just happened? I'm back on the ground in front of the lab and not in some dark room magically bound. Not missing an arm.

"What's going on?" I ask, confused and groggy. The numbness in my leg from the lamia bite is still there as I try to stand.

"Namen came. He knocked you into the wall and out, and then went after Anubis. He touched Anubis and said something to him. After that, Namen disappeared. Anubis told us to run before he began to change. He killed one pack member before attacking Jaxson and almost killed him too, but Zara came back in time and is trying to stop him. I barely had enough time to shield myself. He managed to knock her down and then took off. Rayne, she's going to have to kill him. I think he's gone feral like his father."

No. I snap out of my fogginess and to my feet. "Which way, Selene?"

She points to the west and I take off in that direction before calling behind me. "Help Jaxson!"

Chapter Thirty Two

God, I just hope I make it in time to keep Zara from killing him. Maybe he could fight it. Maybe we could lock him up. I reach a street that has a broken streetlight and a few dented cars and know that I'm on the right track. I sprint for about three more streets and then see a building with a shattered window. Inside and well above me, I can hear growls and grunts. After one quick look behind me, I jump through the broken window and follow the sound up many flights of stairs. For all of Zara's strength, she's having a pretty difficult time with Anubis, who is in his man-beast form as I call it, ripping things off of the walls and throwing them at her. She's dodging and striking, but is unable to get close to deliver a blow.

"Rayne, I'll distract him and you stop him," she orders without looking my way but knowing that I'm with her.

"We don't have to kill him. Anubis! Fight it. Control it damn it!"

"If he draws too much attention, we may run out of time and I will have to kill him. We must do what we have to. Rayne, his behavior is just like those beasts during the Dark Days. Now, focus. We are in for a battle." Her aura shifts again and her eyes become red like pools of blood. Then, she disappears into the shadows. Anubis growls as he tries to track her, following the noise she tries to make and the weak strikes she lands. For my sake, she's holding back and giving me a chance to come up with a solution that will end without me taking the life of my ally and possible friend.

I hide behind a table that is now upright and wedged near the wall and call for my own power as I pray that I won't have to kill him. After convincing him to help me, I don't know how I'd live with myself if I failed him now. There's a loud boom and I glance around my cover to see Anubis on the other side of the wall that he just broke through. Glass is still falling around him from the shelves that he's destroyed and he's definitely not happy about it.

He gets up with a loud howl and comes straight at me with blinding speed. His speed startles me but Zara matches his swiftness and tackles him sideways. They tumble to the floor as Zara sends a blow to his muzzle, but Anubis bucks her off of him. Finally, I see my opening as he's focused on her. Regrettably, I slam the sword into his powerful bicep, pinning him to the floor. He yowls in rage as he fights to get up, but to no avail. Katsu is too deep.

"Anubis. Stop. Listen to me. You can fight it; you're stronger than this," I say with urgency, but it doesn't seem to be getting through. He snaps at me and swings with his free paw.

"Please," I beg. "You're an alpha, you can win this battle. Anubis, reach deep." For a second the words seem to reach him, yet the spark of humanity leaves his eyes just as soon as it appears.

Zara stands beside me and examines him.

"Can you glamour him or something?" I ask, hopefully.

She looks deep into his eyes, pausing, studying, and then shakes her head apologetically. "I can't. He's basically a wild animal right now and I can't glamour animals."

Before I can react, comment, or anything, Zara pulls the sword from his arm and pierces Anubis right through his stomach. He becomes more enraged as he tries to buck wildly to free himself.

"No!" I scream at her, trying to rip Katsu from her strong grip, she pushes me away with enough force to knock me to the ground.

"There's no other way Rayne. Trust me," she growls.

Anubis gasps and turns his head towards me, his arm reaching out as he begins to change back into human. "Rayne, I can't control it. Please," he starts, before the wildness returns to his eyes as his change abruptly stops and he turns back into the beast.

Impossibly, Anubis rips Katsu free of his body, doing more damage to himself with a howl. Before either one of us can react, he grips Zara's neck with his enormous hands and hurls her through a glass window, shattering it, the sound echoing through the room, ten floors up and down to the ground below.

With a low growl and a predatory stance, all his attention is now on me. I make the mistake of locking my hazel eyes with his eerie yellow ones and he goes beserk. Anubis slashes me across my face, easily drawing blood and shutting my right eye. I just hope it isn't as deep as it feels.

With blood streaming down my face threatening my vision in my left eye too, I dodge his next strike and toss a chair in his way to slow his momentum. It seems like a good idea until Anubis catches it and throws it back at me, catching my leg and tripping me up. He's on me before I can regain my feet and as his powerful jaws launch towards my neck, I throw up my left arm in sacrifice. The bones crunch and somehow Anubis only manages to shatter it rather than rip my limb apart. Thankfully, my adrenaline doesn't allow me to feel the extent of the pain. However, I'm still helpless under this alpha werewolf that is poised to attack once more.

I dig my fingers deep into one of his eyes and he jumps back in rage giving me a split second to push up from under him. I'm only going to be able to survive with a weapon and as I look on the floor for my blade, Zara is on the window ledge, mad as hell, face back in a snarl and red eyes begging for blood. With remarkable speed, she and Anubis clash again, too fast for my eyes to follow. Then, with a flying kick, Zara sends Anubis into a wall and is on him in the same instant. I watch her head pull back slightly, and then her fangs find his neck. She pumps toxins in his body to make him weaker and soon he can struggle no more. I find Katsu on the floor and warily take three slow steps towards the two of them.

With blood dripping down her lips and Anubis now slumped to the floor, not yet dead but unable to fight any longer, Zara turns to face me with a look that I hope I never see again in my life. Inside her eyes held the promise of destruction, the true monster that is buried deep within her.

I take a step back and then curse myself silently for my stupidity. I'm making myself look like prey. Holding my head up defiantly, I glance at Anubis, no longer as strong, but certainly not back to normal and my heart drops. He looks up at me and growls.

"They don't come back Rayne, not without the blood of an Immortal, and you learned how well that ended last time. Finish this or I will."

I silently say a prayer for Anubis, for his dead mate and unborn child. I ask for forgiveness for still being too weak to save anyone. I make a vow to get stronger, to become a true protector so that I never have to do what I'm getting ready to again. With tears mixing with my bloody face, I slam my katana through the werewolf's heart. He slumps to the ground immediately after I pull her out of his chest. Unmoving, dead, just that quickly.

The hole in my own heart continues to grow.

Chapter Thirty Three

The back of my head begins to pound from when Namen knocked me into the wall. My other injuries follow suit making themselves known. Anger takes me over as I walk back out of the building, wiping the blood of my new friend on the sleeve of my jacket. Zara reaches out to me with our bond, but I shut her out. I even refuse her blood right now. She instead stalks behind me silently, keeping to the shadows, undoubtedly looking for threats that I could care nothing about right now.

Still inside the building, Zara said that she had a friend on the police force that would take care of the body. They were on their way there now. I just hope that the sirens I'm hearing aren't heading to where we just came from. We did a lot of damage. Shit, I *am* damaged. It seems that now, I lost another piece of myself. I just hope that Jaxson will at least make it, that Selene had been able to do something for him.

Like a Zombie, I tread back down the road. As I get closer to the abandoned research building, I begin to feel the magic, Namen's magic sting me all over. He was here, after we left. Zara feels it too and she grabs my arm, pulling me into the shadows.

"Look up ahead," Zara whispers, pointing in the distance in front of us. The car that Taryn was driving is wrapped around a pole, a limp body hanging out of the driver's side, unmoving.

I run to the car, hoping against hope that the kids are still alive. Instead, ten pairs of dead eyes stare back at me. Taryn, her pack mate, and three innocent children. There is so much blood. This time, I can't fight it, I scream in rage, seeing red, cursing the evil that is Namen. Behind me, I feel Zara's bloodlust rise. She's fighting to keep her composure, but I can tell that she's walking a tightrope in a hurricane.

"Don't you dare," I warn her. "Don't you fucking dare lose it on me too. I don't care Zara, I will kill you myself."

I turn and meet her gaze and she snarls at me, even though her mind is telling me that she's fighting it. I take a step towards her, determined. She tilts her head at me questioningly. "What... are you doing?"

I grab her firmly into an embrace, her short body small and almost frail feeling against me. She tries halfheartedly to pull away, but I don't let her.

"I need you right now. So, you either bite me or you suck it up so we can help the people that I care about."

She breathes in my scent. "I'm sorry, you told me to help them, but I felt you in trouble and I made a choice. I can control it, but this isn't helping. Let's move, but I need you to walk behind me so that I won't chase you."

I pull away, and Zara takes off in the direction where we left Selene. She's making another call about these bodies. There has been far too much death tonight and absolute failure on our part. I refuse to believe that it's even possible for things to go even worse than they did tonight.

When we return, Selene is still on the ground with Jaxson, his head on her lap.

"He's alive, barely. I can hear his heart beat. Anubis ripped a large hole into his stomach. Maybe my blood will help him speed up the process, but he has to change to heal. He's going to be out of it so we need to lock him up in case he loses it too." Zara then rips open a vein in her wrist and feeds Jaxson the blood. His mouth barely moves as he consumes her life force. Finally, after Zara seems satisfied, she gently drags his giant body to the car. We silently walk to the car and get him in.

I ride with Zara as Selene follows us to another one of Zara's safe houses. I hold my left arm as close to my body as possible. Zara promises that she'll help heal my shattered arm as quickly as possible once we are safe, regardless of my protests. She tells me that my face will probably scar a little. I cringe at the thought.

We move fast and get Jaxson in the house and into a large, kennel looking thing but with much stronger metal, and lock him in. Selene then spells it so that he still won't be able to leave if he breaks free. That drains the last of her power and she walks out, completely exhausted.

The three of us make our way back outside just as we hear Jaxson scream in pain as he changes form. I glance back behind me and shake my head at the way the night has gone. It was the wolves that suffered the most and it was all because of my insistence.

"What happened to Anubis?" Selene asks quietly.

I shake my head and tell her as tears well up, "I had to stop him. He was on a rampage."

"What about the others at the house? What do you want to do?"

"They're gone. That's why Anubis and Jaxson reacted that way. That's probably why it was so easy to get to Anubis, he was vulnerable," Zara explains. "We can go in a little while, I just want to make sure Jaxson is going to pull through. He's alpha now and we still need him."

"Okay," I pause, thinking as I wipe away my tears. Something flashes in Zara's eyes and she looks at Selene then at me.

"I'll go watch him and let you two talk. Come get my blood when you're finished," Zara says before touching my good shoulder and walking back inside. When she opens the door, we can hear the snarls coming from Jaxson's cage.

I wait until I'm sure Zara isn't in hearing distance and then I take a deep breath and run my blood crusted hand through my short hair. I think I'm ready to grow it back out. It takes all my strength to turn back to Selene. I'm ill prepared to have this talk, but it can't wait much longer. Not after what I learned.

"I didn't get the gate closed," Selene sighs as I turn towards her. "Maybe we can try tomorrow or something. I don't know."

"Right now, it doesn't matter. Listen Selene, something crazy happened to me before, after Namen knocked me out, I don't know. All I know is that he told me something that changes everything," I pause and sigh again, searching her eyes, seeking out the lies she's been telling me, what she's been keeping from me and my anger threatens to overflow.

"What did he say?"

"Selene, why? Why didn't you tell me about him? I can't believe you. Is that who you were searching for when you left me leaving the club the other night when I was almost taken?"

Selene lifts up her head and looks confused, but unconsciously takes a step back as if she's afraid that I will lash out.

"What do you mean Rayne?"

"Selene, damn it! You have a fucking twin and you never told me!" I shout before I bring my voice down. "Did you know that he was working with him?"

"Santos…"

I turn on Selene, pointing accusingly. "No, let me tell you exactly what Namen said to me as he was torturing me in my mind or in his lair, or wherever the hell I was naked and alone with him. He told me that your twin was one of his best lieutenants and that if I went after him, he'd personally send your brother to kill me."

I watch the shock and hurt flow across her face. She reaches for me, but I snatch my hand away. "Santos would never... He couldn't have."

"You know what I think, I think that he's the one who killed Anubis's pack. While Namen was waiting for his chance, he sent your brother to murder them. I think that you knew what your brother was capable of. He's no better than Namen then, Selene. Fuck! How could you not tell me you had a brother! How could you not tell me that he could possibly be some freaking psycho. The evil twin! Are you serious?"

This couldn't really be happening. My arm throbs even more and I know that I only have a few more minutes on my feet before the adrenaline leaves me and my strength is robbed.

"He was in a lot of trouble last I saw him Rayne, but I promise you, I never thought he'd be a part of this. Please." There are tears in Selene's eyes, but I don't care. She still isn't telling me why she never told me about him. It makes me feel that she's keeping even more things from me and I don't like it.

"Maybe I can talk to him Rayne, we can figure this out," Selene cries.

"No! Let me make this perfectly clear Selene Marquez. If I ever see your brother, if he ever threatens me, happens to even be in the same vicinity as me, I *will kill* him."

"He's my fucking brother Rayne, my twin! Meu sangue."

"And he's a murderer. For all I know, he had a part in my family's murder," I spit with so much venom that I fear that I will lash out and hit her.

"If you can say that to me so easily, if you can make such a promise to me, to kill my brother, where does that leave us Rayne?" Selene cries more this time, her beautiful face full of despair and pain.

I turn away and shake my head. Unable to look into her eyes as the hurt of her betrayal washes over me like a monsoon. It's suffocating me and I grab the front of my shirt hoping it will loosen this choking feeling. She's the last person I'd expect this from. A brother, a potential threat. Where *does* that leave us? My heart slowly begins to break as I have no answer to give.

Be sure not to miss the second book of the Rayne Whitmore Series: *Killer Rayne*

I've been through more than I've ever imagined I could survive. But, this thing is far from over. Namen has decided to change the whole game. The lawyer leads me out of the interrogation room just as the detective grabs my arm.

I glance at the tall man that interrogated me and despite my anger; I still manage a little smirk at the fact that I'm obviously a true threat to him now.

Namen, you bastard, you played your hand perfectly.

"Namen says to tell you smile for the cameras," the detective whispers smugly. I pull my arm away and tilt my head towards him in defiance.

"You know, I'm going to make sure that you're the first human that I kill," I warn.

"There's too many witnesses now. You won't be able to make a move now that the whole world is looking at you. You think you have friends. This police force belongs to Namen Young."

I brush up against the detective and lift my head so that my lip is touching his ear. I'm close enough that I can smell his cheap cologne mingling with his sweat. He fears me and I like it. "Well then," I whisper softly, "I guess I'll have to kill you all."

Dedication

Writing takes incredible insight and patience that I truly didn't appreciate until I finally sat my butt down and got this book done.

Normally, people dedicate their books on the front; however, since this is my first novel, I wanted to save the best for last. People who come into your life and help shape you and teach you to dream bigger are few and far between. I'm just thankful that I've met my share.

First, I am grateful to my parents, especially my mother for not only reading to me, but for reading with me. I love my father for never being surprised when I did something great because he's always known what I was capable of. My brothers helped expand my creativity. Those teachers that saw something in me pushed and challenged me in ways that changed me forever. They also taught me the value of giving back. The love of my life has been the best teammate that I could ask for through it all.

Last, I thank you for choosing to go through this amazing journey with me, helping me get one step closer to my dreams. I hope that you enjoyed reading as much as I did writing this story.

About the Author

Alanna is pretty sure that she loved books from the minute she was born. Raised in Omaha, Nebraska, there wasn't much to do but read anyway. With the encouragement of her mother and a few clever teachers along the way, she turned her love for reading into a love of writing stories, poetry, and music. Although she went to college and obtained a degree in Criminal Justice, Alanna always finds her way back to her first love. She dreams that her own books will give someone the same excitement she feels when she reads a great story.